THE PERFECTION IN
LOVE

~~~

Ronke Abidoye

Published by

The Queen of the King Enterprises

www.thequeenoftheking.com

Paperback: ISBN 978-0-578-78531-8
eBook: ISBN 9781005814984

Cover Art by Rabia Aamir

~~~

For all the couples who have overcome racial and cultural boundaries to find love.

For Cameron Boyce, who exited stage left too soon yet will live on in our hearts forever.

To the One whose Name is Love, whose Love transcends death and planets, whose Love burns hotter than a freaking supernova. Lord, this is for You.

PART ONE

♥ ...4... ♥

CHAPTER 1

"Henry, I am going to kill you!"

It was a cloudy summer day in Phoenix, one of those rare ones that came once every two weeks. While most people chose to leave their house for a picnic or a fun day at the amusement park, Oyin and Henry Wilson lounged by their outdoor pool enjoying the cool desert air, engaged in an intense blinking contest.

Oyin stared at her husband, determined not to lose. A week of laundry was riding on this. She could see Henry's face begin to color, a telltale sign that he was about to break. She just had to last a fraction-of-a-second longer than him.

He blinked. "Darn it!"

Oyin squealed and raised her arms triumphantly. "Yes!"

"I don't know how, babe, but you're cheating."

Oyin laughed. "I'm pretty sure that's impossible."

"Then, how come you always win?" Henry asked, his blue eyes searching her face suspiciously.

Oyin laughed some more. "No tricks, Hen. I just really hate doing laundry."

"I don't like it either!"

Oyin stuck her tongue out playfully. "Well…then you should have won."

"Oh, you're going to wish you didn't say that. Do you want to take it back?"

Oyin scoffed. "Do your worst, Mr. Wilson."

She only had a split-second warning before the feeling of weightlessness attacked her senses. Then half a second later, gravity kicked in and plunged her into the shockingly cold pool. She bobbed to the surface, sputtering, her eyes already stinging from the chlorine.

"HENRY, I AM GOING TO KILL YOU!"

Henry snickered from a safe, dry distance. "I'm sorry.

Oyin growled and launched herself out of the water, murder in her eyes.

Henry's eyes widened, and he sped into the house, Oyin hot on his heels.

By 7 am the next morning, the sun was proudly perched in the sky, determined to burn out every speck of coolness from the previous day. Saying a quick prayer, Oyin rolled out of bed to brush her teeth. By the time she returned, Henry was awake, so they read their allotted Scripture chapters of the day and prayed.

"And we pray today, Lord, that You bless our union. Help us grow in our love for each other and in our love for You," Henry prayed, concluding their morning devotion.

"Amen," they chorused.

"Hen, remember how I said Mummy and Daddy wanted to come spend a couple of weeks with us this summer?"

"Yeah, didn't you say they were coming next month or something like that?"

Oyin shook her head and smiled. "Yes, when I told you two weeks ago, it was 'next month,' but it's two weeks from today."

Henry's eyes widened slightly. "Really? That close, huh?"

He continued quickly, "I mean, of course, they are always welcome."

Oyin smiled. "Well…it's a good thing you think that because they are coming a little earlier than expected."

Henry nodded. "Um, okay. How early?"

Oyin gave a little wince. "This Saturday early. Baby K texted me before I went to bed last night."

Oyin's eyes roamed her husband's face, searching for his reaction…and nothing, which only meant he was trying to hide how he felt.

She was just about to bring it up when he cut in. "Did she say why they changed their plans?"

"She said something about trying to avoid the summer vacation travel crowd since they are traveling with buddy passes."

Henry nodded again. "Okay. It's fine. Like I said, they are welcome anytime."

"Okay, I'm glad you are okay with it."

Oyin stood up. She was definitely going to bring the issue up again, probably after church. But for now, she simply walked to the bathroom.

She popped her head back into the room a minute later. Henry was still where she left him, in a half-sitting, half-kneeling position, thumbing through his phone.

"Wanna join me in the shower?" she asked as she put a shower cap over her newly done braids.

Henry looked up and grinned. "Yes, please."

Oyin shook her head and chuckled. "We only have an hour to get to church, and we live on the West Coast. I am only trying to conserve time and water."

"Sure," he smirked. "You know you want this."

She rolled her eyes. "Do I?"

Henry laughed and wiggled his eyebrows in response.

It took them less than an hour to get ready, and soon, they were on their way to Restoration International Church (fondly referred to as RIC), which was a fifteen-minute drive from their house. They were about five minutes into the drive when Henry spoke.

"I don't think I said it before we left home, honey, but you look crazy beautiful this morning."

Oyin felt her face grow hot. "Thanks, babe. You don't look too bad yourself."

He grinned one of those grins that made her heart pause because it, too, wanted to appreciate God's work on Henry's face.

"And I love that your name literally means *honey*. You bring sweetness to my life every day." Henry found her hand on the console and raised it to his lips.

Tell your spouse one thing you love about them every day.

It was one of the few pointers from their pre-marriage counseling sessions that they tried to practice.

Oyin shook her head, smiling. "That was a good one. I'm not sure I could come up with anything today that could rival that."

So, naturally, they had made it into a competition.

Henry smirked, "So, you concede?"

Oyin stuck her tongue out at him in response and squeezed his hand, which still cradled hers.

He brought sweetness to her life, too.

"I love you," she mouthed to him.

It wasn't long before they arrived. Henry parked the car, and they walked hand-in-hand to the entrance, waving at some of their friends who were just driving in. A familiar voice greeted them as they walked into the lobby.

"There's my favorite couple."

"Hi, Pastor Greg," Oyin smiled back.

"Good morning, Pastor Greg. I bet you say that to all the couples," Henry joked.

Pastor Greg beamed, "I do. You caught me. So, *OH*, how are you guys doing on this Lord's Day?" Pastor Greg asked.

Oyin shook her head at the couple nickname that Pastor Greg had given them, as she always did.

It was cliché, but it was neat, and though she'd never admit it, she liked it. It fit, just like she and Henry.

"We are doing well, aren't we, babe?" Henry asked, glancing at her.

Oyin nodded. "Yes, we are."

Pastor Greg nodded. "Great! I want to keep hearing that, okay?"

They both nodded.

"Okay. Off to your duty posts! You to ushering..." he pointed at Henry.

"...and you to the kids' department." He wagged another finger in Oyin's direction.

Oyin simply giggled.

Henry's bible study group at the University of Arizona had introduced Henry to Pastor Greg and RIC as soon as Henry had graduated. While Pastor Greg had not been their official pre-marriage counselor, he had been a pillar of comfort during their engagement. He was like a second father to Henry, and it didn't hurt that he had the same first name as Henry's dad.

"Have fun with the kids." Henry leaned in and pecked her cheek.

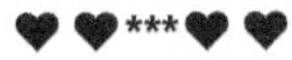

"Hey Daddy," Oyin smiled into the phone later that day. "How is my *oyin*[1]?"

Oyin looked over the island at Henry and chuckled at his horrific attempt to dice onions. "We are good, daddy. How is Mummy? And Baby K?"

Baby K was Oyin's unofficially adopted sister. Her parents, who had been elders in Daddy's church in Lagos,

---

[1] *oyin* – translates to honey (in Yoruba)

died in a car accident when she was only thirteen. She had gone to live with Daddy, and that was how Kike Ogunlomo became "Baby K" — a pet name that Daddy had given her so that she could feel like she was part of the family, the baby of the family, in fact.

"We are all fine. We all miss you. We can't wait to see you this weekend," Daddy replied.

"I miss you all, too. And we can't wait to see you too. How long were you planning on staying, again?"

"I am not sure; ask your mother. Here, talk to her."

Oyin put her phone on speaker and went to help Henry, whose face was already the same color as his auburn hair. She gave him a quick peck and took the knife from his hands. "Check the pasta," she mouthed to him.

"Good afternoon, Mummy."

"My child… How are you doing?" Mrs. Irene Johnson said in Yoruba.

"I'm fine, Mummy," she replied in English, mentally urging Mummy to respond in English. She couldn't make the request explicitly in either language. Mummy would take offense, and so would Henry for different, but equally infuriating, reasons.

"How are you? How was church?" Oyin asked, instead.

Mummy responded, *again,* in Yoruba. "Fine. It was fine. We thank God."

Oyin sneaked a look at Henry. He was otherwise occupied, rubbing his eyes to rid them of the deadly eye-watering serum of the onions. She stifled a chuckle at the furiousness of his motions.

"So, Mummy, how long are you planning on staying in Phoenix?" She made a point to ask in English.

"Two to three weeks. You know we have to go to Atlanta for Bosede's wedding, and your Daddy needs to get back to Lagos to prepare for the new semester."

Mummy was not getting the point; her entire sentence was in Yoruba. Even the numbers!

She tried a different tactic. "You are on speaker, Mummy. Henry's here."

"Oh. Henry, my dear. How are you doing?" Mummy switched to English seamlessly, not missing a beat.

Henry, whose face was finally returning to its normal color, responded in his best Yoruba accent. "*Mo wa, ma'am.*"[2]

Oyin glanced at him and smiled gratefully.

Where others would have turned up their noses at having to navigate an entirely new culture, and sometimes a new language, he embraced it for her. It was not always smooth-sailing, as a sizeable percentage of their few arguments had emerged from their differing cultures. But Oyin knew that no other man, regardless of his nationality, could ever love and understand her like Henry did.

"So Oyin tells me that you are coming this weekend. What time would you be arriving in Phoenix?" Henry asked.

"I don't know the flight details offhand, but I will *Whatsapp* Oyin."

"Oh, okay, ma'am."

"Oyinkan, talk to you later."

"Yes, mom. Bye!"

The phone call ended with a beep, and Oyin glanced at Henry, only to find a slight frown marring his features.

"Babe, what's up?"

"She doesn't like me," he said tightly. Then he clenched his jaw and looked away as if he had not meant for that to come out.

---

[2] *Mo wa* - I am good (in Yoruba)

"My mom?"

Henry did not respond; he continued to avoid her gaze instead.

Oyin was incredulous. "Why would you say that? I thought you were over that. I thought *we* were over this."

As Oyin added the diced onions into the thick pot of sauce and turned the stove knob to *Warm*, she errantly noted that Mummy would have a fit if she knew that her daughter was adding onions to a fully cooked sauce. Oyin shook her head to dismiss the thought and turned to look back at Henry.

Henry finally looked at her after a few moments and shook his head. "You wouldn't understand."

Okay, that hurt.

Oyin moved closer to her husband, who had since taken the pasta out of the pot and set it out to drain. "Okay, help me understand, then. Where is this coming from?"

He opened his eyes and stared at her until a resigned look crossed his face. "Never mind. Forget I said anything."

Oyin turned off the stove and came to stand in front of him. "Henry, we've had this conversation. You can't say things like that, and then expect me not to worry. You got really weird this morning, too, when I mentioned they were coming. I really want to know what this is about."

"And I *really* don't want to talk about it," Henry said.

"Sweetheart…" Oyin put her hands in his hair and began to massage his scalp gently.

She could feel him begin to relax beneath her ministrations.

Henry sighed. "It's just…I mean, there was the whole Dee thing."

Oyin's hands stilled.

Henry continued quickly. "Which, I promise, I have gotten over. But the sting of being unwanted remains, Oyin.

Every time I see or talk to her, I just don't...I - it is not very comfortable. It's almost like she is purposely -" he stopped.

"Purposely...?" Oyin prodded.

Henry said nothing for a few moments, his eyes decidedly fixed on a spot above her head.

But Oyin held her ground. "Finish your sentence, Henry."

"...trying to exclude me," he finally finished.

Oyin inwardly sighed. Mummy's use of complete Yoruba did not go unnoticed by Henry. But there was no way Mummy could have known that the phone was on speaker. So Mummy could not have intentionally "excluded" him from the conversation...right?

"Baby, I explained the whole Dee thing to you. Bringing you home as my fiancé was totally out of left-field for her. She just needs a little time. I don't think she means to exclude you, Henry."

Henry sighed again. "You don't get it. Never mind. Forget I said anything."

Oyin frowned. She was beginning to get irritated.

"I'm trying to understand here, Henry. You are not making it easy."

"There's no point. I don't want this to be a thing. Well, *continue* to be a thing."

She untangled her fingers from his hair and took a minuscule step backward.

Henry frowned at her actions. "Oyin, I don't want to argue. Can we just forget this and move on?"

Oyin didn't respond. Two could definitely play at the game.

She moved away, instead, and walked to the double-door fridge. She brought out two bottles of water and set them on the marble kitchen island that typically doubled as their dining table. Plucking a wide plate from the drying rack, she began dishing out their food.

"Oyin?" Henry called.

Ignoring him, she went on filling the plate with pasta, sauce, and then sautéed vegetables.

"Babe..." Henry called again.

Oyin placed the steaming plate of food on the island and sat on one of the tall stools that lined the island.

Then, she looked up at him. "Yeah?"

"Sea otters?"

Oyin glared at him. "I can't believe you right now."

Henry stared at her, unblinking, as an unsure smile started to form on his lips.

"Fine, sea otters," she conceded.

Henry smiled victoriously and moved to sit at the island.

Oyin said grace over the meal, and they dug in.

"Oyin, I'm sorry. I'm not trying to be difficult. It's just..." Henry started, after a few minutes of tension-filled silence.

Oyin looked up at him.

"I don't want to be that husband, you know? I would never want to be the cause of a conflict between you and your parents."

Oyin let out a sigh and nodded. "I know. But it's frustrating when I'm trying to help, and you won't meet me halfway."

"Sorry."

"Okay."

"And you know you can't just be throwing sea-otters out there whenever you like. It's annoying!" Oyin added, jabbing her fork in the air at him.

Henry scoffed playfully. "You are the one who brought up the idea of a safe word. Don't blame me."

Oyin narrowed her eyes at him half-joking, half-serious. "Whatever."

Henry chuckled lightly. "So, are we okay?"

He reached across the island to grab her idle hand.

Oyin looked at their entwined hands and then up at her husband. "Yeah, we are."

♥ ...15... ♥

CHAPTER 2

Marital Bliss...

Henry smiled at the sleeping form of his wife. It seemed he had been - they had been - doing a lot of smiling since they had exchanged vows.

He knew he was blessed to be married to Oyin. Sure, they had their arguments, but he would not trade a moment with her for anything money could buy.

"Thank You, Lord," he whispered as he gently caressed her arm that had curled around his waist overnight.

Her eyes opened slightly, in response to the touch, but soon closed back.

Henry chuckled softly. It was a Saturday, the only day he and Oyin got to sleep in.

But they could not do that today, he realized suddenly. His in-laws would be arriving in just four hours.

Just another thing that their presence threatened. The thought flashed through his mind. He shook his head as if to physically rid himself of the thought. He could not, *should not*, be bitter. Oyin had warned him that Nigerian customs were different from American traditions. He just had not anticipated how different.

On their first date, she told him story after story of her childhood. They were in stitches throughout the evening, and when the evening came to an end, Henry had left for his apartment without his heart.

Oyin's groundedness was one of the major reasons he had fallen in love with her, and he knew that he had her parents to thank for that. He also knew that her parents had a justifiable reason to be overprotective. She was their only biological child, after all. It was understandable that they wanted to have a big part in her life. He just wished that their part did not threaten his. He knew that Oyin would never do anything to hurt him or even make him uncomfortable. But *knowing* - gosh knowing - was so different from *feeling*.

The first time Oyin had brought him to meet her parents, she had made sure that they kept their Yoruba speaking to the barest minimum. But Henry had seen the look on Mrs. Johnson's face that day. She looked like she had been cheated. He had downloaded a Learn Yoruba app that very same night.

It was not an easy language to understand, even more difficult to speak, but he wanted Oyin to be proud to call him her husband. He wanted his in-laws to be proud of him, too. The first time he had told Oyin he loved her in Yoruba, she had smiled so brightly that it had made him feel like he had given her diamonds.

The object of his thoughts stirred as she began to wake up. He quickly shut his eyes, pretending to be asleep. If she knew he was awake, she would ask what was wrong, and he didn't want to lie. She had made him promise never to lie to her. If he really did not want her to know something, he could utter the safe word – *sea otters*. But Henry thought that calling it a safe word was ironic, considering the fact that it was anything but. Their argument on Sunday was a prime example.

Just then, Oyin snuggled closer to him and sleepily began trailing lines on his chest with her finger.

"You awake?" she mumbled.

He gave a noncommittal grunt.

"Let's pray?"

"Okay."

"Thank You, Lord, for another day. Thank You for giving us each other and thank You for giving us You. As we go on today, may our lives reflect You. Amen."

"Amen," he repeated.

Making no attempt to move, Oyin said, "We should probably get up."

He chuckled. "I don't see you standing up."

"Yeah. I said we should. I didn't say we would."

They lay for an hour, drifting in and out of sleep until Henry's alarm clock cut through the silence and jarred them awake. Henry looked over at the clock. It was almost 7 am.

"Baby, it is almost 7 am. If we are going to get ready and make a quick meal for your parents before they arrive, we should probably start now."

"Okay," she grumbled. "Let the day begin."

Henry felt like punching something. He and Oyin had been waiting for over an hour, but they were not there yet. Oyin had slept off in her exhaustion, her head on his shoulders. He knew he should not get angry at them. Their flight had been delayed for half an hour at Houston. They could not possibly have had any control over that. But still.

After he and Oyin had finally gotten out of bed and completed their morning devotion, Oyin had sped into the kitchen to make brunch, while he rushed to prepare one of the guest quarters.

Three hours later, they were ready and on their way to the airport. Henry had driven as fast as he could, considering the speed limit. It was rather annoying to arrive at Sky Harbor International Airport, only to wait.

Oyin had fallen asleep almost immediately. She seemed almost grateful for their delay, as it afforded her more time to sleep. He grinned.

Of course.

For the umpteenth time, he looked at the screens above him that showed flight status updates. The expected arrival time was in 20 minutes. He gave Oyin a slight nudge.

"Babe, they would be here soon. You want to get something to eat?"

"Hmm...yes, please."

"Maybe some bacon croissant sandwiches?"

She moaned. "Oh…I love you because you know me so well."

He laughed as he stood up. Extending a hand to her, he said, "Love you too, babe. Shall we?"

Henry drummed his fingers on the wheel. Next to him, Oyin chatted away with her mom while her dad dozed off. They were speaking rapid-fire Yoruba, which made it even more difficult for him to understand, but he didn't really care. Whenever Oyin spoke Yoruba, it always sounded endearing. Maybe it was because he knew that she would never say anything negative about him just because he could not understand her. Maybe it was because everything about her was just so lovable.

"Baby, did you hear what happened?" Oyin asked.

"Huh?" He turned to face her.

"Baby K just introduced her fiancé to Mummy and Daddy."

He looked at his mother-in-law through the rear-view mirror. "And how did you like him, Mrs. Johnson?"

She waved her hands noncommittally. "He was okay."

Oyin whispered, but loud enough for her mother to hear. "He is Nigerian, but not Yoruba."

Henry's interest doubled. "Really? What's his name?"

"Daodu."

"Da-woo-du?"

Oyin giggled. "Close enough."

Henry sneaked a peek at his mother-in-law. She was watching them intently. When his gaze met hers, she smiled tightly and looked away. His stomach turned.

Soon, they entered their neighborhood, and Oyin's dad perked up. "This is a very nice neighborhood. Tell me, Henry, do you have nice neighbors too?"

"Yes, sir. It is also very quiet, as you can probably tell," Henry replied.

"And how much do you think these houses would go for on the market?"

"I don't know a lot about real estate, seeing as I am an engineer." He chuckled. "But ours cost about 2.5 million."

Oyin's dad's eyes widened, and he whistled a peculiar tune that Henry could only interpret as "Wow."

Henry's face reddened. He didn't like it when people made a fuss about his or his parents' wealth. Honestly, they were just really blessed. His dad had his own successful architecture firm, and his mom was a successful chef in her own right. It was one of the many reasons his parents loved Oyin so much. She was an architect who knew how to cook. Not to mention the fact that she was so darn adorable.

After a few beats of silence, Oyin spoke up, "We're here."

Just then, Henry could have sworn that he heard Oyin's mom make a sound that sounded a lot like a snort.

He drove into the four-car garage and parked the car. He looked back at his in-laws, and while Oyin's dad had an astonished look on his face, Oyin's mom looked visibly unimpressed. His face grew even warmer.

Henry got out of the car and walked quickly to the trunk to offload it. Oyin appeared next to him, all smiles. "Here I am. Put me to work."

He turned to face her. "It's fine. I got it. Take your parents inside." There was a certain edge to his voice and, judging from Oyin's raised eyebrow, she had heard it too.

"You and me, we are going to have a talk later," she said, brooking no argument.

Giving him a glare, she picked up the two carry-ons and walked briskly into the house.

He sighed. *This was not how it was supposed to go.*

Lord, he prayed, *please help me navigate this situation.*

CHAPTER 3

Quintessential Overbearing

Mrs. Irene Johnson took another bite of her fried rice. Just like everything else in this house, it was amazing. She looked over at her son-in-law and her daughter. It was obvious to anyone with eyes that Oyinkan loved him. But did he love her like she deserved to be loved?

"This fried rice is really good, Oyinkan."

Oyinkan looked up and smiled. "Thanks, mom."

"Is this shrimp you put in it?"

Oyinkan smiled again. "No, mom. I used diced chicken breast instead because of Daddy. I didn't forget that he does not like seafood."

Dele chuckled from beside Irene. "*Ose, oyin mi*[3]. You know how your mom is."

Irene pursed her lips and said nothing in response. Oyin would not be there when Dele started complaining of an upset stomach in the middle of the night, yet Irene was the quintessential overbearing mother for asking.

Irene suppressed a sigh. It was just safer to change the subject.

"Your house is very beautiful. Pictures and WhatsApp video-calling do not do it justice. How many bedrooms?" Irene asked.

Oyinkan looked to Henry to answer. His face reddened instantly.

––––––––––––––––––––

[3] *Ose, oyin mi* – Thank you, my honey (in Yoruba).

"Five bedrooms, ma'am," he replied.

Irene narrowed her eyes infinitesimally. There was something about Henry that rubbed her the wrong way, something she could not put her finger on. Oh, she was sure that he liked Oyinkan—at least enough to marry her. But she did not trust him, did not trust his intentions. She decided that she would be watching him very carefully on this trip. She had to. No one else was.

"Hmm," was all she said out loud in response to Henry.

Next to her, Dele narrowed his eyes at her response and spoke up. "So, how is work going, Henry?"

"Quite well, sir." His face slowly began to return to its natural color. "I might be up for a promotion soon."

"Oh, that is good news!"

Dele then turned to Oyinkan accusingly. "You didn't tell us, Oyinkan. We would have been praying along with you."

Henry's face reddened *again*. There and then, Irene decided that she really didn't like the color red.

Oyinkan's eyes flashed, but she said nothing and just shrugged.

Henry looked at his wife. "I hadn't told Oyin just yet. I just found out recently."

Dele continued. "Oh, that's okay." He waved his hand in the air in a dismissing manner. "These women, they always want us to be telling them everything all the time. What if we forget?" he said with a conspiratorial grin.

Irene harrumphed.

Ose o [4], *Dele*, she thought sarcastically.

"There is a reason for that, and you know it. How would you like it if the tables were turned?" Irene asked her husband.

---

[4] *Ose o*, Dele - Thank you, Dele (Yoruba)

Dele leaned closer to Henry, as if to whisper, but not really, "Another thing that they do very well – guilt-tripping."

Irene glared at her husband. She wanted to pull him by the ear away from the table.

What was he thinking?

Dele glanced at her with mirth-filled eyes. "Oh, no. I recognize that look."

Irene knew her husband was just joking. It was his nature—a trait that Oyinkan inherited. But not in front of Henry. He did not need another reason to disrespect her.

Just then, she felt a gentle stirring in her spirit, as if the Lord were saying, **"When has he ever disrespected you?"**

She ignored the feeling. It didn't matter whether it had already happened. The point was that it was bound to happen. Henry couldn't help it if he tried; he wouldn't know respect even if it slapped him in the face.

Irene turned the television off and lay back down on the bed. It was almost 10 pm, but sleep eluded her. She had to sleep. Oyinkan had told them after dinner that they had to be in church by 9 am. She and Henry had responsibilities, and so they had to be there about 30 minutes before services. She tried to get more comfortable, but she still couldn't sleep. It wasn't the bed. It was probably the plushest bed she had ever slept on, but she still couldn't sleep.

She decided to get some warm milk. Maybe that would help her sleep. She came out of the rather large room and walked into the short hallway. The house truly was gorgeous and big! So big, she and Dele basically had an apartment of sorts to themselves. She was grateful that her daughter would get to live a comfortable life, but she didn't like that it came with Henry. He...just wasn't good enough for her.

Irene rounded the corner and padded down the long hall that seemed to go on forever. Just as she was beginning to think she should have paid more attention when Oyin had given them a tour of the house, she heard voices. Apparently, Henry and Oyinkan were still awake. She strained to hear what they were saying.

"...ever," Henry said.

"Babe, I know. Okay? I get it. But we are supposed to be a team," Oyinkan said.

"I know."

"When you feel affronted, I want to know. Whatever you're feeling, I want to know, especially if I can help."

Henry said something that Irene did not catch.

"Did you just find out today?" Oyinkan asked, in a slightly raised voice that Irene knew meant she was getting angry. Oyinkan was a very levelheaded person, and she did not get angry easily. She had always said that anger was not worth all the energy that it took her to express it.

"Yeah."

"That's just very convenient," she spat.

"What is that supposed to mean?"

"My parents get here, and all of a sudden, Olive is coming here too?"

"Oyin, there is more than enough space for everyone."

"That's not the point, and you know it. She is in love with you. Forgive me for not wanting her in my matrimonial home."

Irene's eyes widened.

"Oyin, you are blowing this way out of proportion. We've been best friends since we were in diapers. She is not in love with me. I told you. She is basically my sister."

"Is she now?"

"Babe…"

"Henry, don't "babe" me. Anyone with eyes can see that she loves you. I told you I was not comfortable with you guys' relationship, and you said she would not be around that much."

"Oyin, I have not seen her since our wedding, which was a year ago!"

There was a long silence, and Irene feared they might come out of the kitchen and discover that she had been eavesdropping. Making an about-turn, she tiptoed back to her room. Irene did not find sleep until 3 am.

CHAPTER 4

Olive Skin and Couple Things

Oyin was so frustrated. Olive was coming to visit them. Olive with her perfect olive skin, red hair, and blue eyes. With their matching hair and eye color, she and Henry looked like the perfect couple—everything matching. Ever since their argument on Saturday, she had barely talked to Henry. Anytime he wanted to start a conversation, she would just walk out of the room. She knew her mom suspected something, but she was not going to tell her. Mummy would blow it out of proportion.

You mean just like you are doing now? She heard the still, small voice in her spirit.

Admittedly, she was being a little petty. Marriage was not like courtship. It was a whole new ball game. Before they got married, whenever she had an argument with Henry, she would withdraw from him. It always drove him crazy, and Oyin knew that was why she was doing it now.

She looked up from her computer screen where she had AutoDesk open. It was only 11 am on Monday, and she was already tired. She knew that her fatigue stemmed from the state of her relationship with Henry, a situation that was mostly her fault. They didn't usually pray together on weekdays because they had different work hours. But even on Sunday, she had dressed up and left the room before Henry was fully awake, opting to do her morning devotion alone. Though praying together on Sunday mornings was more of an unofficial affair, judging from the look on

Henry's face when she saw him later that morning, she knew that he knew she had purposely gone out of her way to avoid praying with him and that it hurt him.

Looking back, Oyin realized that her actions were quite childish.

Where was the Christian in her?

Letting out a sigh, she picked up her phone. She couldn't help it. She was so insecure when it came to Henry. And though she would never admit it to another living soul, she still had some walls up with Henry, preventing herself from utter heartbreak if he, one day, decided she was not good enough for him anymore.

She hated that there was some part of her that felt this way, but that part recognized the fact that Henry was way out of her league. He had the whole package – rich, tall, handsome (*very handsome*), and God-fearing. And she couldn't help but feel like it was all a fluke, even over a year down the road.

The day he asked her to marry him was one of the best days of her life, second only to the day she got saved. He was a prince out of a fairytale, her very own Prince Charming. Even through their cultural differences, he had come out shining by trying to learn the Yoruba language, trying to learn Yoruba traditions, and traveling to Nigeria multiple times to meet the rest of her extended family who never seemed to remember that his name was Henry, not *Oyinbo*[5]. She knew it couldn't have been easy for him. But he did it all, never complaining.

Oyin was scared that Perfect Olive would come, and Henry would realize that he had made a huge mistake in picking her. And while Henry loved God too much and was

---

[5] *Oyinbo* – translates to foreigner/white person (Yoruba)

too noble to divorce her, his heart would be Olive's. And to Oyin, that was worse than a thousand divorces over.

Since Saturday, the end of their conversation was on a constant loop in her head, reminding Oyin that Olive's place in her husband's life was not one that could be easily dismissed.

"Oyin, you have to understand. Olive is a reminder of the good old days. Her visiting is not just about her. It's about home, about my life back in California."

Her heart had plummeted at that statement.

"I thought I was home."

"Babe, don't take it like that. I didn't mean it that way. Oyin..."

She had walked away at that. She knew that Henry had not meant it the way she took it. But it hurt hearing it out loud.

Unlocking her phone, she found his number and pressed 'Call.'

He picked on the fourth ring, though she definitely wasn't counting.

"Hey," she whispered.

"Hey," he responded, something like relief in his tone.

"I ..."

"I..."

They began talking at the same time, and Oyin giggled.

"Ah...It's so nice to hear that sound again. I missed you, Oyin. Your laughter makes the day worth it."

Oyin couldn't help it; her heart swooned. Everything was forgiven. He had the best one-liners in the world. "I know. I missed you too. I'm sorry I overreacted."

"No!" he protested. "You were right to react that way. I just...I didn't mean that my home was not with you. I just meant my life back in California."

"I know...that's why I'm sorry."

"Me too. I love you. Please don't ever do that again."

Oyin giggled. "Okay. Even though I'm sure, you will soon get tired of my face."

She had not meant for that to come out. She chuckled quickly, hoping Henry would take her sentence as a joke and not push any further.

"And, you will be tired of mine," he retorted playfully.

"Never! I'm sure you will still be as handsome as you are now," Oyin said, a relieved smile playing on her face.

"That's true--" Henry acquiesced confidently.

"Babe!" Oyin exclaimed, chuckling.

"--But you will be even more beautiful, and guys will still be trying to steal you from me," he finished.

They laughed.

There was a contented silence, and then Henry spoke up. "Sweetheart, if Olive's being here gets too much for you, you let me know. Okay?"

Oyin nodded. "Okay."

"I love you."

"I love you too."

Oyin dropped her phone and smiled.

"Thank You, Lord," she whispered.

Oyin giggled. "Okay, Mr. Know-it-all. Let's see what you got!"

Henry rolled his eyes. "Babe, my cooking is better than yours. Admit it."

Oyin scoffed. "Su-u-u-re."

"This *Alfred* food you are making, is it good?" Daddy called out from the breakfast nook that was big enough to have passed as the dining room in a smaller house.

Henry chuckled.

Oyin rolled her eyes. "It's alfredo, Daddy. And yes, it's good."

"Heh, I'm just asking. I don't want to eat something that will be making me go to the toilet," Daddy said matter-of-factly.

Henry chuckled again. "Mr. Johnson, don't worry. I'm sure you will enjoy it."

Daddy dropped the journal he was reading and sat up. "Which one is Mr. Johnson? *Oyin mi*, tell your husband. My name is Daddy, and Oyin's mom is Mummy. That way, there will be no confusion when your children start calling me Granddaddy," he finished with a playful wink.

Henry's eyes widened. "Of course, sir. Daddy, I mean."

Daddy sat back on the chaise lounge with a satisfied smile on his face, and Oyin wanted to run and hug him. She just realized how unwelcome Henry felt. And it must have been hard for him, she reckoned, considering the amount of love she had received from his family. This was a wonderful step in the right direction.

"Where is Mummy?" Oyin asked. She hopped onto the kitchen island and adjusted until she could see both Daddy and Henry without turning her neck.

"Oh. She went to see a friend. One of her friends lives near downtown Scottsdale. She called an Uber."

Oyin glanced at her husband as she responded to Daddy. "She could have waited for me to come back. I would have driven her. Or even, Henry?"

Daddy gave a dismissive wave. "She didn't want to bother you. She might not even like that you are making dinner when she is around to make it. You know how she is."

Oyin smiled at her husband. "It's okay; we cook on most nights."

Henry snorted. "You mean I cook on most nights."

"Yeah, well, who makes breakfast and weekend lunches? This girl!" Oyin pointed both her thumbs to her chest.

Henry continued to stir the contents of the pot. "But I help."

"So do I. I'm helping right now," Oyin retorted playfully.

He glanced back, a smirk on his face. "You mean by sitting over there, thumbing through your phone?"

"Of course. You need a pretty sight to keep you focused. I'm your muse."

Henry laughed. "That you are."

Oyin blew her husband a kiss. "Thanks for the meal, babe. You're the best."

She glanced over at Daddy. He was watching them, a happy-proud look on his face.

Henry had noticed, too, judging by the slight tinge of pink at the tips of his ears. She winked at him.

Thank You, Lord, she thought for the umpteenth time that day.

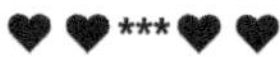

Oyin grunted as she stocked up the second guest bathroom. Olive was to arrive in a couple of days, and while she and Henry were back to the way things were before their Olive argument, she couldn't help but feel that Olive's presence was going to lead to even more Olive-themed arguments.

Great. Just what she needed, with Mummy and Daddy around.

She was tempted to go tell Henry that Olive's presence was already getting too much for her, and she hadn't even gotten here yet.

"Hey," Henry said from the doorway.

Oyin jumped, sending the bottles of soap and lotion in her hand to the floor. "Babe, don't scare me like that."

Henry chuckled. "You're the one who's jumpy. Don't blame that on me."

Already ruffled by the Olive issue, Oyin grumbled ill-humoredly.

Henry's eyes lit up as he continued to grin. "Sorry, sweetheart. Just came to see if you needed help."

Oyin looked up at him. "Um…yeah. I'm literally gathering stuff off the ground, stuff you made me drop."

He must have seen something in her face because he immediately sobered up and bent down to help. "Okay."

They worked together in silence, stocking the bathroom, and airing out the room. Oyin made a mental note to tell Agatha, their cleaning lady, to change the bedsheets and vacuum the floor before Olive's arrival.

"This Olive thing bothers you a lot, doesn't it?" Henry asked suddenly.

Oyin looked at her husband as he gazed back at her intently. Her stomach dropped. She knew she could say yes, and in Henry's kind and loving way, he would ask Olive not to come. But she couldn't do that to him. She shouldn't do that to him.

Henry was a good man. He put up with her, her idiosyncrasies, and her family. She would put up with Olive. She had to.

Ugh.

"To be honest, Henry, it bothers me. A lot, actually. But it's okay if she comes. She's your friend, and you should have her here if you want."

His eyes did not get any less intense. "Are you sure?"

"Yeah. I mean, I am not jumping with joy that she is coming. But my parents are here. It will be hypocritical of me to say that your 'best-friend-since-diapers' shouldn't come."

He smiled slightly. "Okay."

She moved to hug him. "It's okay, Henry. Really, I will be okay," she murmured into his chest.

He leaned into her embrace, tucking her head beneath his chin. "Okay."

"Ow, babe! The braids still hurt!" She punched his chest lightly.

He raised his head quickly, a blush coloring his face. "Sorry, sorry. I didn't know they still hurt."

Oyin giggled. "They don't. Just wanted to see you blush. You are so cute when you are embarrassed."

Henry gave her a sly smile. "You know, there are other ways to get me to blush." He wiggled his eyebrows for effect and looked pointedly to the bed.

"Henry!" Oyin exclaimed. "My parents are in the house."

Henry laughed and picked her off the ground with the familiarity and ease that come from repetition. "I am sure they know where babies come from."

Oyin laughed in response, as she wrapped her arms around his neck. "I love you, crazy man."

Henry grinned. "And I you, weird girl."

"Did we just get a new couple thing?"

"We definitely just got a new couple thing."

CHAPTER 5

Two Different Directions

Henry tapped his knee impatiently. Where the heck was she? He wanted to strain his neck, but he did not want to seem overeager. Oyin was already uncomfortable with the thought of Olive coming. He did not want to add fuel to the fire in any way. He glanced at Oyin next to him. She was deeply engrossed in her sketch.

His phone chimed as a text notification popped up.

Already at Gate C4. Where are you?

He broke into a grin. She was here!

He turned to Oyin. "Babe, she's here."

Oyin looked up at him with unfocused eyes. He knew that look; Oyin was dreaming up the next Sistine Chapel.

"Oyin…" he said again, gently.

"Hmm…"

"Olive's here."

Oyin blinked. "Oh, okay. Oh! Olive! Right! Where is she?"

He was about to reply when he spotted Olive a few feet from him. He waved furiously. "Olive!"

She looked at him, and her face broke into a grin. "Henry!"

She walked over to them as quickly as her heels would let her. As soon as she was close enough, she dropped her bags and flung herself into Henry's arms.

Henry hugged her tightly, raising her in mid-air.

It was really nice to see her again.

The sound of a throat clearing behind them caused Henry to untangle himself from the embrace. Olive did the same, wiping tears from her eyes.

With just as much gusto, she flung herself into Oyin's arms. Oyin's eyes widened, and she patted Olive's back awkwardly.

Soon, Olive extricated herself from the embrace. "It's so nice to see you both. It's been way too long."

Oyin laughed. "It's only been a year."

Olive chuckled in response. "Yeah, in Henry and Olive terms, that's like forever. I don't think we have ever gone this long without seeing each other. Have we, Beave?"

Henry grinned at the sound of the familiar pet name. Just as quickly, his grin fell as he took in Oyin's expression.

She looked…hurt?

Suddenly, he wasn't so excited anymore. He cleared his throat. "Y-Yeah. I don't think so either."

Oyin smiled way too brightly. "Well, let's head on to the parking lot. Henry, I can drive so you and Olive can catch up."

Henry tried to read Oyin, but he was too late. Her wall was already up. Anyone who didn't know better would think she was genuinely smiling. But he knew better.

"Are you sure? I don't mind driving," he said in a bid to placate her.

"Yep. I'm good. I would like to drive." She stretched her open palm to him. "Hand 'em over."

Biting back a sigh, he placed the keys to his Ford Mustang in her palm.

He laughed from the passenger seat, next to Oyin. "You can't be serious."

Olive nodded vigorously from the backseat. "I am."

He turned to Oyin, whose forehead was in a crease as she tried to maneuver them on the busy highway. "Babe, are you hearing this?"

Oyin glanced at him. "Hmm? I wasn't listening."

"Oh, Olive was just telling me about this guy at a dinner party who was following her around, practically begging for her number. So crazy."

Oyin gave a half-smile. "That sounds terrible. I'm sorry, Olive."

Olive waved her hand dismissively. "It's okay. I'm just waiting for the one, you know? The others are just wasting their time."

Henry laughed. "Wow. You sound so mature. Good for you," he said mockingly.

Olive swatted his arm playfully. Then she let her hand linger on his arm.

Seeing as she was sitting in the back seat and he was in the front passenger seat, it was a bit physically uncomfortable for him.

Oyin's words rang in his head. *She's in love with you.*

Uncomfortable...in more ways than one.

After what felt like an eternity, Olive dropped her hand. She winked at him. "You've been working out. Nice."

Henry's face felt warm.

Was that flirting? That wasn't flirting, right? Oyin was right next to him—that could not possibly be considered flirting. Surely, this was not the first time Olive had commented about his muscles. And that was okay. Right?

Ugh. He was so confused.

He glanced at Oyin. She seemed unaware of what just happened.

He breathed a sigh of relief. One less thing to worry about.

"So, Oh-yinn…" Olive said, putting emphasis on the first syllable instead of the second. The mispronunciation of her name was one of Oyin's pet peeves.

Henry jumped in quickly. "It's Oyin. Say it like you are singing it."

"Oh. Oyin. Got it. Sorry." She smiled sheepishly at Oyin.

Oyin just nodded with a slight smile.

Henry grimaced, resisting the urge to put his hand over his eyes. Oyin was being uncharacteristically quiet—that was never a good thing.

"So, your parents are around now?" Olive asked.

Oyin turned into their neighborhood. "Yeah. They are visiting for a few weeks."

Olive's eyes lit up. "So, how has it been to have them over?"

Oyin frowned slightly. "It's been okay, mostly. I guess. Henry would have to tell you more on the subject."

Oyin turned into their driveway and paused for the garage door to open fully.

Olive's mouth popped open. "Okay, wow."

She turned to Henry. "Your parents are buying my wedding gift. I can't believe this house. It's so nice!"

Henry chuckled. "Yeah."

The car came to a standstill in their garage, and Henry jumped out. He helped Olive out of the backseat, and then walked around to help Oyin out, but she was already out of the car. She threw the car keys to him.

She gave him a half-smile as he caught the keys in one hand. "Hey, I am going to check in with work; my phone has been buzzing incessantly for the past few minutes. Can you show Olive to her room and make her comfortable? I will see y'all in a bit."

Without waiting for a response, she turned to look at Olive, addressing her. "We have some leftovers in the fridge if you are hungry. Henry actually made his famous beef stew last night."

Olive smiled, a faint look of surprise on her face. "Oh, okay. I will definitely have some. Thank you."

Oyin smiled slightly in response. "Okay. I will catch up with you guys in a bit. Welcome to our house, Olive." She turned and walked into the house.

Henry watched her retreating figure till he couldn't see her anymore. He felt like he was being pulled in two different directions, and whichever way he picked would damn him.

Biting back a sigh, he turned to Olive. "Let's get this party started, shall we?"

Her smile was less bright than it had been moments before, her eyes unreadable. "You really love her, don't you?"

Henry's heart dropped. Maybe Oyin was right?

He chuckled awkwardly. "Of course, I do. I married her."

Olive nodded, her face blank. "Right. Of course. Just making conversation."

"So," she nudged him playfully, her smile back in place. "You want to give me the grand tour, Mr. I-now-own-a-mansion?"

Henry picked up her luggage, mentally berating himself. It was all in his head. *He* was all in his head. Of course, Olive didn't have those kinds of feelings for him. Oyin wasn't right. She couldn't be.

This was Olive, for goodness sake. He had seen her make a snot bubble big enough to fill her mouth.

"Yep. Come see how the grown-ups live," he responded.

She swatted him again. "Oh, shut up."

They entered the kitchen and its accompanying larger-than-a-nook area first, from the garage.

"So, this is the kitchen," he said in an exaggerated game-show host voice. "In this place, food is made by those who know how."

Olive giggled. "So, I get game-show host Henry? I like game-show host Henry!"

Henry continued, "And this," he motioned to the adjoining nook area, "is where back-seat cooks and commentators sit while the real work is being done. So, naturally, this is where you would sit in this scenario, Ms. Olive."

Olive snorted. "You are so stupid."

Henry laughed. "Follow me."

He walked her through the house, showing her the dining room, the living rooms, the family room, and the den.

"Wow. I didn't realize how big this house was. So many rooms," Olive commented.

"Yeah, and I have not even shown you the bedrooms. It's funny. We didn't realize it either until we came back from our honeymoon. For weeks, Oyin felt guilty. She even began drawing up a plan of how to repay them."

"Hmm…how many bedrooms?"

"Five. Four baths, and three walk-in closets. Thank God for Agatha. The whole house is just very rich-people-esque."

Olive looked at him strangely.

"What? What'd I say?" Henry laughed.

Olive shook her head at him. "Rich-people-esque?"

Henry chuckled. "Yeah, those were Oyin's words. I just borrowed them."

He came to a stop in front of the bedroom that had been set up for Olive. "Well, here we are. This room is the farthest from the living area of the house, and the closest bedroom to the outdoor pool. I thought you would like it. The pool is just right through that sliding door."

Olive smiled. "Yeah. I love it. It's nice to know you still remember."

Huh?

"Of course I do," he replied, confused. "Why wouldn't I remember that you love to swim?"

Olive frowned slightly. "It's nothing, Beave. Forget I said anything."

Henry opened his mouth to respond, but Olive spoke up quickly. Too quickly for it not to have been an attempt to cut him off and discontinue the conversation. "So, are you just going to stand there with my bags, or are you going to come in?"

Henry hesitated.

Navigating his new dynamic with Olive as a married man was hard enough without having to worry about her possibly being in love with him. Was it wrong to be alone in a room with Olive because he was a married man or because she was maybe in love with him?

But he didn't have time to ponder that question without seeming rude. He walked in and placed her bags next to her bed.

This was the first time in his life that he had felt unsure with Olive. With Olive, it had always been simple and easy. Oyin's words were making him doubt the intentions behind Olive's every word and action, and ...it just wasn't fair.

He didn't want to, but he could feel the stirrings of anger and resentment.

Olive made a purring sound that brought him back to the room. "I might never walk again if it means leaving this bed."

Henry chuckled lightly despite himself. "Make yourself comfortable, Olive. I'll see you in a bit."

❤ ❤ *** ❤ ❤

He found Oyin in their personal study curled up on the loveseat, her LapDesk on her lap as she furiously sketched away.

When he was just a few inches away from her, she looked up, her eyes bright with passionate excitement at whatever it was she was creating. "Hey."

That smile…

He forgot how to be angry.

He dropped next to her. "What are you up to?"

Oyin smiled. "Just sketching some ideas that came to me. It's for the Burrows project."

"I was going to startle you and steal a kiss or two in your confusion."

Oyin giggled. "Oh, really?"

Henry nodded. "Yup." A mischievous glint crept into his eyes. "But I don't want to kiss you again. It's too late."

She smacked his chest. "Ha-ha. Be deceiving yourself."

Henry chuckled. He loved her weirdly worded sentences—she called them *Yorubanized* English (another one of her weirdly worded phrases), but Henry chose to file them under *Oyin's Endearing Quirks*. They were so endearing that he found himself speaking like that once in a while.

Henry was trying to remember one that he had used recently when he saw Oyin move closer out of the corner of his eye.

He eyed her suspiciously. "What are you doing?"

"Just trying to show you what you're missing out on."

Henry pulled her closer. "So, does this mean you are not angry?"

"Why would I be angry?"

"I don't know. You just seemed upset at the airport and on the drive home."

Oyin turned to face him and automatically weaved her hands into his hair. "No. It's okay. I mean, I was. But that is not on you. It's just me. I am having a hard time getting used to the idea of you and Olive being best friends. But the Lord is working on it, don't worry."

"But baby," he drawled. "She was there while we were dating." Henry moved even closer to her so that their foreheads were almost touching.

"That's true. But we weren't married then. And I also wasn't sure...you know...about this. Dee was also in the picture, remember?"

"Believe me, I didn't forget," Henry said with a slight growl. "So now that we are exclusively together, it feels worse?"

"Yeah." Oyin moved the half-inch to place her forehead against his. "Something like that."

"Tell me how I can make it better."

Oyin smirked. "You can kiss me."

Henry smiled as his lips met hers. "Yes, ma'am."

CHAPTER 6

The Outing

Henry loved his Saturdays. It was a day when he could relax, sleep in, eat junk food, and spend precious time with his wife. This Saturday was not supposed to be any different. Everyone would have breakfast and then retire to do their own thing. But Oyin was not having that. She thought it would be nice if they all went out to something fun. They had had an argument on the issue the night before:

"Babe, I know you love your quiet Saturdays. But we haven't taken my parents out to do anything fun since they came here. Even Olive, for that matter. Tomorrow is literally the only day that we can."

"Yeah, but it's not like they sit at home bored," had been his weak retort.

"But they came to spend time with us, Henry, not watch all the Nigerian movies on Netflix."

He did not think that Oyin's parents, especially her mom, wanted to spend time with him, but he had kept that to himself.

Instead, he tried to find some way to exclude himself from the outing. He wasn't about to subject himself to Oyin's mom's judgmental looks.

In the end, Oyin had won the argument, not by some expert intellectual manipulation. She had simply kissed him.

Henry smiled to himself at the memory of what had followed, as he sat at the kitchen island, watching as Oyin informed every one of the plans over breakfast.

"Honestly, I think we should just go out and have fun. It doesn't even matter where we go. What does everyone think?"

Oyin's mom smiled. "Where are the good places we can go around here?"

Olive piped up. "I think we should go to Berry's Country Club! The girls can get massages, and the men can do whatever it is men do when women are having fun."

Henry laughed. "Wow. Thanks for including us, Olive."

Olive grinned and winked. "You are welcome."

"My *oyin*, I am all for going out. But Henry and I cannot sit around while you women have all the fun. We would like massages, too. *Abi*[6], Henry?" ~~Mr. Johnson~~ Daddy said.

Heat flooded his face as everyone turned to face him. "Y-Yes, sir. Of course, sir."

He mentally face-palmed.

Smooth, Henry.

He loved the fact that Daddy had so casually included him in the conversation, even using a Yoruba word. He wished he had said something witty and casual back. Instead, he had sounded like he had not understood what Daddy had said.

Great. Another weapon in Oyin's mom's "Disapprove of Henry" arsenal.

Weapon Number ∞: He does not understand simple Yoruba words, like abi.

---

[6] *Abi* - Right? / Isn't it? (in Yoruba/Nigerian Pidgin English)

Oyin giggled, and she rubbed his arm comfortingly. "Daddy, don't put my husband on the spot. Babe," she tapped his arm, "you don't have to get massages if you don't want."

Henry glanced at Daddy. "I mean, I don't mind getting massages, but I agree with Daddy. Let's find a place where we can all have fun together."

Daddy smiled widely at him, and a dimple, reminiscent of the one on Oyin's left cheek, popped out. "Exactly. Thank you."

Henry bit back a relieved sigh. It was just a smile, but it felt like everything. Riding off of that high, he glanced at Oyin's mom. Her face was scrunched up in a frown as she looked between Daddy and him.

He swallowed as their eyes met. He gave her a slight smile and looked away. He felt queasy. He didn't understand why she didn't like him.

Do you like her? He heard the Spirit whisper.

He didn't have time to dwell on that, as Oyin tapped his hand distractedly. "It's decided, then."

Henry whispered to Oyin. "What's decided?"

Oyin looked at him, her eyes dancing with laughter. "The ladies are going for massages. You and Daddy are going to play 'white man's ball.'"

"Wait, what? Why can't we go for massages too? And what is 'white man's ball'?

Oyin giggled. "Sorry, babe, it is already decided. You and Daddy are playing golf. Your protesting is a little belated; where were you?"

He rolled his eyes and grunted. "When did golf become 'white man's ball?'"

Oyin just giggled even more.

After only twenty minutes, Daddy gave up. "I can never learn how to play this game. It is not a curse."

Henry laughed again as he clutched his sides. "Daddy, I agree."

Daddy turned to him and gave him a mock glare. "The game is senseless. What is the point of using a stick to hit a ball when God gave us hands and feet?"

Henry started laughing again as he remembered the comedy show that had been the last thirty minutes. For some inexplicable reason, Daddy and the golf club didn't seem to be on the same wavelength. The only time he had successfully hit the golf ball, the stick had followed, flying across the field and almost hitting a caddie. Other times, the grass, the air, basically anything that was not the golf ball, had been on the receiving end of Daddy's swing. Henry had tried to hold his laughter at first, but after the caddie incident, Henry could no longer hold it in. It was just too funny!

At some point, Daddy had blamed the terrain for interrupting his mojo, so Henry had driven him to another area of the golf course. Daddy did not get any better.

Half an hour later, Henry had aching sides and teary eyes as proof of how much fun he had had, even though he had not played at all.

"Henry, *oya,*[7] come and take your stick." Daddy finally threw the golf club to him in defeat and stalked off to the golf cart.

Still chuckling, Henry took the offending club and put it with the others. He jogged to meet Daddy in the cart.

"Are you not playing again?" Daddy asked

---

[7] *oya* - a colloquial that means come on (in Yoruba/Nigerian Pidgin English)

"No. I think we have both had enough of golf for today," Henry said, biting back a laugh. Apparently, he was not successful in hiding his mirth as Daddy narrowed his eyes at him and looked away.

Henry laughed silently as he placed the bag in the cart and entered the cart to drive. A few weeks ago, if Oyin's dad had narrowed his eyes at him, laughter would have been the farthest thing on his mind. But today, it felt okay to laugh.

"So, Henry, when are you and Oyin planning to give me grandchildren?" Daddy said suddenly.

At least, it felt sudden to Henry.

"I – I mean…we, um…" he sputtered, heat rushing to his face.

Daddy chuckled. "Why do you always get red in the face?"

Henry flushed even deeper and said nothing.

"So, when now?"

Henry cleared his throat. "We haven't really talked about it, sir. But I know we want to spend a little time just being a couple before we start thinking about it."

"Hmm. Just don't wait too long. We are not getting any younger."

Henry smiled cheekily. "We will take that into consideration, sir."

Daddy rolled his eyes. "You are not serious."

For the sake of everyone in a ten-mile radius, Daddy did not handle a golf club for the rest of the day. He and Daddy had driven around the golf course for a while to pass the time as they waited for the ladies to finish up their massage sessions.

"So, where are we supposed to meet the ladies?" Daddy inquired.

"I think Oyin had said something about a green lunchroom. Let me text her to confirm."

He slid out his phone from his pocket to text Oyin.

"So, how does one get into a club like this? Do you pay for membership every month or..."?

Henry blushed. "My dad sits on the board for this club, so we do not pay for membership."

Daddy raised an eyebrow. "Really?"

Henry tried to bring his face heat under regulation and simply nodded.

He did not want Daddy to see him as a boy still attached to his father's purse strings. "I mean, we do not come that often."

"I thought your parents lived in California."

"They do. This club is part of a chain of clubs headquartered in San Jose, California."

"I see."

Before Henry could decide whether Daddy was intimidated or unimpressed or simply unaffected by this revelation, his phone rang. It was Oyin.

"Hey, babe?"

"Hey," she responded. "We are already at the Green Room getting a table. Where are you guys?"

"Didn't you see my text?" he inquired.

"No, babe, are you on your way?" she asked, a little curtly.

Henry stifled a sigh. He was not having a conversation-into-an-argument with Oyin with Daddy next to him.

"We'll be there in a couple of minutes."

"Okay."

"Alright. Bye. Love you."

She sighed. "Sorry. Love you, too. See you in a bit."

In less than two minutes, Henry and Daddy walked into the Green Room and spotted the ladies immediately.

As soon as Oyin saw him, relief flooded her face, and she beamed at him.

"Over here, Henry!" she waved.

Daddy whisper-yelled next to him just as they approached the table. "If only someone was happy to see me as Oyin is to see her husband."

Oyin's mom gave Daddy a mock-glare and then, miracle of all miracles, actually stuck her tongue out at him.

Daddy laughed, a full belly laugh that made everyone else at the table dissolve into chuckles.

Henry was seated next to Olive, as that was the only seat available apart from the one next to Oyin's mom, which Daddy sat in.

Olive whispered to him in a mock-serious tone. "I am happy to see you, too. Just FYI."

Henry rolled his eyes. "Yeah, right."

Olive nudged him playfully and proceeded to rest her head on his shoulder. "I am heartbroken you don't believe me," she said dramatically.

Henry just chuckled and shook his head at her. Then he looked over at Oyin. "What looks good on the menu, babe?"

The rest of the day passed by quickly, and unexpectedly, Henry had a lot of fun. What made the day extra special, Henry mused that day later in bed, was the fact that he had been able to bond with Daddy.

Before Oyin's parents had arrived, Henry was ready for them to leave. But now, he didn't mind them—or rather, *him*—staying a while longer.

"Why are you smiling?" Oyin asked as she climbed into bed, her face free of makeup and her eyes red, *presumably* from the prolonged contact with water.

"Just thinking about happy things."

Oyin chuckled dryly. "Like how much you love me?"

Even though she was smiling, there was a seriousness in her eyes—like she really wanted to know if he loved her.

He frowned slightly. "Babe, you know I love you."

After a beat, he asked, "Where is this coming from?"

Oyin shrugged and started to get comfortable on the bed, all the while avoiding his eyes.

"O?"

"Yes," she said, still not looking at him.

"Look at me."

"I don't want to," she said.

"Why?"

"Because."

Henry sighed. "Babe, come on."

She finally looked at him, but only for a second. "Are you happy now?" she asked gruffly.

"I'm only trying to make sure you're okay."

She said nothing.

Henry grunted. He loved Oyin, but sometimes she drove him crazy, especially when she began to withdraw from him like she was doing right now. It really annoyed him that it had only taken a few sentences from a surly Oyin to bring him down from cloud nine.

He flipped over to face away from Oyin and reached up to turn off his bedside lamp.

After a few minutes, Oyin spoke, "Henry?"

"Yeah," he answered curtly.

Usually, when Oyin pulled away from him, it made him very upset, where he was more sad than angry. But tonight, he was more angry than sad.

"It's your turn to pray tonight."

He had hoped that Oyin wanted to apologize or at least fix the situation in some way. The fact that she ignored the tension made him even angrier.

He took a deep breath and tried to let go of his anger, knowing that whatever he said to God in his angry state of mind would not go past the ceiling.

"Lord, we thank You for today. Thank You for our loved ones, and for giving us laughter and love today. We ask that Your loving protection will be ours this night. All this we ask in Jesus' Name. Amen."

"Amen," Oyin whispered.

Henry decided that he was not going to be the one to initiate a conversation. If she did not want to address the situation, so be it. He clutched the covers tightly around his shoulders and closed his eyes.

"...Do not let the sun set on your anger."

The Lord was just going to have to forgive him this once.

CHAPTER 7

Essential Assessment Skills for Couple and Family Therapists

Olive sighed as she absently thumbed through her *Essential Assessment Skills for Couple and Family Therapists* textbook. She was getting nowhere. She had decided to go for her MFT program because she loved love. Family was the most important thing to her, even though she had not really had the white-picket-fence kind of family. Her mom had skipped out early in the game before Olive was five. Her father had tried his best, but in trying to be both parents, he had ended up being none.

From the first day Olive had seen Henry's family, she knew she wanted something like what they had. A few years later, she found out who she wanted it with. But he had never seen it with her.

When Henry first introduced Oyin to Olive as his girlfriend, she thought he was just experimenting – as horrible a thought as that was.

That all changed when he began to mistakenly refer to her as 'Oyin.' Olive had found it so annoying that he had found it easier to say 'Oyin,' a name he had only known for a few months than to say 'Olive,' a name he had practically heard all his life.

Then, one day, to further rub salt into the gaping wound in her heart, he had asked her what kind of ring she thought Oyin would like.

That day, her heart had shattered into a million pieces. For years, she had hoped and waited for him to smile at her with something other than friendship in his eyes. His question had destroyed every ounce of hope she had left.

She had taken the heartbreak pretty well, even attending both of their weddings. She had drawn the line at being involved in the planning, though. When Henry had asked about her aloofness, she had claimed preoccupation with her graduate school applications. He had not probed further, too focused on his bride-to-be and her family.

Now, over a year later, she was still as in love with him as she had ever been. And boy, she had tried so hard not to love him. When Henry had called to invite her over for a couple of weeks, claiming he missed her and needed a familiar face, she had jumped at the opportunity to see him.

She missed her best friend. And a part of her heart, the part that was still in love with him (so, the whole thing), hoped that maybe he realized that he, too, was in love with her.

She looked at the time. It was 12:58 pm. They were supposed to be back from church by now. She sighed as her stomach grumbled. This was the part of Henry that she did not understand, which Oyin apparently did. How could a normal guy like Henry actually believe that there was a Higher Being somewhere who controlled affairs on earth?

She shook her head. Not her. She would stick to her empirical facts, intelligent reasoning, and personal improvement. Thank you very much. She could not deny, though, that his beliefs were what had set him apart from other guys from middle school all the way to college. In late middle school, when guys became more interested in lady parts, Henry had always been a gentleman. Even in college, he exuded a maturity that drew girls to him. Every girl wanted a nice guy, and Henry was it. He had been it for her, too.

Feeling a little guilty at having these thoughts in Henry's matrimonial home, she shook her head as if to physically ward away the thoughts. She stood from her bed, grabbed her laptop and phone, and headed to the kitchen.

Before long, she was seated comfortably at the kitchen island, a plate of hot food to her right, and an empty Microsoft Word Document in front of her.

She had not been staring at the page long when she heard the steady whirring of the garage motor. She looked at her food and laptop. Could she make her escape before someone saw her?

The very-near sound of Oyin's snort-filled laughter answered her.

Great. She could not leave without them spotting her.

Oyin and her father walked in just then, arms linked, as they laughed. On seeing her, the laughter in Oyin's eyes faded, and Olive swore Oyin stood a little straighter.

"Hey, Olive," Oyin said.

"Hey." Olive looked over at Oyin's father. "Hi, Mr. Johnson."

The grin on his face became even wider as he walked closer to her. "Hello, miss. I have been wondering when I will actually get to speak to the other lady guest in this house."

She smiled tentatively. "I'm sorry. My room is all the way in the back of the house. But we did all go out together yesterday, though I did not ride with you."

Olive had ridden Henry's bicycle to and from the club yesterday, rather than ride in Oyin's BMW with the rest of the group. It was only a 15-minute bike ride, and she had made it her workout for the day.

"Oh, it is okay." He waved away her excuse. "You spent all morning with my wife. And since we are one flesh, you have indirectly spent time with me, *abi* Oyin?" he asked with a cheeky grin on his face.

Oyin simply shrugged and walked to open the fridge.

Oyin and her mother had barely said a word to her during their massage sessions, but okay...

Olive eyed him amusedly. "Okay. I mean, sure."

"I am just joking. You can call me Uncle Dele. Pleasure to directly meet you," he said, a grin still on his face.

"Olive. You can call me Olive."

"So Oyin tells me you don't go to church. Why?"

Well, he was definitely direct. And why were Oyin and her dad talking about her?

Olive's smile slipped a little. "I am agnostic."

He simply raised an eyebrow. "Really?"

Olive nodded. "Yes."

She was not about to discuss religion with her nemesis' father, so she began to pack up, hoping he would get the message.

He did. "Okay, well. I will be praying for you."

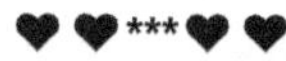

There were two things that Olive noticed as they all sat around the dinner table eating Chinese takeout. One, Oyin's dad, Uncle Dele, seemed to have a perpetual smile on his face. Second and most importantly, Oyin and Henry were not talking to each other. Sure, they talked to one another, but it was out of necessity. Olive knew she should not be glad at this development; in fact, she was sure she wasn't. But for inexplicable reasons, a small smile played on her lips.

There was nothing wrong with smiling.

"So, Olive. Have you decided what your thesis is going to be about?" Henry asked.

She frowned slightly. "No."

She continued. "I thought I knew what I wanted to do, but things just didn't seem to click. So now I am back to square one."

Uncle Dele chuckled. "Don't worry about it. It is when you are least expecting it that God will whisper the right topic to you. You just have to be calm and listen."

Okay...

She looked at Henry, trying to read his expression.

He had been feeding her similar sentences for years. Some days, she wanted to believe him—that there was someone who cared for her, enough to die for her. But she couldn't—there was too much bad in her life, in the world.

She looked back at Uncle Dele and gave a smile, albeit a fake one. "Of course."

"What was the previous topic that didn't click?" Oyin asked.

What was with everyone wanting to talk to her?

The day before, they had not talked much, what with the natural awkwardness that came with being semi-naked in the same room with strangers. It wasn't until the meal that Olive felt comfortable enough to talk and laugh, and that was only with Henry. She did not think that Oyin or her mother liked her very much.

She would never admit it, but Uncle Dele's welcoming attitude had meant a lot—it had opened a tiny crack in the tough shield around her heart.

Refocusing, she saw that everyone was staring at her, waiting for an answer.

Oh! What was the question?

"Um...it was on the difference in marriage norms in the 19th century and 21st century," she said, recovering quickly.

Oyin smiled. "Oh, I love the 19th century. That was the era of romance, in my opinion."

Olive nodded. "I thought so too. But when I began to research, I got blocked. That was when I realized I am much better working on observable case-studies—relationships here and now."

"That makes sense," Oyin said.

"So, have you found couples to use for your case study?" Uncle Dele asked, interested.

Olive remembered Henry saying something about Oyin's father being an academically renowned professor in Africa.

"No. I have not really been thinking about it. Instead, I have been trying to find a way to circumvent. I mean, what couple would be willing to be lab rats for my thesis?" Olive chuckled.

"How about Oyin and Henry?" Oyin's mom spoke for the first time that night.

Olive was not sure what to make of her. She seemed to be reserved, but Olive was positive that nothing escaped her notice.

Wait…what?

"I…I'm s-sorry?" Olive sputtered.

"Oyin and Henry." Oyin's mom pointed a finger at them. "I'm sure they will be happy to help."

That was actually not a bad idea.

"What do you guys think?" Olive looked at the couple in question. They were not looking at each other. In fact, they were actively avoiding each other's eyes.

Olive bit back a smile. Her initial diagnosis had been correct. There was trouble in paradise.

She was only happy because a correct diagnosis was a notch in the belt of a counselor-in-training. No other reason, whatsoever. None.

Stop smiling, Olive.

Finally, Oyin shrugged, glancing at Henry. "It's fine with me."

Henry shot her a look. "Me too."

Hmm…this was going to be interesting.

"Are you sure about this?" Dr. Marigold asked.

"Of course, I am sure. It makes perfect sense."

"At the risk of sounding like a jerk, I've gotta ask. Are your intentions behind this purely scientific?"

"What is that supposed to mean?"

"Olive, you know I had reservations about your going to Phoenix. You are trying to get over him. I don't think studying his marital relationship is healthy for you."

Olive clenched her jaw tightly. "Let me be the judge of that."

She did not realize that being in a graduate class with a bunch of her peers would end up being a support group of sorts, with her professor and mentor, Dr. Marigold, acting as the class sponsor.

One day, after a 4-hour long class where she had talked about Henry, they had all left the class with tear-stained faces. Dr. Marigold had, since then, began to pay special attention to her emotional health and treat her like a porcelain figurine placed dangerously close to the edge of a shelf. It irked her to no end, and she hated the part of her that was glad that someone cared.

Dr. Marigold sighed. "I am just concerned, Olive. That's all. But if you're sure?"

"I'm sure."

"Okay. Write up a proposal and get it to me by the end of the week. I will look over it, and we will go from there."

Olive breathed a sigh of relief. If her mentor was not on board, her thesis would not see the light of day.

"Thank you, Doctor Marigold."

"Dave," he said firmly.

Olive was not sure how professional it was to call her mentor by his first name. But he had been asking her for so long, a couple of days after what Olive had dubbed the "confession class," and she did not want him to change his mind about her thesis.

"Thank you, Dave."

She dropped her phone on the desk and tapped her touchpad to wake her laptop. She just had to figure out exactly what part of their relationship she wanted to study.

CHAPTER 8

Proverbs 31

Oyin sighed as she dropped the phone receiver. This was an irritating déjà vu moment. The only difference was Henry had made an effort—efforts! —to talk to her the last time. Every time that she had ever withdrawn from him, really. But it had been three days since that ill-fated conversation.

Three days!

Her stomach twisted in anger and jealousy. Maybe the sting of her withdrawal did not hurt as much because Olive was around.

What made the situation worse was that she and Henry were never really alone. And when they finally were, one of them was sleeping.

Oyin missed her husband, but she was not going to break first. If he didn't want to talk to her, if he'd rather talk to Olive, then so be it.

Or you could talk to him. She heard the Lord say.

Oyin shook her head. He was the one at fault. He was the one who brought Olive into their matrimonial home. He was the one flirting with her at the lunch table, in front of her parents! He was the one who needed to address the issue. But if he would rather not, two could play the game.

"I'm sorry, Lord. I don't want to offend You, but he doesn't get to flirt with Olive in front of me and have it be okay. You understand, right?"

The peace she was expecting did not come.

She sighed again.

Oyin tapped her hand on the wheel impatiently as she waited for the traffic light to turn green. Today at work had been awful. She loved her job. She loved creating new designs; she loved the autonomy and freedom. But most of all, she loved seeing her clients' faces light up when they saw a design that they loved. She had felt none of that today.

"Lord Jesus, I need Your peace."

Nothing.

Thankfully, there hadn't been much to do. The next deadline was months away. So, she had done some high-level micromanagement and eaten a solo lunch. Henry hadn't called to flirt with her as he usually did when he got a chance.

Her stomach had been in knots all day. As she pulled into her driveway, the knots grew even bigger.

She parked her car in the garage, picked up her purse, and headed for the kitchen. She hoped a glass of cold water would help ease the knots in her stomach.

She was not prepared, however, for the sight that greeted her as she entered the kitchen. Olive and Henry were sitting very close, looking like the picture-perfect couple, straight from the covers of *Thriving Family*. Henry was smiling at something Olive had said.

Her stomach decided to abandon knotting and started cartwheeling.

"Hi." She hated how tiny and injured her voice sounded.

They both looked up. While Olive at least had the decency to blush, Henry, Mr.-I-blush-easily, did not even flinch.

"Hey, Oyin. We were just working on my thesis. Come on in." Olive said, with a smile.

Henry said nothing.

Oyin gritted her teeth.

Come on in?

She resisted the urge to shout, 'It's my house, my matrimonial house. Not yours!'

She pasted a smile on her face. "It's okay. I just wanted to grab a bottle of water. If you need me, I will be in *my* study."

The slight reddening of Henry's face indicated that he had understood the jab.

It was their study. She knew that her word choice would hurt him. It did.

Good.

She walked around them to the refrigerator. As she retrieved her water, she noticed the refrigerator was messy, even though Agatha had been scheduled to come in earlier in the day to clean.

Forgetting herself, she absentmindedly asked. "Babe, do you know if Agatha came today?"

Realizing the term of endearment that she had just used, she clamped her lips together. Henry turned to face her, and the intensity in his eyes almost made her take a step back.

After a very long moment, he answered. "No, she didn't. She called. She would be here tomorrow."

"Oh. Okay."

With a death grip on her bottle of water, she headed out of the kitchen.

Then she heard Olive speak, and she stopped in her tracks. "Are you guys okay?"

Henry cleared his throat and said tightly. "Why? Why wouldn't we be?"

Olive chuckled. "Don't bite my head off. I am just asking."

Not wanting to hear anymore, Oyin walked briskly towards their bedroom, where the effects of the kitchen's bad acoustics couldn't be heard.

Not long after, she was curled on her favorite loveseat, flipping through her Bible. She hadn't read the Scriptures in a few days, and she needed to catch up. Looking through her reading timetable, she opened to Proverbs 31 and began to read.

Her eyes absently traced the words on the page while her mind replayed the image of Olive and Henry together. Then she reached verse 10.

A wife of noble character who can find? She is worth far more than rubies.

She felt the Lord gently touch her heart with the words. She was not a worth-more-than-rubies wife to her husband. She wouldn't even talk to him.

She continued.

Her husband has full confidence in her and lacks nothing of value. She brings him good, not harm all the days of her life.

Oyin paused. She couldn't remember the last time she had complimented him or told him she loved him, probably before Olive came. It seemed all she had been bringing her husband since last week was harm. Almost as if she was punishing him for Olive's presence.

Oh no.

Henry had been uncomfortable with her parents' coming too. But he had handled it way better than she had.

"Lord, I have not been a very good wife. Help me be better."

And the peace finally came.

❤ ❤ *** ❤ ❤

Immediately after she finished her Bible reading, Oyin decided she was going to make dinner. Usually, Henry did it, but tonight, she wanted to be a Proverbs 31 woman for her husband. Humming, she tidied their rooms and headed to the kitchen.

Henry was already there, chopping onions.

"Hey," she said.

He looked up at her. "Hey." He continued chopping onions.

Then silence.

She cleared her throat awkwardly. "What are you making?"

"Potato salad," he said without looking up.

"Oh. Can I help?"

He looked at her again, seemingly unconcerned. "Suit yourself."

Oyin paused.

Why was he being like this?

Anger rose in her, but she attempted to keep it at bay.

She was trying here! Why won't he meet her halfway?

"Beave!" Olive's voice cut through the awkward silence that reigned in the kitchen.

"There you are!" Olive walked briskly towards the kitchen sink where Henry stood. She had not noticed Oyin.

"Dr. Marigold approved the proposal. He was impressed that I got it to him so quickly," she beamed.

Henry smiled a huge smile that showed his dimples, a smile Oyin had thought was reserved for her.

Apparently not.

"That's good news, Olive."

Oyin's heart hurt. She felt like she was being eaten up from the inside. Tears gathered in her eyes, and it was all she could do to not let them fall.

She backed up and walked away from the kitchen as quickly as she could, angrily brushing the tears that had begun to leak from her eyes.

"Oyinkan, is that you?"

At the sound of her mother's voice, Oyin walked even faster. She could not allow Mummy to see her crying. That would lead to questions she was not ready to answer and 'I-told-you-so' laden looks.

She entered their bedroom and slumped on the bed. She knew, rather than heard, Mummy was following her and would soon come into the room.

She cleaned her face as quickly as she could and sat up on their bed. Two seconds later, Mummy walked in.

"Oyinkan."

"*Ekaasan*[8] mummy." Oyin knelt on the bed as a sign of respect and sat back down.

"*Ki lo se e?*"[9]

Oyin sniffed. "Nothing. Why?"

"You are lying. Your eyes are red. What's wrong?"

"Nothing that can't be fixed," Oyin said, even though she was not entirely sure she believed that.

Mummy narrowed her eyes. "Is Henry maltreating you?"

Oyin's heart thudded painfully. "Mummy, this is between Henry and me."

Mummy shut the door behind her, drew closer, and sat on the edge of the bed.

"Oyinkan, this is for your own good. If there is something that needs to be done, talk. Talk now before your daddy and I leave!"

---

[8] *Ekaasan* - Good afternoon. (Yoruba)

[9] *ki lo se e* – What's wrong with you? (Yoruba)

Oyin was too emotionally tired to get upset at Mummy's insinuations. "Mummy, there is nothing to talk about. I'm tired now, and I just want to sleep."

Mummy's eyes widened. "It is not even eight o'clock yet. Hmm! Oyinkansola! Oyinkansola!! Oyinkansola!!!"

"How many times did I call you?"

"Three times," Oyin said in a deadpan voice.

"I don't want to cry over you!"

She should have defended Henry. She should not have let Mummy think *whatever Mummy was thinking*. But Oyin was too angry at him to care. If he would rather be with Olive than his wife, then he deserved all the snide remarks and looks Mummy would give him.

Oyin looked up. Mummy was still talking. "…I told you. But you never listen to somebody. Now see, you are in your room with red eyes."

Oyin sighed. "Mummy, I love you. But I just want to sleep."

To show Mummy she was serious, Oyin lay back on the bed and covered herself with a coverlet.

Mummy huffed. "*Mo sa ti so temi.*"[10]

"Yes, Ma."

Mummy turned on her heel and left the room, closing the door a little too forcefully.

And just like that, the tears started again, like they had on Saturday every time she remembered the image of Olive's head on her husband's shoulder.

"Lord, I can't be a Proverbs 31 wife. I tried, but I can't."

For the first time since Oyin married Henry, she cried herself to sleep, fully clothed.

---

[10]*Mo sa ti so temi* - I have said my piece

CHAPTER 9

Let's Hope It Doesn't Come to That

Ọ̀rọ̀ àgbà bí o sẹ láàrọ́, bópẹ́ títí a sẹ lọjọ́ alẹ́.[11]

Mrs. Irene Johnson brushed her teeth furiously, holding the sink with her unengaged hand with just as much fury.

She could not believe that what she had feared from the get-go was actually happening. On the other hand, she *could* believe it. But that was the problem, wasn't it?

She had told Oyin, told Dele, told Baby K. But no one listened. They thought she was being paranoid. Even called her closed-minded and racist. But she knew. She knew. She just knew.

This was what she had been telling them. The cultures were just too different. There would be a lot of misunderstandings. Who knows how many times Oyin had run to her room crying?

That Henry boy thought he had everyone fooled. She had almost fallen for his act. Almost.

This was exactly what Ore, her friend, had been talking about. And Ore would know. Her nephew had been married to a white woman, and of course, they were separated now.

Irene huffed. She would make it a point to call Ore tomorrow to find out how they were faring.

---

[11]*Oro agba bi o se laro, bope titi a se lojo ale* - The words of the old and wise always ring true, no matter how long it takes (Yoruba)

"Irene, take it easy in there. I can hear the sink groaning *o!*" Dele shouted from the bedroom.

Irene *hissed* [12] as she rinsed the toothpaste out of her toothbrush. She was in no mood tonight for Dele's jokes.

She needed to find out what was going on and how she could fix it.

Dele chuckled as he saw her walk out of the bathroom. "Why are you frowning now?"

Irene narrowed her eyes at him and got into her side of the bed.

"So, you are not going to talk to me?" Dele asked, switching their conversation to Yoruba.

Irene sighed. "Dele. I'm not in the mood. Leave me alone," she responded in Yoruba.

Dele looked at her, the amusement fading from his features. "What happened?"

"Oyinkan was crying earlier this evening."

Dele sat up abruptly. "What? Do you know what happened?"

"No, she won't tell me. But I know it is Henry, Dele. I just know."

"Don't say that. You don't know for sure. It could be anything."

Irene rolled her eyes. "You've come again. Why else would she be crying?"

Dele sighed. "I don't know, Irene. But don't go jumping to conclusions."

"When I was telling everybody, in the beginning, I was being closed-minded. Now see."

---

[12] The word *hiss* here refers to a sound Nigerians make that typically expresses disapproval. The *hiss* sound is produced by sucking air through the teeth.

Dele lay back down on the bed. "Irene, I've said my own. Don't destroy your daughter's marriage with your own hands."

He faced the other side and left Irene to her thoughts.

Could she really be jumping to conclusions?

Irene settled into bed. No, she was not jumping to conclusions.

The next morning, Irene was no closer to figuring out what was going on. It was driving her crazy. She spent all morning deep cleaning the kitchen because chores helped her think, but she still didn't know. She didn't think that Henry was beating Oyin. But what could he have done that would have made Oyin cry? Oyin was not one to shed tears easily. In fact, even when she had been spanked as a child, she would scream and scream, but actual tears were few and far between.

Irene huffed. She was going to get to the bottom of this even if it meant Oyin leaving Phoenix with her and Dele.

What God has joined together, let no man put asunder.

The rebuke came—as clear as day.

"Well, Lord. Hopefully, it doesn't come to that stage."

By noon, every surface in the kitchen gleamed. Irene threw the last wad of paper towels in the trash and heaved a sigh as she looked around. If only real life could be as easily cleaned up.

She made a mental note to tell Oyinkan that their house-help did not need to come clean anymore.

Just then, Dele walked into the kitchen area, whistling.

"Irie-Irie," he greeted.

Irene just gave him a tired half-smile, slumped into the nearest stool, and laid her head on the kitchen island.

"What's wrong?" Dele asked, taking the stool closest to her.

"I'm just worried about Oyinkan."

Dele sighed and rubbed his hand on Irene's back soothingly. "I know. But I think you are making a mountain out of a molehill. Whatever it is, I'm sure they will work it out."

Irene frowned. "But you didn't see her, Dele! Her eyes were so red, and immediately I left the room. She started sobbing. Oyinkan does not cry!"

Dele's face mirrored hers, and he gave a small sigh. "I know a little about Henry. And from what I've seen, I don't think he would intentionally hurt her. Who knows, maybe Oyin is just on her period."

He tried to chuckle, but it came out more like a grimace.

Irene shook her head as if to ward off the tears that were gathering in her eyes. "I'm just scared, Dele. We have been hearing all these stories. Remember Bisi, my friend from U.I? She was just telling me that her daughter is living separately from her husband, after repeated abuse. And those ones are both Yoruba! What if that happens to Oyin, too? How would we know? How would we be able to intervene? All the way from Nigeria!"

Dele shook his head. "That won't happen to her. We prayed. Oyin prayed. And we asked God to take control. We have to trust that He would take control."

Irene nodded. It wasn't necessarily that she didn't trust God to take control, per se. This was just too close to her heart. Oyin was her only living biological child—the only proof that she wasn't a fruitless, barren woman. She couldn't take the chance that God may deem it fit to take Oyin too.

A shudder passed through Irene's body at the thought of that.

"Maybe we should talk to them," Dele proffered.

Irene looked up. Yes. Maybe that could work. "Yes. We can just talk to them and tell them what we are seeing."

"We don't even have to say anything specific. Just frame it like we are giving them advice before we leave."

Irene smiled at her husband.

Yes. This would work.

"Thank you, Dele."

He smiled at her, his dimple popping out. "Oyin is our daughter, Irene. Everything will be alright."

CHAPTER 10

The Withdrawal Thing

Henry ran his hand through his hair for the umpteenth time and *hissed* in frustration. Even that simple action reminded him of Oyin—how she liked to run her hands through his hair and mess up its carefully coiffured style. When she first began doing it, he had always complained. But after a while, he grew to enjoy it and didn't even bother to style it anymore.

He missed her. Boy, he missed her. But she didn't seem to care. His yearning was hanging off of him, begging for her to notice. But all he got were short, to-the-point conversations.

She had walked into the kitchen the day before, radiant as the sunset cast a glow on her beautiful umber skin, and she looked like a haloed angel. It was all he could do to hold on tightly to the knife instead of gathering her in his arms and kissing her like he really wanted to.

Since when did he have to hold himself back from his wife?

Henry hated this feeling. It was reminiscent of the first year of their courtship when he wasn't sure how she felt about him. There had been another guy in the picture, and Oyin had seemed indecisive. He had wanted to give her his everything then, but he didn't want to come on too strong and scare her off.

She had married him. He had won the girl. But once in a while, when she withdrew from him like she couldn't care less, it made him wonder if he was the loser. Maybe he was the loser who married someone who didn't love him as much as he loved her.

Henry unbuttoned his collar, took off his tie, and threw it on his desk, near a picture of him and a smiling Oyin. He had about ten pictures of them in his office. Did she really not see how much he loved her? He'd do anything for her. Hadn't he already proved it? Learning how to speak Yoruba—basically adopting a foreign culture. For her. All for her.

Since Saturday, all he had gotten from her were stupid conversations about Agatha and the food. He wanted her to talk *to* him.

What had been the bile on an already indigestible cake was getting to the room the night before, only to find her lying diagonally on their bed. It had been a slap in the face. Sure, they had their disagreements, but they always, always, slept in the same bed. But apparently, her sleeping form couldn't stand his presence.

He had had two options: wake her up and ask her to readjust or find somewhere else to sleep. He had opted to sleep somewhere else.

His desk phone jolted him out of his reverie. He was in no mood to talk to anyone, but only the office assistant ever called his desk phone directly.

"Hey, Cindy."

"Hey. I was wondering if it was okay to send tulips to Mrs. Wilson. The flower shop near her office is out of white roses."

Henry cleared his throat. Flowers?

"Wait. What day is it? It's Wednesday already?"

Cindy chuckled. "Yes, Henry. So, do you want me to send tulips?"

His lonely, Oyin-starved heart cried yes. But his head knew better. There was no point. Nothing he did was ever enough.

"Um, Cindy. Not today. Maybe next week."

Cindy's silence said it all. Ordering flowers for his wife every Wednesday had been the first 'unofficial' duty he had given her.

"Henry, is everything all right?" Cindy asked.

"Yes, Cindy. Thank you."

He dropped the phone receiver with a loud thud.

When did everything get so out of hand?

All Henry wanted to do as he drove his Mustang into their garage that evening was sleep. He was emotionally and physically exhausted. It had been a taxing day, yet he had a feeling it was going to be an even more taxing evening.

He looked to see if Oyin's BMW 3 series was in its spot. It was; she was home early. Usually, he got home before her. That was why he ended up making dinner most nights.

He sighed and got out of the car.

Maybe she wanted to surprise him? Maybe she wanted to reconcile?

Henry shook his head at his thoughts. He hated how much he ached for her; he couldn't, for the life of him, do the withdrawal thing like Oyin could.

He grabbed a bottle of water from the fridge and headed to their rooms. With every step, his stomach tightened a little more. If Oyin was home, it was very likely that she was in their rooms, either in the bedroom or the study. He did not think he could stand the awkwardness and angst of being alone (and conscious) in the same room with Oyin without actually talking to her.

He sighed and entered the bedroom, dropping his briefcase on the futon near the door. Oyin was sitting on the bed, legs crossed Indian style. As he shut the door, she looked up from her laptop.

"Hey."

He cleared his throat. "Hi."

She looked back to her laptop, seemingly unconcerned with his presence in the room. In fact, he would have thought she couldn't care less, if not for the steady drumming of her fingers on her touchpad. It was a nervous tic – one she did when she was very uncomfortable. It annoyed him how well he knew her.

He waited a few seconds to see if she wanted to say something. She didn't. He bit back a frustrated grunt at himself for hoping. But just as he moved to enter the closet, she spoke up.

"Mummy and Daddy would like to have a chat with us if that is okay with you."

Great. Like he wasn't stressed enough.

He pasted a smile on his face. "Sure."

"When?"

Henry resisted the urge to bang his head on the wall. Why was this more important to her than what was going on between them?

"Whenever is fine."

"Okay. If now is fine, I can tell them to come to our study."

Henry walked into the closet and started changing. "Okay."

Not twenty minutes later, they were all sitting in the study. Daddy and Oyin's mom sat on the loveseat where he and Oyin liked to curl up. He and Oyin sat, almost a foot apart, on the two straight-backed chairs across the room. The irony of the situation was not lost on Henry.

"So, does anyone want to lead us in prayer?" Daddy asked.

Henry shook his head. He and God weren't exactly on the best terms recently, what with the whole not-talking-to-his-wife thing. He really didn't know how Oyin related to God whenever she did her withdrawal thing. Since Sunday, he had felt a divide between him and God, as Matthew 5:23-24 kept ringing in his heart:

"Therefore, if you are offering your gift at the altar and there remember that your brother has something against you, leave your gift there before the altar. First go and be reconciled to your brother; then come and offer your gift."

Oyin's mom spoke up. "I'll pray then. Father in Jesus' name, we ask for Your guidance and wisdom. Amen."

"Amen," they chorused.

Oyin frowned slightly at her mom, but her mom didn't seem to notice as she continued. "So, Oyin and Henry, how are you doing?"

Oyin looked at him and then glanced away quickly. "We're fine, I guess."

Oyin's mom looked at them dubiously, a penciled eyebrow raised. "Are you sure?"

Henry was beginning to get irritated. He probably should have told Oyin that he couldn't have this chat now. The last thing he needed was Oyin's mom's officiousness.

Oyin's mom continued when none of them answered. "Well, Henry, can you explain to me why Oyin was crying the other day?"

She had been crying?

His first instinct was to go to her and wrap his arms around her. But he pushed that thought away.

He looked at Oyin. "You were crying?"

Oyin didn't look at him. But she nodded once.

He wanted to ask why. He wanted to ask what had upset her so much that she cried. Oyin never cried.

Instead, he replied to Oyin's mom, "I don't know what happened, ma'am. As you can see, I didn't even know she was crying."

Oyin's mom huffed. "What do you mean you don't know? Ehn? Answer me! How can you not know?! Is she not your wife?!"

Oyin's mom's voice was a whisper away from a full-on scream, and Henry was not sure how to respond, as his ire began to rise. He did not trust himself to speak respectfully to her if he did respond.

Daddy put his hand on Oyin's mom's arm to calm her down. "Henry, we just want to make sure that you and Oyin are fine. Irene saw her crying, and we were worried. That's all. Maybe you did or said something that you didn't think would upset her so much?"

Through all this, Oyin just sat still, her head bowed. Henry's irritation at the situation doubled. Couldn't she say something in his defense? Couldn't she tell them that she was not crying because of him, instead of letting them think he was some kind of wife-mistreating savage?

Heat began to flood his face. He felt cornered. He had done his best to be a wonderful, doting husband to Oyin. He had tried to be the best son-in-law to her parents, better than any other (Yoruba) son-in-law they might have preferred. But it wasn't enough. It was never enough.

And where did her parents get off butting into their marriage, anyway? Whatever happened between him and Oyin was supposed to stay that way – between them!

He was done. "Daddy, I..." He took a deep breath. "I didn't do anything to her. I didn't hit her. I didn't call her names. I didn't cheat on her. I have tried to be a good husband, so I don't know where this is coming from. But I'm sorry it wasn't enough."

There was more, so much more, Henry wanted to say. Instead, he just stood up and made to leave.

"Henry, wait," Oyin called.

She was the last person in the world he wanted to talk to. Funny how much difference a couple of minutes could make.

She stood up to meet him, placing a hand on his trembling arm. "Mummy and Daddy, thank you. Let me just talk to Henry."

Henry didn't wait to see if they responded or not; he walked briskly out of the room, with Oyin following closely behind him.

He marched into their bedroom. Oyin walked in and closed the door behind her.

He whirled to face her. "What the heck, Oyin? What the actual heck?!"

"I didn't say anything to them. I swear!" She moved a few steps toward him, her hands raised in a surrendering fashion.

"What the hell is that supposed to mean?! What is there to say to them?" he asked incredulously, getting even angrier.

"I am saying that it is not like we ganged up on you. I didn't even know what they were going to talk about."

"You could have defended me. You could have shut down their assumptions and insinuations. Instead, you said nothing. You just sat there while your mom yelled at me, and all but called me a wife-abuser."

Oyin's placating expression twisted into a frown. "I didn't know what to say. It's not like you weren't the reason I was crying. It's not like you've not been ignoring me all this while."

Henry couldn't believe what she was saying. *He* ignoring *her*? He'd all but begged her to talk to him these past few days, what with all the moping he'd caught himself doing.

"Wow! That's rich! So, this whole situation is my fault? You've done nothing wrong?" Henry asked, in a sarcasm-flavored tone.

Oyin's frown deepened, and she walked even closer to him. Her finger poked his chest as she emphasized every word. "You're the one who has been flirting with Olive in front of me! You are the one who hasn't talked to me in days! You are the one who didn't send me fl-flowers to-today."

Her voice broke as tears began to form in her eyes. "Y-You've n-nev-never not sent me fl-flo-owers."

Henry's anger began to dissipate as he stared into her tear-filled eyes. He'd always thought that she had the most beautiful chocolaty eyes, but at that moment as they filled with tears, they turned auburn. A lone tear ran down her right cheek, and before he realized what he was doing, he had raised his thumb to wipe it away.

It was like his fingers had been aching to touch her, and once he'd done so, he couldn't tear his hand away from her face.

Oyin closed her eyes and leaned into his touch. More tears fell from her eyes, and his heart gave a painful thud at the sight of each one.

Oyin opened her eyes and gave a wry chuckle. "I'm a blubbering mess."

Henry gave her a small smile. He didn't know what to say. A couple of minutes ago, he was so angry – angrier than he had ever been in his life. But now, all he could think about was how nice it was to be this close to Oyin again.

"I missed you, Henry," Oyin said, and then brought her lips to meet his, as her fingers found their way into his hair.

All his anger disappeared, and happiness flooded his Oyin-starved heart.

Henry woke up with the familiar weight of Oyin's head on his chest. He squinted into the darkness, trying to determine what time it was. His stomach grumbled, reminding him that he had skipped dinner. A sheepish smile graced his face. He and Oyin had been otherwise occupied.

His eyes widened. Uh-oh. It was quite possible that his in-laws had still been in the study. He could only hope that they had left after he and Oyin left.

Or…

He shuddered at the thought.

Remembering what had caused him and Oyin to leave the study sent a plethora of emotions coursing through him. He was glad, ecstatic even, that Oyin had been the one to reach out to initiate intimacy. It showed him that she wasn't as indifferent about him as her actions claimed. But there were other issues that they needed to address in order to move forward. And he needed to talk to God. It wasn't right that his relationship with Him should suffer because his relationship with Oyin was suffering.

"Lord, I'm sorry," he whispered.

Just then, his stomach grumbled again. Next to him, Oyin began to stir, probably from the combination of the sounds. She opened her eyes and looked at him.

"Hey," he said.

Oyin hid her face in his chest. "Hey," she mumbled.

His lips lifted in a half-smile. "Are you being shy right now?"

Oyin mumbled something, her face still buried in his chest.

"I didn't hear you."

She rolled away from him and covered her face with the coverlet.

"Sorry. Ijustfeelembarrassed," she rushed the words out.

Henry moved closer to her and pried the coverlet from her face gently. "Hey. What do you mean? Why?"

An embarrassed smile played on her lips, and her cheeks felt hot to his touch. "I was all over you like an animal in heat."

Henry tried really hard not to laugh, but he failed. He rolled away from her, clutching his stomach.

Oyin punched his back lightly. "It's not funny! Stop laughing!"

That made him laugh harder, and soon his eyes began to water. It felt so good to release all those pent-up emotions.

After a few seconds, he sobered up. "Sorry, babe. I can't believe you're embarrassed about that. We've been married for over a year now!"

"I know. But still…" she mumbled.

Henry pulled her closer to him. "Hey, I'm glad you did. It was what I needed. To remind me that I wasn't alone in this."

Her stomach grumbled just then, as if in response. They both chuckled.

"I guess we are both hungry. You wanna go raid the fridge?" Henry asked.

Oyin nodded. "Okay."

A couple of minutes later, they were seated at the kitchen island, sharing a huge bowl of cereal.

"Breakfast at midnight. We are breaking all the rules," Henry joked.

Oyin smiled. "Yeah." Then her eyes grew serious. "We should talk."

Henry's blue eyes turned azure as he stared at her. "Yeah, we should."

Then no one said anything.

"Do you have feelings for her?" Oyin blurted out suddenly, cutting through the awkward silence.

What?

Henry frowned. "What? What do you mean?"

"Olive," she said simply.

Henry narrowed his eyes at her. What kind of question was that? They were married, for goodness sake!

She continued. "Because if you do, that's okay. I mean, I understand the appeal. She's beautiful. She's smart. And you've been friends for a long time. And she comes from your world, from home, like you said…"

Henry's eyes widened. Wow.

He cut in. "So, this is what you think? Oh my goodness, Oyin, I can never win with you, can I?"

A thought occurred to him, and his heart began to slam in his chest in anticipation of her response.

"So what happened…um, what we, what we did in the room…me and you…" He cleared his throat and continued. "Was that about Olive?"

Her eyes widened, and Henry got his answer. He suddenly lost his appetite. "Wow. Just wow."

He dropped the spoon on the island, and it resounded with a clang. He felt empty. He felt disgusted. He felt sick. He felt…he didn't know how he felt.

"Henry, wait. Don't leave. Please let's talk."

What was she talking about?

Then he realized that he had stood up and put some distance between himself and Oyin subconsciously. "I don't know what to say to you right now, Oyin. Actually, scratch that. I do know what I want to say, but I don't want to say something I will regret later. So, I'm going to leave."

Tears gathered in her eyes. "Henry…"

Henry tried not to snort in derision. "I'll be taking the futon. You can have the bed."

At those words, the tears fell from her eyes and into the abandoned bowl of cereal, and she pressed her lips together in pain.

Henry did not wait to see any more. He walked briskly out of the kitchen.

He didn't want her to follow him, yet his heart further broke at the absence of the sound of footsteps behind him.

CHAPTER 11

Be-Kind-to-Oyin Elixir

Olive clapped her hands in delight.

Yes! Finally, something was going her way. If all things went according to plan, she could be done with the rough draft of her thesis by the time she left Phoenix.

She had decided to study the progression of Oyin and Henry's relationship from courtship to marriage. While she was excited at getting to do some actual fieldwork for her degree, she was also wary of digging that deep into their relationship. Truth be told, she feared what she'd find. But what could she do? Turning back was not an option.

Olive picked up her phone and texted Henry.

> *Hey, we should get together for an interview ASAP.*
> *Tell her, too.*

Dropping her phone on the desk, she powered on her laptop and began typing out interview questions.

It wasn't until early afternoon, three hours after she had texted him, that Henry replied:

Sure. I will talk to Oyin and let you know.
When do you have to leave?

Olive grimaced. She had just received an email from ~~Dr. Marigold~~ Dave that she had to return to school a week before the official start of the semester.

> *In less than two weeks. I have to leave earlier than expected. Would it be possible for me to get a sit-down with you both today?*

Let me talk to her.
I will let you know.

A couple of minutes later, her phone chimed.

Yes. When I get back from work.
Oyin is at home right now…
If you want to go ahead and talk with her first.

That was weird. She had not seen Oyin, or anyone else for that matter, when she had gone to fix herself lunch.

Oh. Okay.

Olive didn't think she could be in a room with Oyin alone. It wasn't that Oyin was a bad person. It was just awkward. Henry was the glue between them, and without him, they were just two women who would never be friends in a different situation. It definitely had nothing to do with the resentment she felt towards Oyin having all that she had ever wanted.

Yeah...she would rather wait till Henry got back.

Her phone chimed. It was a text from Dr. Marigold…er, Dave.

How is it going?

Olive smiled uncomfortably. He was her mentor, and while cordial, their relationship was supposed to be formal. She did not like the vibe she had been receiving from him recently. It seemed like he wanted more than a mentor-mentee relationship.

It's going well, sir.

She added the sir for her own peace of mind, and to make it clear how she regarded their relationship.

I'm glad to hear it. I understand that you are going to study the course of their relationship. But have you thought about what exactly your hypothesis would be?

I don't just want this to be an observational case study. I want you to take it a step further. What exactly can the psychology community learn from your study, from their relationship?

Olive nodded as she read through the messages. That made a lot of sense.

What do you suggest?

You can view their relationship considering already existing relationship theories or use their relationship as the grounds for developing a new theory.

Olive grew excited. This was going to be so much fun. But what theory would she use? Then it hit her.

What do you think about using attachment styles?

Just as Olive hit Send, Dave's message came in:

How about using the Bowlby attachment styles?

Olive laughed. Attachment styles it is.

Perfect. Keep me updated. And Olive, take care.

Olive frowned slightly at the last message, but she quickly dismissed it. She needed to get working on focused questions to determine Oyin and Henry's attachment styles.

This was going to be so much fun!

"Thanks for this, guys," Olive said as she set her laptop on the kitchen island.

Oyin and Henry sat across from her in stony silence. Oyin looked positively awful. Her eyes were swollen and red like she had been crying for hours. Olive glanced at Henry to garner insight about the situation. But his eyes were fixed on the wall above her head.

Olive sighed. She hoped they were okay.

Olive started. *Wait…what?*

When did *that* happen? When did she become okay with their relationship? It was probably the MFT therapist in her that did not want to see yet another troubled relationship. Right?

Olive stored that thought away for future examination in the privacy of her room.

"So, what do you want us to do?" Henry asked impatiently.

Olive shot him a 'really?' look, and he clamped his lips shut.

"I have a few questions for both of you and a bunch of written questions I want you to fill out and return to me. How's that sound?"

"Fine," Oyin replied. Henry just nodded.

Olive narrowed her eyes at him. What was up with him?

"Okay. I am going to record these conversations, so I am going to use your last name. Is that okay?"

They both nodded.

Olive hit *Record* on her phone.

"Mr. Henry Wilson and Mrs. Oyin Wilson. Introduction," she said into her phone.

"Mrs. Wilson, how long did you and your husband date before getting married?"

Oyin cleared her throat. "A year and a half."

"And when did you think that he could be your husband?"

"Almost as soon as we met."

Henry turned to look at Oyin for the first time that evening. She, on the other hand, studiously avoided his eyes.

Olive was surprised. She hadn't realized then that Oyin was that into him. In fact, when Henry had asked Olive what she had thought of Oyin, she had told him that Oyin didn't seem that into him. That was when he had confessed that Oyin was also 'talking' to another guy. It was, therefore, surprising to hear her say that she had thought Henry could be her husband that early into their relationship.

"Mr. Wilson, when did you know that she was the one you were going to marry?"

"The day we met," he said simply.

She remembered that day. Henry had texted her, excited about the possibilities with Oyin. She hadn't taken him seriously until he had started shopping for rings ten months later. During some of her weak moments, Olive had berated herself for not taking him seriously. Then, she had thought, she would have been able to nip the situation in the bud.

"Interesting," Olive said. "Well, there are more questions like this in the forms, just a bit more detailed."

They both nodded.

"Mr. Wilson, when did you know you were in love with Mrs. Wilson, and when did you tell her?"

Henry stole a quick glance at Oyin, and their eyes met, as she had been looking at him. They shared a weak smile.

Olive wrote that exchange down in her notes. The purpose of the in-person interviews was to note the couple's body language to determine if their words matched their actions and unconscious reactions.

"Um…The first day I saw her, I felt drawn to her. It wasn't until a couple of days later that I felt the Lord was telling me that she was my wife. That was when I went to introduce myself to her. So, to answer your question, it might have been a love-at-first-sight situation for me. I told her on the day I proposed, which was about fifteen months into our relationship."

Henry's eyes had taken on a faraway look. There was a slight smile on his lips like he was reliving said day. Olive cleared her throat and his eyes refocused.

Realizing what had happened, a slight blush crept up his neck and tinged his ears. Oyin just gave a small smile and shook her head.

"Okay. Thank you. How about you, Mrs. Wilson?" Olive asked as she typed furiously.

"The day we met, which was the first day I saw him, I also felt drawn to him. But…there were other circumstances in place. So, I was more resistant than he was. It took a while for me to admit it to myself, but I think I must have fallen in love with him a couple of weeks after we met. And I think he knew that because he pursued me so relentlessly. I officially told him after I introduced him to my parents as my fiancé."

Olive's mental mouth popped open. Henry was going to marry her without knowing for sure that she loved him? That was unbelievable!

"Thank you," was all she said out loud, though.

"We are moving to the next section. Attachment Styles." Olive said into her phone.

She turned back to them. "So Mr. Wilson, do you consider yourself as someone who is secure in their relationship?"

Henry furrowed his brow. "I'd like to think so."

"What about you, Mrs. Wilson?"

"I believe so."

"Okay, thank you."

Olive hit Pause on the Recorder. "Here is where it gets a little dicey. But I would need both of you to be as honest with me as possible."

They nodded.

She hit Resume. "Mrs. Wilson, if you were to hear from an outside individual that Mr. Wilson was cheating on you, what would be your first reaction?"

Oyin blinked. "Um…um, I don't know. Disbelief, I guess."

"And you, Mr. Wilson?"

Henry colored. "Heartbreak."

Olive noted Henry's choice of words. Based on his response, it meant that he was more willing to accept that Oyin could cheat on him.

"Mrs. Wilson, when you are upset with your significant other, what is your initial impulse? To fight or to retreat? A mixture of both?"

Oyin snuck a glance at Henry. "Retreat."

"Mr. Wilson?"

"A mixture of both, I would say."

Olive nodded and put a mark next to that question. She would ask it again in the written questionnaire.

"Lastly, on a scale of one to ten, how much arguing do you think you do as a couple? The question is for you, Mrs. Wilson."

Oyin frowned in thought. "Maybe 6?"

"And you, Mr. Wilson?"

"6."

"Okay. That's good. Thank you very much."

Olive pressed Stop on the Recorder app on her phone. "Thank you, guys. I'm gonna email you the questionnaires. Do you think you could have it filled out by Monday at the latest?"

"That's fine. I think," Oyin responded.

"Yeah," Henry said, getting up.

"Okay. Well, thanks again, guys."

Henry nodded before he disappeared around the corner. Oyin remained seated, however. Not knowing what to say, Olive began packing up her stuff.

"Um…Olive?" Oyin called.

Olive looked up. "Yeah?"

"I was going to order Chinese takeout for everyone. Do you know what you want?"

Olive looked at Oyin. Her eyes were less swollen than they had been before the interview, but they still remained sad.

Ignoring her question, Olive asked, surprising herself yet again, "Are you and Henry okay?"

Oyin sighed and dropped her head in her hands. "I did something stupid."

Olive's heart skipped a beat. She hoped it was not infidelity. She couldn't not tell Henry if it was.

Oyin continued. "But we'll be fine. Thanks for asking."

Olive nodded in sympathy. "Okay. And I can do the ordering. You go rest."

Oyin looked surprised. "Are you sure?"

Olive wondered what be-kind-to-Oyin elixir she had consumed because she answered with a 'Yes.'

Oyin stood up. "Thank you, Olive. My mom and dad want fried rice and chicken tenders. One plate is enough for them. Henry and I will have the rice noodles. And there is a cash drawer next to the stove. The menu is also in there. Thank you so much. Seriously."

Olive nodded. "Of course."

Oyin walked off, turning the same corner as Henry did.

CHAPTER 12

Listen to Me.

She found him sitting in a lounge chair by the pool. He looked so sad, and all she wanted to do was make it better. His gaze was fixed on the pool, and Oyin was not sure if he even heard her come out. She walked closer to him and was only a few steps away when he spoke up.

"I really don't want to talk now."

Her heart dropped to her stomach, and a sob lodged in her throat. "Henry, please."

He put his head in his hands. "I just need time to figure out how I am feeling, okay?"

She took the remaining steps and sat down on the chair closest to him. "Okay. I get that. But how about how I am feeling?"

Henry turned to face her. "I always consider your feelings. I always try to make sure you're feeling comfortable. That's what started this, remember? This time, I'm asking that you consider mine. All I'm asking for is time."

Oyin's heart ached. Why won't he just let her explain? She hated this unrest in their relationship. They had barely argued before her parents and Olive's arrival. Now it seemed like that was all they did. "Would you at least let me explain about yesterday?"

Henry heaved a deep sigh and scrubbed his hands over his face. "Sure."

Oyin knew that these signs meant he was frustrated, but she forged on. "So yesterday…it's not what you think."

"How do you know what I think?" He shot back, a frown marring his face. His blue eyes were so intense, and in conjunction with the blueness of the pool, it almost made Oyin dizzy.

Oyin paused to clear her thoughts. "It wasn't about Olive. I mean, it was, but not really."

Henry closed his eyes, his frustration palpable. "Oyin…"

She continued, undeterred. "I hadn't thought about it until you asked. It wasn't like I…was thinking of her or anything. When you mentioned it, it was then it occurred to me that maybe…like, that could have been why."

Henry opened his eyes and sighed.

Oyin continued. "It haunted me through the night, and I had to call in sick for work. But as I thought on it through the day, I realized that it wasn't just that. It couldn't have been just that."

"I pushed you away, and I wanted you back. I really missed you. We are good together, Henry. And I wanted to prove that to you and myself."

"And Olive," he added.

"And Olive," she granted.

"Okay. I understand," Henry said after a few hair-pulling moments.

A smile began to spread across her face. "You do?"

He took one of her hands in his. "Yeah. I'm sorry I overreacted."

Oyin's eyes widened. "No, you didn't. You have nothing to be sorry for. I'm the one harboring the green-eyed monster. I'm sorry, Henry. I really am."

Henry smiled at her, the smile that she loved so much. "It's okay, baby."

Oyin returned his smile and leaned in for a kiss. When their lips met, he stiffened. But as Oyin made to pull away to look at him, he held her in place.

"I'm fine," he murmured against her lips.

CHAPTER 13
My Wife

He wasn't fine. Henry lay wide awake next to Oyin. His eyes had adjusted to the darkness of the room, and he could make out the outline of the futon. Henry did not understand what he was feeling. He had always considered himself a level-headed person. But twice in one day, he had behaved irrationally, out of anger. He had walked out on Oyin and on her parents. Right now, he was supposed to feel remorseful for his actions, and happy that for the first time in their marriage, Oyin sought him out and apologized. Instead, all he felt was resentment and anger.

He was angry at Oyin for making a big deal about Olive's presence. He understood the jealousy. He really did. But it still irked him. It wasn't like *he* was always comfortable around her friends and family. It wasn't like *he* had not felt jealous of Dee. But he had stuck with it. He had not made a fuss. But the one time she was not comfortable, the one time she did not have everything her way, everything went up in flames.

He had done so freaking much for her! He had learned Yoruba for her; he had contributed thousands of dollars to make both weddings happen because God forbid a Yoruba girl does not have a traditional wedding. He had gone above and beyond for her, even when it was inconvenient, even when he'd rather not. But she couldn't do the same for him.

He was so angry at Oyin's parents for getting involved in their marriage. He had known that Oyin's mom had a bias against him from the first day he met her. She thought he would be less of a husband to Oyin because he was white. He had tried to get her to like him. He had been respectful to the point of deference. Yet, even after almost two years of knowing him, she still saw him as the white outsider, the one who was going to ruin her daughter's life, for no reason other than the color of his skin. It was so stupid and racist. He was tired of trying. He was done.

He was angry at Olive for whatever she was doing that was making Oyin jealous.

Henry sighed. He hated this. A couple of days back, all he wanted was for Oyin to come to him, to talk to him. She had done that. She had told him that she loved him, that she missed him, everything he had wanted to hear. In the moment, it had been so wonderful to hear. But as the night went on, it began to make him angry. It had taken all of his self-restraint to be polite through dinner. It annoyed him that she had so starved him of her love. He gave her himself in every way. But she doled out such small portions that hearing her say she loved and missed him was such a big deal.

Henry gently took her head off his chest. He needed some air. The room felt too small for all the thoughts and emotions coursing through him.

He should have realized Oyin would wake up. She was a light sleeper.

"Hey."

He sat up. "Hey."

"Are you okay?" she asked, her voice groggy with sleep.

"Yeah. I will be right back."

She smiled as sleep began to overtake her. "Okay."

He stood up and walked to the balcony. He closed the doors behind him, rested on the railings, and put his head in his hands. The Phoenix night breeze wafted around him, and he felt slightly better.

Henry.

Henry had been a Christian for most of his life. He had become born again when he was nine, and he had forged on since then. He probably ticked every box for the quintessential millennial Christian: went on mission trips, served in his church as an assistant youth pastor... In fact, he had wanted to apply to Pepperdine University, but he had felt like the Lord was leading him to the University of Arizona instead. When he had met Oyin in his junior year, he had finally understood why. But in all of his Christian years, he had never heard the Lord as clearly as he did that night.

"Lord."

You don't have to carry it alone.

A verse floated into his mind, one of his dad's favorite verses, Psalm 94:19.

When my anxious inner thoughts become overwhelming, Your comfort encourages me.

He fell to his knees. "Lord, I need You. Please."

That night, Henry poured out his hurts and anxieties before the Lord. And the Lord heard him.

CHAPTER 14

The Calm Before The...

Henry rolled over and hit the snooze button on the noisy alarm. He rubbed his eyes vigorously and looked at the time. It read 6 am.

He groaned and put his arm over his eyes as he began a mathematical word-problem equation in his head. If he slept for twenty more minutes, got dressed, and grabbed breakfast in thirty minutes, he should still be able to make the fifty-minute traffic-laden trip to the office and get there just in time for that meeting with…

"Henry, you might want to go grab a shower. It is a couple of minutes after 6 am," Oyin said, next to him.

At the sound of her voice, the events and emotions of the past 36 hours hit and coursed through him at whiplash-inducing speed.

He waited to feel some sort of bitterness or resentment toward Oyin, ready to tamper it down and sound as pleasant and engaging as he possibly could. Oyin was adept at deciphering his feelings just from the sound of his voice, and if she thought he was still upset, she would ask, and an argument could begin – he did not want that.

He waited…no anger surfaced.

Henry smiled outwardly as he laughed in relief and gratitude internally.

Thank You, Lord.

He felt Oyin scoot closer and touch his arm. "Why are you smiling?"

With the ease that comes from repetition, Henry removed the arm that covered his eyes and pulled Oyin on top of him in one swift motion.

Oyin yelped at the sudden movement and hit his chest playfully. "What are you doing?" she laughed.

Henry pecked her nose. "My, are you full of questions this morning."

Oyin retorted. "I am not the one being weird. You are going to be late. You should be in the shower by now."

Oyin nodded as an idea occurred to her. "Ah…I see now. You are using me as an excuse not to get up. It's not going to work. Don't you have that meeting with Tim at 8:30 this morning?"

She made to get up, but Henry pulled her back down, his left hand snaking around her waist. "Yeah, but you have to admit, you are a pretty attractive excuse."

Oyin gave a small laugh. "So, am I to take this to mean that we are okay?"

Henry nodded, his nose brushing against hers. "Yeah, we are."

Oyin gave him a long, lingering kiss, which he returned enthusiastically.

"Good," she said when she stood up. "Now, get up, lazy bones!"

Henry smiled. "As you wish, madam."

And just like that, it didn't require a complex math equation for Henry to get out of bed.

"Thank You, Lord," he whispered again as he scrambled out of bed.

It took Henry fifteen minutes, ten less than usual, to shower, throw on his suit, which Oyin had uncharacteristically laid out for him on the bed and attempt to style his hair.

Oyin was going to ruffle it up anyway, so what did it matter?

That thought brought a smile to his face as he walked briskly down the hall. The same smile died on his lips as he walked into the kitchen to grab a juice, and he sighted his in-laws.

They sat at the island, coincidentally in the same two stools that he and Oyin liked to sit and eat.

At the sight of them, heat flooded Henry's body, and he looked around helplessly, hoping that Oyin would materialize and act as a buffer.

No such luck.

Henry did not think his in-laws had seen him, but he couldn't be sure. If they had and he turned back, it would look like he was trying to avoid them, even though he was – but they did not have to know that. If they had not seen him, and he went into the kitchen, he was subjecting himself to an awkward interaction.

Lord, I am going to need some help here.

Like the answer to a prayer, Oyin rounded the corner and saw him. "Babe! Why are you still at home?"

Oyin's voice reverberated across the hall, and his in-laws looked up at the sound of her voice.

Henry heated up again as he now had not one, not two, but three pairs of eyes peering at him curiously.

He cleared his throat. "Yeah…I am still here. I was just going to grab a juice."

He gave Oyin's parents a bow that dipped into a half-prostrate. "Good morning."

Oyin's dad smiled slightly in response. "Henry, how are you doing?"

"Fine, and running a little late," Henry replied as he moved into the kitchen area and in the direction of the refrigerator. He could feel Oyin's eyes following him, and though he couldn't see them, he would have bet money that her eyes were narrowed.

"Good morning Henry," Oyin's mom said quietly, a little too quietly.

Henry opened the refrigerator, his arm gripping onto the door handle a little too tightly.

Oyin's dad seemed like he could easily forgive him for walking out on their conversation. Oyin's mom, on the other hand, was an entirely different issue. She already did not like him. He had probably hit the final nail in his coffin in her eyes.

Henry mentally sighed. He would never be good enough for her.

"Good morning, ma'am," he greeted again.

He grabbed the first bottle his hand touched and closed the refrigerator quickly, ready to hightail it out of the kitchen.

"You have taken care of yourselves? We have some yams. I was going to make yam and egg for everyone – I didn't know you were going to wake up so early. Sorry," Henry heard Oyin say to her parents, as she hopped onto the island and sat close to her dad.

"O, I am heading out. Goodbye, sir and ma'am," Henry said, giving a polite smile as he made to leave.

"Okay." Oyin hopped off the island. "Let me walk with you?"

Henry nodded and extended a hand out to help her descend the island. She took it, a smile playing on her lips.

"I'll be right back, Mummy and Daddy."

Still holding onto Henry's hand, Oyin walked towards the door adjoining the garage.

"I took the day off. Want me to bring you lunch?" Oyin asked, as she turned the door handle and walked into the garage. The lights automatically came on, sensing her movements.

Henry smiled. Though Oyin had met some of his colleagues, she had not actually come to their offices before. The thought of Oyin walking into his office and everyone knowing that she was taken - not just taken, but his - made Henry's heart skip a beat in anticipation.

"That would be amazing."

Oyin smiled, her yummy-chocolate eyes crinkling at the corners. "Yeah?"

Henry opened the back seat of his Mustang and unceremoniously dumped his briefcase onto the seat. He took a couple of steps to close the distance between himself and Oyin and pressed his lips to hers.

"Yeah."

Oyin giggled. "Okay."

Henry rested his forehead against hers and chuckled. "I really should go."

"You really should," Oyin said, her eyes saying the opposite.

Henry reluctantly moved away and got into the driver's seat, put on his seatbelt, and turned on the car, his eyes never leaving hers.

"I love you," he mouthed.

Oyin made a heart sign with her forefingers and thumbs, a goofy grin on her face.

"I love you too," she mouthed back.

Henry backed the car out of the garage, a similar grin on his face.

It was the sound of his office door opening that made Henry drag his eyes from the computer screen.

Cindy walked in, Oyin in tow carrying a picnic basket. "Here you go, *Oh-yin*. It is a pleasure to finally meet the recipient of those weekly flower deliveries."

Oyin smiled politely. "Thank you, Cindy."

Cindy beamed at Oyin. "Of course, it is my pleasure." She walked out the door, but not before giving Henry a conspiratorial wink.

Henry shook his head at Cindy's antics and walked around his desk to give Oyin a peck. "Hi."

Oyin wove her free hand into his hair to pull him closer and deepened the kiss.

Many seconds later, it was necessary to come up for air.

"Wow. I should have had you bring lunch a long time ago," Henry said, out of breath.

Oyin smiled shyly as she walked out of his embrace to place her basket on the small center table in the corner of his office. "Hey."

Henry looked at the picnic basket and raised his eyebrows at Oyin, his eyes full of mirth.

Oyin grumbled as she sunk into the settee across from the center table. "Shut up."

Henry chuckled lightly as he sunk right next to her. "I didn't even say anything."

"It was the only thing I could find to pack food in, so shut up and eat your yams."

Henry playfully slung an arm around her shoulders. "Anything for you, babe."

Oyin chuckled as she pushed his arm off her shoulder. "You are annoying."

Henry unpacked the basket, shooing Oyin's hands when she tried to help. "You made the food; I'll set the table."

"You definitely get brownie points for that one."

"That's what I am counting on." He laughed.

Soon, Henry had two warm plates of yams and scrambled eggs on the table. Oyin blessed the food, and they dug in.

Henry broke the companionable silence a few bites later. "Your parents are mad at me, aren't they?"

Oyin looked sideways at him. "Probably."

Henry bit his lip and looked away, a nervous expression creeping onto his face.

Oyin gently placed her hand on his knee. "It's fine."

Henry sighed. "It really is not."

Oyin rubbed his knee affectionately. "Hey, don't worry about it. Let's enjoy our lunch. We can talk about this later."

Henry sighed and nodded. He wasn't trying to be difficult, but it had been a tough couple of days, and he hadn't exactly been on his best behavior when he had spoken to Oyin's parents.

A few minutes later, he spoke again. "Should I bring it up and just apologize to them for walking out?"

Oyin sighed exasperatedly. "Henry, honestly…"

Henry cut in, a slight frown on his face. "They are your parents; you can afford to be like that."

Oyin gave him a stern look. "Let's not go down this road, please. It's my day off; I made yams, and I brought some for you. I obviously don't want to fight."

Henry sighed. "You're right."

"I know I am. We need your head in the game if you are going to get that promotion."

Henry smiled slightly. "Yeah."

Oyin rested her head on his shoulder. "So, how did your meeting with Tim go? Did he like your proposal?"

Henry's eyes lit up. "It went well. I think he really liked it. He had some tough questions, but I think he was satisfied with my answers."

"Speaking of which," Henry turned and gently took Oyin's head off his shoulder, "you should come meet him and the rest of the team."

Oyin shook her head, a shy smile coming upon her face. "No."

"Come on. It will be fun. You have already met Thomas and Jeremiah. I am dying for everyone else to meet you and be seriously jealous of me."

Oyin scoffed playfully. "Yeah, right."

Henry stood up, pulling her up with him. "Come on, babe. You know how much of a catch you are."

Oyin giggled. "Yes, you never stop telling me."

She sighed dramatically. "Fine, I will go with you. Let's just clean up here first."

Henry gave an overly dramatized bow in response. "Your wish is my command, my lady."

Oyin smiled as she bent down to clear the plates. "So stupid."

CHAPTER 15

The Idiosyncrasies of Irene

Irene put the last clove of garlic in the thick pot of stew. From the breakfast nook area, Dele read, his reading glasses sitting comfortably on the bridge of his nose. Irene had no earthly idea why anyone would need a sitting area with couches near the kitchen. What, were they afraid they would die from the walk to the actual living room? Considering how big the house was, Irene definitely understood the importance of having a sitting area in every room of the house. Not.

"*Ku ise o* [13], Irene," Dele called out, his voice an almost-yell.

Irene smiled. "*Ose*, dear."

"Did Baby K WhatsApp you?" Dele called out loudly again.

"Dele, it would be easier to have a conversation if you were sitting closer *o*," Irene remarked.

"I know. But this chair is very comfortable. When you finish, come and sit down. We can talk then."

Irene shook her head and turned to chuck a kitchen towel at him. "You are not serious."

From the other side of the room, Dele dodged the towel and laughed uproariously in his Dele-like manner.

---

[13] *Ku ise o* – Yoruba word that means *well done*. Nigerians use "well done" as a greeting to someone who is hard at work on a chore or task.

Still shaking her head, Irene moved to the double sink to wash the stickiness of the garlic extract off her hands.

"I keep forgetting that this tap is automatic," she said with a *hiss*.

Dele chuckled. "*Ara-oko*[14], just put your hand under it."

Irene rolled her eyes. "Thank you. I am well aware."

She continued. "Why does anyone need a touchless tap anyway? It's a waste of money."

Dele frowned slightly. "Irene…" he chided gently. "It's her matrimonial home. Let her do it however she wants to."

Irene dried her hands with a wad of paper towels. "She is still my baby, Dele."

"I know, but at what point do we *hands off*?"

"We don't," Irene said simply.

Dele sighed with the weight of an old argument. He switched to Yoruba. "We have trained her; it's time for her to use that training."

Irene pursed her lips. "Why don't you tell that to Eli, the high priest? His sons were not children anymore, yet God expected him to put them right."

"This is not the same thing, and you know it. What has Oyin done now that requires us to 'put her right?'" Dele retorted, his fingers bending in air quotes.

Irene eyed him angrily. "You know what. And you know you don't like it too, so don't make me the witch that is always complaining."

Dele sighed resignedly. "Irene, it has been a year now. They are obviously happy together. Leave it be."

E gba mi o[15], Irene thought.

---

[14] *Ara-oko* - Bush girl (Yoruba)

[15] *E gba mi o* – Yoruba word that translates as *help me*, but in this situation and typically, it is used as an incredulous exclamation.

"Didn't you see Oyin crying the other day?"

Dele had a patronizing look on his face, and Irene was tempted off to wipe it off with a slap. Here she was, expressing a valid concern, and he was looking at her as if she was a child throwing a tantrum.

Dele put his book on the corner stool next to him and beckoned to her, his hand bent in the universal sign for "come here."

That further frustrated Irene; she almost pulled her hair out.

I am not one of your students, she wanted to scream.

Instead, she planted her feet firmly on the ground and crossed her hands over her chest.

Dele sighed again as if she was the problem. Why did everyone not see what was going on here?

"I actually did not see Oyin crying. You told me –"

Irene cut in. "Are you saying I am lying?"

"No. I am just saying I didn't see her crying. That being said –"

King of kings and Lord of lords, I might kill this man.

"Okay, forget Oyinkan's crying or no crying, did he or did he not walk out when we were talking to him?"

Dele nodded. "He did."

"How can we expect him to respect Oyinkan when he does not respect us?"

"Irene," Dele sighed. "That boy has been nothing but respectful to you since Oyin brought him home, and you know it."

You know that. The Holy Spirit prodded gently.

Irene slammed the door on the Voice. Not now.

"The respect that you are claiming he has for us is not the same and will never be the same as if he was Yoruba. That fact is very well evidenced in his walking out the other day."

Dele narrowed his eyes infinitesimally. "So that's what this is about?"

Irene sighed, irritated. Where were his ears all this while?

"Mighty God, Dele, that's what it's always been about!"

Dele shook his head and sighed. "So, what do you want to do now?"

Irene wanted to stomp her feet in frustration, but she could already see Dele's reactionary signature lip curl – the one he gave to his undergraduate students.

"Dele," she took a deep breath, "I just want my daughter to be happy."

"Why do you think she is not?" Dele asked.

Rather than repeatedly throw all the sharp objects within reach at Dele's general direction, Irene picked up her phone from the island and walked out of the kitchen, her fisted palms trembling.

"Irene?" Dele called out. Her retreating steps were the only answer she gave.

"Irene, come off it. We have not finished this conversation."

Irene refused to turn back to "finish" the conversation. She was not the overbearing mother/mother-in-law in this narrative. She only wanted what was best for Oyin. And she was tired of being the one who had to say something.

"Irene, *kini gbogbo eleyii bayii? Iwo ni mo ba soro* now.[16]"

Irene stopped.

"I know, but I wouldn't want to separate you from your comfortable chair. When you finish, come, and then we can talk, *Baba iyawo Bournvita.*[17]"

---

[16] *kini gbogbo eleyii bayii? Iwo ni mo ba soro now* - What is the meaning of this? I am speaking to you! (Yoruba)

Irene continued to their rooms, half-expecting Dele to follow.

He didn't.

It was just as well, Irene thought many minutes later, as she lay on the bed, a little less angry. She wasn't sure what other hurtful comments she would have hurled at Dele, just because she knew that they would hurt. She knew the *Baba iyawo Bournvita* comment had been a low blow, downright cruel, but she couldn't help but feel that there was some truth to it.

Dele had shared her reservations regarding Henry from the beginning. And when Oyin had adamantly refused to consider anyone else, she and Dele had spent countless hours in prayer and fasting. Then, Dele saw Henry's house, saw the material wealth that Oyin was living in, and suddenly, *she* was the officious one.

Irene was tired. Tired of being scared out of her mind that she would suddenly receive a call in the middle of the night from someone she had to struggle to understand confirming her worst fears. Why, oh why, couldn't Oyin have fallen for someone else? For Dee? He was a good boy from a good home. His family history was not a mystery. He was third in line for the throne of Oba of Lagos.

Sighing deeply, she rolled onto her side. She knew Dele wanted the best for Oyin just like she did. But how could he possibly think Henry was the best for Oyin?

O su mi, Oluwa[18].

---

[17] *Baba iyawo Bournvita* – Yoruba insult that means *Opportunistic father-in-law*. It is a play on the title of a Nollywood movie, *Iya Oko Bournvita,* that was about an opportunistic mother-in-law.

[18] *O su mi, Oluwa* - I am fed up, Lord (Yoruba)

Though Irene's back was to the door, she heard when the door opened, and Dele walked in. Irene refused to turn around. He could think she was sleeping...or not.

"I turned off the stove for you. I wasn't sure if it had finished cooking," Dele said tentatively.

Irene's eyes widened a fraction. In her anger, she had forgotten she was cooking. That was very unlike her.

"*Ose,*" Irene said.

Dele walked closer and sat on the bed. "Irie, what do you want me to say?"

Irene sighed. If she was being honest, she was not really angry at Dele. Frustration was a more apt description, but the real source of her discontent was Oyin's marriage.

"I cannot, in good conscience, continue to oppose that boy, Irene. They seem happy together, isn't that what we want for her?"

Irene sighed again; Oyinkan was not happy.

+Argument today, tears tomorrow, silence the day after. Not to talk about Henry's friend who mooned over him. Anyone with eyes could see that.

Dele continued when she did not verbally respond. "Okay, how about this? How about you and I talk to Oyin before we leave? Make sure she is happy. *Iyen nko?*"[19]

Irene finally turned to face Dele. "I don't want another talk like the last one. I just might slap that boy if he walks out on me again."

Dele rolled his eyes. "He does not have to be there. That way, Oyin might feel more comfortable to tell us if anything is wrong."

Irene sighed again. It was a good plan, and it would have to do.

---

[19] *Iyen nko?* - How about that? (Yoruba)

After her conversation with Dele, Irene had made her way to the kitchen to finish her cooking. Thankfully, the *ayamase* stew did not burn.

Irene had planned to make *ayamase* for her Oyinkan before she left. It was one of Oyinkan's favorite meals, and she knew that Oyinkan would never go to all through the trouble to cook it. And Henry, well…it didn't matter. He would not be able to appreciate it.

Just as she took the rice out of the pot to drain, she heard the whirring of the garage motor. Irene hoped against hope that it was Oyin who had just returned. She couldn't handle Henry alone. By some unspoken agreement, Dele had always acted as a buffer between her and Henry. After the whole walking-out thing, she needed (or Henry needed, depending on how you look at it) a buffer now more than ever. Of course, Dele had decided that a late afternoon nap was in order and was therefore unavailable.

The ridiculousness of the situation hit Irene like a gut punch, and she felt tears prick the corner of her eyes.

This was not the relationship a mother is supposed to have with her son-in-law.

She couldn't stop herself from thinking that this would never have happened with Dee.

Finally, the door opened, and Henry walked in.

Irene knew the moment he realized that she was the one in the kitchen and that she was the *only* one in the kitchen by the progressive reddening of his face.

She waited for him to speak.

"Good evening, ma'am," he said.

Irene nodded at him, not trusting herself to speak and not really knowing what to say.

She turned away and busied herself cleaning up the mess *ayamase* had left behind. She hoped he'd leave. She had nothing to say to him. When she had taken the time out of her day to talk to him, he had the effrontery to walk out.

For some reason, Henry wasn't leaving. Irene could feel his eyes boring a hole through her back, but she refused to make it easy for him.

He cleared his throat. "Um...ma'am. I was hoping to talk to you."

Really? You don't say!

Irene turned to face Henry in a deliberately dramatic manner and simply raised a perfectly penciled eyebrow.

As expected, Henry was red. Irene almost rolled her eyes.

"I... I just -" Henry cleared his throat. "I wanted to apologize for the other day. I was having a bad day. I should not have walked out, and I am sorry."

Much against her will, a small part of Irene's heart softened towards Henry. Maybe it was the fact that this was the first time she had held a solo conversation with Henry. Maybe it was the fact that he was not too proud to apologize. Maybe because, at that moment, for the first time, Irene could see how much her answer—her good opinion— meant to him.

"It's okay," was all she said, though.

Henry gave her a small smile, but she could see him almost sag with relief.

"I made *ayamase,*" she heard herself saying, "It's Oyin's favorite Nigerian food. It's a little spicy, but it's very good."

Henry's smile grew tentatively. "Yes, I know it. I like it. Oyin and I sometimes buy it on the weekend. Thank you, ma'am."

"You literally just texted me; how can the kitchen be smelling so good already?!!" ~~Olivia~~ Olive (Her name was

Olive)'s words crashed into the shaky something-of-a-foundation that was being built between her and Henry.

Won de [20].

"Oh! I'm sorry. Did I interrupt something?" Irene turned to see Olive halted just inside the kitchen entryway, not because she was uncertain (she was too self-assured for that) but in confusion.

"That's because I am not the one cooking, Olive. Oyin's mom is."

Irene didn't know why, but Henry referring to her as *Oyin's mom* annoyed her.

"Oh." Olive walked into the kitchen. "It smells really good, ma'am."

Irene resisted the urge to narrow her eyes at Olive. Hadn't she been in the house when she was bleaching the palm oil to make the stew? There was no way Olive did not know she was cooking. What? It smelled bad before, now it smelled good?

Isn't that how ayamase works?

Seriously, Lord, you can't be taking everybody else's side...

She didn't have the time or patience for this. Irene turned back to the sink to finish cleaning up.

"Thank you," Irene replied to Olive simply because politeness will not have it any other way.

Fueled by the determination to get out of the kitchen, Irene was done cleaning up in a couple of minutes.

She looked up, just as she placed the last dish on the rack. Olive had already crossed over to where Henry was, and

---

[20] *Won de* - Literally means *they* have arrived (Yoruba). Here, it is used sarcastically to comment on an unwanted appearance.

they were both sitting in the kitchen living room area, smiling as they conversed.

Irene's heart thudded in pain for her daughter. Their faces said it all. Irene *hissed*. And here she was, thinking that maybe Henry was not so bad.

Irene picked up her phone, turned on her heel, and left the kitchen. If their trip ended with Oyin leaving with them, so be it.

CHAPTER 16

Oyin Tried

As soon as Oyin put the car in 'Park,' she smelled it. Her heart gave a little drumroll, and Oyin had to laugh at her own ridiculousness.

Henry loved *ayamase*...a lot. She hoped this would be a good step in the right direction for his and Mummy's relationship because if there was something Mummy loved, it was someone who appreciated her cooking.

At that moment, Oyin was filled with awe at the Lord's working. Despite her inability to pray about the rift between her parents and her husband, God still heard the groanings of her heart and was working.

Oyin rested her head on the steering wheel.

Thank You, Lord. Thank You so much.

She got out of the car and walked into the house, a smile playing on her lips.

Oyin tried. She tried. She really did, but she could not stop her smile from slipping at the sight that greeted her again.

Henry and Olive were sitting together, *again*. So engrossed in each other that they did not hear her come in, again.

It means nothing. It means nothing, Oyin. She repeated to herself.

Forcing the smile back onto her face, she called out to Henry. "Hi, baby."

Henry looked up, and a wide smile engulfed his face. "Hey, babe."

"Hi." She smiled back.

"Hi, Olive."

Olive looked up as well. That was when Oyin saw that they had been watching something on Olive's phone.

"Hi, Oyin."

Oyin tried not to read anything untoward on Olive's expression. Surely, the minuscule narrowing of Olive's eyes was a side-effect of staring at a small screen for so long. Surely, the slight upturn of her lips was an attempt at a smile, not a sneer. Surely, that expression in her eyes was not anger at Oyin's interruption.

She was trying so hard not to read anything on Olive's face that she did not realize that Henry had walked over to her. He took her purse from her hand and gave her a quick peck on the lips.

"You went out after you left my office?" he asked.

Oyin snapped her attention back to her husband. "Yeah. Had to go into work for a few hours. We got a new client, and everyone is excited."

Henry nodded. "Cool. I wanna hear more. But first, tell me what you smell?"

Oyin rolled her eyes. "Your favorite stew?"

Henry acquiesced. "My favorite stew."

Oyin chuckled lightly. "I guess we have my mom to thank for that. She's the best."

"I just might drop you and marry her, if only for the food."

Oyin burst out laughing. "Okay, Henry. That sounds like a great idea that will go over well with my mom and dad."

She continued. "Speaking of which, I should go get them for dinner."

She looked around him to Olive. "The stew my Mom made is really spicy. Is that okay with you, Olive? We have some sautéed veggies in the refrigerator that you can eat with your rice if you would prefer."

"I think I would like to try the stew. It smells really good. Thank you for offering, though."

Oyin gave a small smile. "Of course."

She turned back to Henry and took her purse from him. "I am going to head to the room to freshen up." That's when she noticed that he was still in the outfit he wore to work. "You haven't changed yet?"

Henry colored slightly. "No, not yet. I have been hanging with Olive since I got back."

"Oh, okay. See ya in a few minutes."

Oyin tried not to let it bother her. Olive was not a threat to her marriage. Henry loved her, and she loved him.

As Oyin stepped out of the kitchen, instead of heading straight to her room, she made a turn to her parents' room.

As soon as she stepped into her parent's room, Oyin squealed and rushed to hug her mom. "Thank you, Mummy!"

Mummy laughed, and she brought her arms to hug Oyin back. "You are welcome, my dear."

Mummy stroked Oyin's braids. "*Pele* [21], love. Have you eaten? Did you like it?"

Before she could answer, Daddy cut in from the desk where he sat at with yet another journal article in hand. "So, am I just a wall painting here? Is that all it takes to win your love? Food?"

---

[21] *Pele* literally means Sorry (Yoruba). It is also used as a greeting to show care or concern about a person's wellbeing.

"*Jealousy-Jealousy*. Dele, what does the Bible say about jealousy again?" Mummy answered, instead.

"That God is a jealous God. Read your bible, *iya ijo*.[22]"

Oyin rolled her eyes at her parents' bickering that was as old as their marriage. She went over to her dad, genuflected, and kissed him on his forehead.

"Good evening, Daddy."

Daddy made as if to wipe her kiss away. "I don't want your secondhand affection."

Oyin rolled her eyes again and laughed.

Mummy laughed, too. "Oyin, don't mind him. Come and sit with me. We have not really had time to talk very well."

Oyin moved away from the desk and sank onto a spot on the bed that was close enough to Mummy but not far from Daddy, where she could see them both, and more importantly, they could both see her.

"Oh, I actually just came to thank you for the *ayamase* and call you to have dinner with us."

"Oh, okay."

A look passed between her parents that Oyin neither liked nor understood.

"What?" Oyin tried to bury those hackles, but they wouldn't budge. They rose all the same.

Daddy, ever the observant one, quickly replied to reassure her. "Nothing. We just wanted to talk to you before we leave tomorrow."

We all know how well that went the last time.

"Talk to me about what? I don't understand."

They shared a look again, and Oyin's heart thudded. "What's wrong with Baby K? Where is she?

---

[22] *iya ijo* - church lady (Yoruba)

"What do you mean what's wro... oh, nothing is wrong with Baby K. She is fine. Everybody is fine," Daddy replied.

"Everybody is fine, Oyinkan. We want to talk to you about you..."

Oh, Lord Jesus, not this again. I thought everything was fine.

Henry had promised to apologize to Mummy and Daddy for walking out. What else?

"Okay," Oyin sighed. "Can we eat first? Henry and Olive are kind of waiting for us."

Oyin knew, rather than saw, Mummy purse her lips and roll her eyes.

It was Daddy who responded. "Of course, my dear."

Probably propelled by the prospect of the dinner palette, everyone was at the dinner table in twenty minutes with heaping plates of rice and *ayamase*.

For the first few minutes of the affair, after Henry had said grace, one could have heard a pin drop. For some of them, they were too busy savoring the taste of the stew. For some others, the spice of the stew made speaking impossible. Oyin had her suspicions as to who fell in which category, so a wry smile played on her lips.

"This is really good, Mummy. Thank you."

Mummy smiled. "You are welcome."

Henry spoke up. "I second that. This has to be the best I have ever tasted."

"Even better than your wife's?" Daddy's eyes twinkled.

Henry looked over at Oyin and blushed. "Oyin does not really -" Her eyes widened, and she gave a little head shake.

Henry clamped his lips shut, a slightly alarmed look in his eyes.

"Oyin, let the man talk!" Daddy mock scolded.

"I didn't even say anything!"

"Henry, speak, please...Oyin, does not really what?"

Henry looked over at Oyin, a question in his eyes. Oyin just rolled her eyes in response.

"Oyin does not like to cook *ayamase* stew..." Henry finally said.

Oyin groaned. "Before anybody says anything, I just want to say in my defense, it is a lot of work!"

Daddy chuckled and shook his head at her. "Lazy girl. You are lucky your husband is white and can cook. Henry, don't mind her. Just call whenever you want *ayamase*, I will gladly borrow you my wife for a few hours."

"Please don't pimp me out without permission; thank you," Mummy cut in, a mock-serious expression on her face.

Oyin rolled her eyes and chuckled, as everyone at the table dissolved into laughter.

Later, whenever Oyin remembered this moment, she wondered at the blissful ignorance of those people, people who had laughed together before everything went to hell.

PART TWO

CHAPTER 17

The Foreboding

"Advising" Oyin on her marriage without her husband in the room was a bad idea. Dele Johnson could feel it in his bones. The sense of foreboding was so compelling that more than once during dinner, Dele almost told Oyin not to come to their rooms after dinner. He knew that Irene would not publicly contradict him, but she would be hurt, and hell hath no fury like a hurt Irene. She had already accused him of taking Henry's side (whatever that meant) for purely materialistic reasons.

Dele breathed out a sigh.

As soon as dinner was pronounced over by Henry's exclamation of being "super full and unable to contain one more bite," Dele could feel his wife's impatient anticipation. It was in the twitching of her fingers in her lap; it was in the pursing of her lips; it was in the vein in her neck that throbbed ceaselessly.

"Oyinkan, don't forget to come by our room before you go to bed," Irene blurted, and Dele almost smiled at how well he knew her.

He was probably the only one that could tell it was a blurt, but it still felt tactless, as if Irene were intentionally excluding Olive and Henry from whatever would be happening in their room.

Oyin looked askance for a moment before she quickly rearranged her features into a tight smile. "Yes, ma."

"Well," Dele said to no one in particular as he got up from the table. "I am going to retire. Good night everyone."

Choruses of "good-nights" followed him as he walked out of the room.

If Dele were a man more attuned to the spiritual realm, he would have understood this sense of foreboding was more than paranoia, and he would have taken Irene in hand. He would have prayed. He would have done something, anything…

Alas, Dele was not. So, he simply walked on to his room, made some finishing touches to his packing, and sat at his desk to read a periodical, while he waited for Irene and Oyin to come through the door.

It didn't seem like long before Irene walked into the room, Oyin close behind. Irene had a battle-ready face, and Oyin had her walls-up face. Dele put his periodical away and sighed inwardly.

It was going to be a long night.

"I don't understand the purpose of this, Mummy. Henry and I are fine."

"Please speak in Yoruba," Irene hissed at Oyin in Yoruba.

Oyin closed her eyes in frustration and repeated herself, this time in Yoruba.

Irene pursed her lips. "So, you are happy?"

"Yes."

"Oyinkan, it is your life. When your dad and I leave, that's it. We can't help you, at least not immediately."

"Mummy, what do you think is going on? Why do you think I am not happy?"

Irene shook her head, disbelievingly. "Are you *also* going to tell me that I imagined seeing you cry the other day?"

Oyin faltered for a second. "No, I was crying. But -"

Irene cut in. "And what happened when we tried to intervene?"

Oyin sighed. "Henry said he already apologized for that, Mummy."

"Oyinkan, listen. I am happy in my husband's house. And I want you to be happy in your husband's house. Are you happy in your husband's house?"

"Yes," Oyin answered unequivocally, without hesitation.

"Is he enough for you?"

"Yes, Mummy."

"Are you enough for him?"

Oyin hesitated, and Dele's heart skipped a beat at the unsure expression that crossed Oyin's beautiful face. Dele did not know whether to yell at Irene for the question or probe even more.

Why was Oyin unsure? Anyone with eyes could see that Henry loved her! What kind of question was that?

But Dele said nothing. He didn't know what to say. So lost was he in his thoughts that he barely heard when Oyin whispered an unconvincing "yes."

CHAPTER 18

The Imperfections of the Human Mind (Part 1)

They had left, but their words, indelible and unforgettable, stayed with her.

"Are you enough for him?"

She was. She had to be.

I am. *He chose me.*

But her mind could not forget the picture of familial perfection that Olive and Henry painted when they were together...without her. Olive and Henry laughing. Olive and Henry sharing an old inside joke that she was not a part of. Henry's face lighting up when he was with Olive. Olive and Henry. Olive and Henry. Olive and Henry. Olive and Henry. Olive and Henry. Olive and Henry. Olive and Henry. Olive and Henry. Olive and Henry. Olive and Henry. Olive and Henry. Olive and Henry. Olive and Henry. Olive and Henry. Olive and Henry. Olive and Henry. OLIVE AND HENRY.

OH. And her heart splintered.

OH for Olive and Henry. ~~Not Oyin and Henry~~

Henry had married the wrong O, and it would seem that he had realized it, too.

CHAPTER 19

The Imperfections of the Human Mind (Part 2)

The sun peeked through the curtains and flirted with Oyin's eyelashes. She sleepily raised a hand to swat it away. Unfazed by Oyin's feeble deterrent, the sun continued to trace patterns all over her face, the balcony curtains aiding its efforts as they moved gently to the tune of the wind. Not bothering to raise her hand again to swat, she turned away from the offending light and burrowed deeper into the bed covers.

Henry smiled to himself as he continued to watch his wife sleep. She had denied being sad that her parents left yesterday, but Henry knew otherwise. When they came back from dropping her parents off at their airport, she had gone straight to their study and sketched until it was time for dinner.

Knowing she was feeling melancholic, he had made one of her favorite meals, cajun pasta salad, for dinner. She hadn't said anything in gratitude, but later that night, she had clung to him in her sleep like her life depended on it, and he had held her back, just as tightly.

Henry sighed contentedly. It was so good to have the house to themselves again. For a second, the fact that Olive was still around and so they did not *really* have the house to themselves flitted through his mind; he waved it away just as quickly. She didn't matter. She was family, and she was not in their business like.... some other people.

The rays of the sun creeping in informed Henry that it was time to get up for church, but he wanted to spend a few more blissful moments in bed with his wife.

His alarm clock had other ideas, however. It blared just then, crashing into the silence of the room, and waking Oyin. She sat up with a jolt, and it was all Henry could do to stop himself from bursting out in laughter.

She *hissed* loudly and angrily as she sat up, not as amused with the situation as Henry was.

"Really, Henry?! Really?!" She turned on him, anger darkening her pretty face. "We've talked about your alarms. That stupid thing just gave me a headache!"

The smile on his lips died as he stared at her, open-mouthed.

She *hissed* again, rubbing her temples. "I promise, if that thing wakes me up like that tomorrow, I will personally smash it."

Um…

Was she being serious?

"Good morning to you, too," he muttered in response.

Oyin turned to look at him, her typically bright chocolate eyes bleary. She raised an eyebrow. "That's all you're going to say? You're not going to say anything about what I just said?"

Henry scoffed. "What do you want me to say, Oyin? Obviously, it does not matter what I say. I have already been tried and pronounced guilty."

Oyin narrowed her eyes and scoffed. "It's *your* alarm, Henry, and we've talked about you lowering the volume or using those earbud-thingies that makes the alarm only sound in your ear."

Henry's eyes widened in disbelief. "You didn't seem to have a problem with my alarm clock ringing the past few weeks. But all of a sudden, you wake up one morning, and I am the bad guy for forgetting a conversation we had months ago."

Oyin shook her head and got off the bed. "I am not having this conversation with you if you are going to be unreasonable."

Henry was incredulous. "I am being unreasonable? Me? I'm the one being unreasonable in this scenario? You've got to be kidding me!"

Oyin eyed him angrily and walked into the bathroom without responding.

What the heck just happened? Did he and Oyin really just argue about an alarm clock? The same alarm clock that had sat on his bedside table for weeks without opposition?

Henry sighed and placed his head in his hands in defeat. This was not how he wanted the day to go. A trickle of fear went down his spine at the thought of constant bickering and repeated arguments characterizing his marital future.

Oh, Lord.

Oyin walked back into the room, a towel around her neck as she wiped off water from her forehead. She stopped halfway to the bed, put her hands on her hips, and looked at him expectantly.

Was she really expecting him to apologize? When pigs fly!

Follow peace.

He stifled a sigh, and his ego grumbled in protest. *Why do I have to be the one to apologize?*

"I'm sorry," he said finally.

"Thank you." She closed the distance and came to kneel next to the bed. "Can we pray?"

Henry didn't think he succeeded in keeping his irritation at her from showing on his face, but she did not comment on it. "Sure."

"Thank You, Jesus, for a new day. We ask for Your blessing on this new day. As we search for You now, may we find You. Be with all our loved ones, especially Mummy and Daddy, as they land in Atlanta today. Amen."

"Amen," Henry chorused, barely hearing Oyin's prayer.

He was having a hard time letting go of what just happened. As usual, Oyin was the picture of poise and indifference. He wanted to scream in frustration.

"Henry, I read the devotional the last time. It's your turn to read." Henry took the devotional booklet from Oyin's outstretched hand, his body on auto-pilot.

There was no mistaking the words in block letters that greeted him as he opened the booklet to the passage that they were supposed to read that day.

LETTING GO

He let out a wry chuckle at the Lord's sense of humor. Oyin looked at him. "What's funny?"

Henry just shook his head, the amusement washing away his irritation and loosening the tension. "The Lord definitely has a sense of humor."

When Oyin saw that he was not volunteering any more information, she simply nodded and did not push any further.

Henry began to read from the devotional, and he could hear the Lord tell him to let go of everything and trust Him, especially regarding Oyin.

Thank You, Lord, his heart whispered back in gratitude.

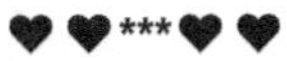

"Have you ever been able to get Olive to go to church?"

Henry glanced sideways at Oyin, who had been silent since they left the church after the services were over.

"Not church, per se," he responded. "We went to youth camp together once while we were in high school."

Oyin nodded in response. Henry glanced at her again before turning his eyes back to the road. "Why do you ask?"

Oyin shook her head. "No, I guess I am just trying to understand her. It feels weird to go to church and leave someone behind, and I guess I am trying to understand why she does not believe..."

And why you are okay with it. Henry heard the unspoken words.

"Olive has been through a lot, Oyin." He switched lanes on the busy highway to get onto their exit. "It's not really my story to tell, but I keep praying – believing that the Spirit will touch her."

They turned into their neighborhood just then.

Henry glanced at her again. She was fidgeting with the ruffles on her pink top. She was uncomfortable, wanting to say something but not knowing how to.

"You never really want to talk about Olive to me."

"What?" came his automatic response.

Oyin met his eyes and said, "I asked if you had completed Olive's questionnaire."

That was not what she said. He could have sworn that that was not what she said.

"No, I have not. Have you?" was his response, though.

"I haven't."

He turned into their driveway just then and glanced at Oyin again. Her fingers were still deeply entwined in her blouse.

He put the car in Park and reached out almost without thinking and covered her hands with his.

At the contact, Oyin lifted up her eyes to his. What he saw in them took his breath away.

Like the words of a well-written poem, Oyin's eyes clearly told of a sadness tinged with insecurity and fear.

Henry blinked once, but that was all it took. Her eyes shuttered, and the canvas was blank again.

"Baby," he cradled her palm in his and interlaced their fingers, "are you okay?"

She nodded. "Yeah, I am fine." She responded quickly, but not before Henry heard her voice quiver.

"I don't understand what's going on, Oyin. Won't you tell me?"

She just shook her head as if to say nothing was wrong, but the fact that she could not verbalize it was telling.

"Is this about your parents? You miss them?"

He almost choked on the words. The idea that his presence was not enough to ease the absence of her parents pricked him. He had left his parents and cleaved to her [23], and she was enough for him. Why wasn't he enough for her?

Oyin just shook her head, blinking furiously as if to wade away any tears.

"Sweetheart," he cooed. He came out of the driver's side and rounded the car to open her door.

He pulled her up gently and hugged her tightly. He did not really know why she was upset, just that she was.

They stayed in that position for a few minutes, Oyin's hands holding onto his shoulders as he ran his palms soothingly up and down her back.

As he felt her begin to calm down and her breathing evened out, he thought a joke was in good order.

"Olive is probably feeling left out of the party that has detained us from coming in."

---

[23] *Left his parents and cleaved to her* - Biblical reference from Genesis 2:24

Oyin stiffened in his arms, and Henry instantly knew he'd said the wrong thing.

"What? What did I say?"

CHAPTER 20

A Physical Conspiration

Olive rubbed her eyes furiously just as she remembered that she had put on mascara that morning.

Ugh!

She hastily pulled her hand away from her face, but it was too late. Her fingers came away with the black sticky substance. She was sure she had streaks across the bridge of her nose as well.

Thankfully, she was the only one in the house. Since Oyin's parents left on Saturday, she was usually the only one in the house. And as much as Olive wanted to be around Henry, she was beginning to feel like a third wheel and not even the lovable kind that the couple keeps around so that the person does not feel left out. She was the I-am-only-tolerating-you-because-you-are-friends-with-my-partner kind.

It was time to leave. Henry and Oyin had given her the filled-out questionnaires. She needed to analyze their responses, determine their attachment styles, figure out what "new" thing their relationship could tell the psychology community, and get out of Dodge.

If this were any other couple, it would have been expedient to be close by to carry out more in-person interviews, as needed. But this was Oyin and Henry, and she did not think she could handle the mixed signals that she was picking up from Henry.

It meant nothing, she tried to tell herself over and over, that Henry sought her face whenever he walked into the room. It was only because he had not seen her in over a year that he spent all evening yesterday with her, choosing her company over Oyin's. But her heart was difficult to convince. It started to flutter whenever Henry smiled widely, something it stopped doing exactly two months after he married Oyin. Her eyes had started to follow him out of the room as they used to before he proposed to Oyin. Her mind, treacherous thing that it was, would not stop thinking about the way his eyes crinkled at the corners when he smiled. Her nose was quick to catch a whiff of his cologne. Her fingers itched to cradle his perfectly sculpted jaw. Her…

No!

Her whole body was conspiring against her, and the sooner she left the house, the better for her sanity. She would leave. She had to.

CHAPTER 21

I love you, okay?

She was going to let this go.

She had to. For the sake of her sanity. For the sake of her marriage.

"Oyinkansola, get a grip!" she shouted into the empty ladies' bathroom on the sixth floor of Ponce De Leon Office Building

Her fingers gripped the edges of the sink tightly as she stared at her reflection in the mirror.

Her features looked like they always had. Slightly pointed nose, small ears that easily got lost behind her voluminous hair, too-bushy eyebrows, but it was the dullness in her brown eyes that betrayed what she was feeling.

In them, she could see pain, raw and sharp, and she knew that Henry saw it, too.

She wanted to shake off the doubt and fear. Henry loved her. She knew this deep in her heart. She knew that it was stupid and pointless to continue like this.

But *knowing* – gosh knowing – was so different from *feeling*.

"What if I ask him and he confirms it, God?" she whispered.

Confirms what? She felt the response prod her heart.

"That he loves her!" she responded immediately, her protest bouncing off the stone-tiled walls.

"That I am not enough for him," she added weakly.

Her phone vibrated next to her on the sink countertop. It was Henry.

She sighed. He was probably on his lunch and was calling to flirt with her, as he typically did when he got the chance to.

"Hi babe," he greeted as she accepted the call.

"Hi," she replied, thankful that her voice had not come out shaky.

"What's up? What are you doing? Are you on lunch yet?"

She cleared her throat. "Yeah…um, yeah, I am. Are you?"

"I am."

He paused, and in that pause, Oyin could hear that he wanted to ask if she was okay again, but he was holding back, not wanting to spook her.

"I am fine, Henry."

Henry sighed. "Are you really, baby? I keep feeling like I am doing something wrong. Like yesterday at the car. You pushed me away and won't say why."

Oyin tensed, her fingers gripping the edge of the sink even tighter as she recalled the incident. She couldn't tell Henry that she was upset that he mentioned Olive's name while they were having a moment, that she was insanely jealous of Olive, who was able to get her husband's attention without trying…that she felt that she was not enough for him. So, she didn't.

Oyin cleared her throat. "I told you, nothing. I simply realized that you were right, and we were being rude to Olive."

This web of lies you are weaving...

Henry paused again. The pause was pregnant like Henry was unsure whether to accept her explanation or push some more.

"Okay," he finally said. "But Oyin, you will let me know if there is something, right? You know you can tell me anything, right?"

Without waiting for her to respond, he continued, "We will pray about it together, and we will be fine. We are in this *together*. I love you, okay?"

Oyin nodded. "Okay."

Just then, Oyin heard sounds from Henry's side that sounded like a door opening and someone talking.

"What is the call about, Cindy?" Henry asked someone in the background.

"Do you need to go?" Oyin asked.

Henry sounded apologetic. "Yes. There is an impromptu call I have to be on. I will see you at home."

"Okay. Have fun."

"And Oyin, we are okay, right?"

"Yes, we are," she responded because she so badly wanted it to be so.

"Okay, love you. Bye."

"Lord," she breathed silently as she placed the phone back on the counter. "Please help me. I can't continue like this. I want to let it go. I need to let this go. Will You help me?"

Taking a deep breath, she stretched out her arms and splayed her hands in a surrendering fashion as if to physically give over her doubts and anxieties to God in exchange for His peace.

Help me. She begged.

"Oyin, you have been holding out, girl!"

Oyin looked up from her computer screen at Nysha, one of the four team members that she shared a corner with.

"What are you talking about, Nysha?"

"Your unbelievably hot, smoking, beautiful husband!"

Nysha was one of those people whose every sentence seemed to end with multiple exclamation marks. Combined with her curvy figure, wild curly hair, and tanned olive skin, Nysha was very much not the stereotypical Indian-American woman.

Oyin chuckled. "Again, I ask, Nysha, what are you talking about?"

Nysha waved a phone in Oyin's face. "This, girl! This!"

Oyin rolled her eyes at Nysha's exuberance and plucked the phone from her hands.

"What are you - oh! Where did you get this from?"

Nysha grabbed her phone from Oyin as if she could not bear to part from it longer than a few seconds. "Facebook! So… my girl, Oleander, went to the U of A. She graduated last year and is now working in Silicon Valley. Anyway, she used to talk about this guy, Henry Wilson. Say how he's like the standard. Hot, rich, single, nice, you know the important stuff. She had, like, the biggest crush on him! Anyway, we get to talking last night, and she is talking about how there are no eligible guys over in California, yadda, yadda, yadda. So, I ask, how about your imaginary boyfriend? And she goes, oh he's married now. So, we look him up and guess who I see standing next to him in his Facebook cover photo wearing white?"

"Me?" Oyin asked when it was clear Nysha was expecting a response.

"Yes, you!" Nysha continued, accusingly.

Oyin resisted the urge to roll her eyes. Nysha was so dramatic!

"You hit the jackpot, girl! Seriously, what did you have to do to get him?"

Oyin smiled. "Nysha, you are too much!"

Nysha laughed, a tinkling sound that bounced off the walls and made Oyin smile even more. "No, you are too much. You have that fine piece of *mhmm* at home, and you are coming here in the morning frowning as if one of your nine cat-lady cats scratched you in your sleep."

Oyin laughed, shaking her head vehemently. "I do not come in frowning!"

Nysha sat back in her chair and raised an amused eyebrow at Oyin's denials. "Um, yes, you do."

"What does she do?" Binta, the only other Nigerian in Oyin's team, asked as she walked over, a bottle of Diet Coke in one hand and a glazed donut in another.

"Come in looking like someone stole her chocolate," Nysha supplied, her large brown eyes looking to Binta for confirmation.

"Mhmm-hmm," Binta confirmed through a mouth full of food.

"Thank you! Here's the kicker, Binta. You should see her man at home. He is F to the I -N – E," Nysha added, clearly enjoying the conversation.

"Show me! Show me! Show me! I want to see!" Binta squealed.

"Girl, calm down." Nysha laughed.

Binta was silent for a full minute - a record for her - as she held Nysha's phone.

"Darn."

"I know, right?!" Nysha said.

"Oyin, please explain to my mind because it cannot understand how your man is this fine, and we are just finding out now."

Oyin did not know what to say. It was obvious that despite the playful joviality of the moment, Binta and Nysha were hurt.

"Have you guys never seen a picture of him, for real?"

The question was directed to herself as much as it was directed to them.

Why did she not boast about Henry?

CHAPTER 22

I said I love you

Oyin's conversation with her co-workers (the closest thing to girlfriends that she had) swirled around in her head as she drove home hours later.

She had made it up to Binta and Nysha by promising to bring Henry to lunch with them sometime soon. What Oyin had been unable to resolve just as easily, though, was why she had not been vocal about her husband. If she was being honest with herself, it was more that she was afraid of discovering the reason.

As she braked at the last traffic light before their neighborhood, she decided that it didn't matter. She was going to be better. Beginning now.

No more feeling sorry for herself. No more feeling inadequate. Henry was *her* husband, darn it!

"Babe! Babe! BABE!" Oyin yelled as she drove into the garage and put her car in Park and opened the car door.

Henry threw open the garage entry door, a look of overpowering concern in his eyes. "Oyin! What? What is wrong?"

Oyin took a second to bask in the warmth that washed over her at being the source of the concern, at being the one he showered his love and attention on before she launched herself at him.

She was sure it was only by God's grace, and those evenings spent cycling that he did not fall over as she barreled into him. Instead, he caught her and picked her off the ground.

"Honey, what is wrong?"

"Nothing," she beamed at him. "Everything is absolutely perfect, and I was too much of a fool to see it before."

"But --" Henry did not get to finish his sentence as she silenced him with a kiss.

Oyin knew she was not the only one shocked by the intensity of the kiss. It was a first kiss all over again, filled with longing and the promise of a better and more trusting future.

Oyin was not sure how long they stood there, just inside the garage entry door, her car beeping because its door was left ajar and the garage motion-sensor lights confused as to whether people were in the garage.

But she was sure that it was not long enough for *Perfect Olive* to come and ask, "Is everything okay?"

Oyin was perfectly content to remain in *her* husband's arms, kissing him like the newly-weds that *they* were.

But Henry pulled away, his voice husky as he replied without taking his eyes off Oyin. "Yes, everything is fine. We are fine."

"Oh. Oh! ...oohhhh." Olive said, stupidly.

Oyin rolled her eyes internally. Oh, for Pete's sake, go away!

It was the stiffening of Henry's arms around her that made her realize she had said that out loud.

"Sorry," she said sheepishly, her turn to sound stupid.

Olive laughed, a forced laugh if Oyin ever heard one. "Nothing to be sorry about. I am obviously interrupting."

To Oyin's disappointment, their lips did not continue their previous occupation as soon as Olive walked away, and it was certainly not due to a lack of desire on her part.

"That was rude. We were rude," Henry started in a careful voice.

It was Oyin's turn to stiffen. "I said I was sorry, and I am sure she gets it. We are newlyweds, for goodness sake. We should be able to kiss whenever we feel like it."

Henry said nothing but was obviously not satisfied. With the mood successfully ruined, Oyin wanted nothing more than to leave the scene behind and disappear into her art.

"Can you put me down, please?"

Henry narrowed his eyes at her. "Oh, so now you're mad?"

Oyin sighed. She had just wanted to kiss her husband without interference or arguments!

"I just want to come down, Henry." Her defeated voice pled.

Henry did as she asked and more. He took a few steps away from her. Then, without looking at her, he said, "I'm gonna go out for a short drive. Should I pick up dinner on my way back?"

"Sure. Whatever you want."

"Okay." He grabbed his keys from the hook and entered his car, but not before turning hers off, closing its door, and placing her keys where they were supposed to go.

Oyin watched him back out of the driveway, her mind reminding her that that was a déjà vu moment. She was feeling a lot different now than she had then.

CHAPTER 23

Mad

Henry Wilson was upset, and he didn't know why. The past few weeks had been an emotional rollercoaster, quite unlike anything he had ever experienced in all his twenty-four years, and it was driving him crazy. He remembered when life was so simple. Work. Church. Home with Oyin. That was it.

His fist collided with the steering wheel in a bid to expel the inexplicable feelings whirling inside him. Anyone who had ever hit a wall in frustration could have told Henry that it was an ineffective way to deal, but it didn't matter because it felt good.

Without realizing it, he was out of their residential neighborhood. He turned into the first fast food place he saw. It was Taco Bell. He parked and placed his head on the wheel.

"God." was all his overwhelmed soul could pray.

A few seconds later, his phone rang.

"Mom?"

"Hi, baby." Mom's familiar soothing voice wrapped around him like a comfort blanket.

"Hi, Mom."

"Are you okay? I was actually just making dinner when I felt the urge to call you."

Henry mentally thanked God for His omniscience. "I am a little overwhelmed, Ma."

"Baby, what's wrong? Talk to me."

"That's the weird thing, Mom. I don't know," Henry said confusedly. "I just have all these feelings, and I don't even know how to unravel them, and it's choking me, Mom."

Mom's voice went from mildly concerned to full-blown mother-hen. "Where are you right now, Henry?"

"Taco Bell. I am buying dinner."

"Is Oyin with you?"

"No. She is at home."

"Oh, okay." Mom paused. "Are her parents still around?"

"No, they already left. But Olive is still around."

There was a longer pause from Mom's side before she finally said. "Olive?"

"Yes, she came to stay with us for a few weeks. I told you, Mom."

"No, you didn't. Hold on a second."

Mom spoke to Dad in the background. "Did Henry tell you Olive was staying with them? Greg, honey, can you put that down for a second..."

Mom's voice was inaudible for a few moments, and then she came back on. "Your dad did not know, either. And Oyin was okay with Olive staying over?"

Henry was incredulous. "What does that even mean? Olive is family, just like Oyin's parents. Olive was my friend before Oyin was my wife!"

Mom's silence said it all.

"You know what, Mom? Forget it. You are supposed to...I don't know...you just...you are not helping matters. Say hi to Dad for me. Bye."

"Henry, wait. Calm down for a second."

"No, Mom. I gotta go. I need to pick up dinner."

"Sweetheart..."

Henry did not hear any more, his thumb already tapping the End Call button.

Everyone was acting like he was cheating on Oyin with Olive! Olive had been in his life for more years than she had not, and he was just supposed to cast her away like a rag doll when he married Oyin? Like Oyin cast off her parents? Like Oyin cast off her sister? Heck no!

Henry had no idea what he ordered, and he also might have given the drive-through attendant a very generous tip in his inattentiveness.

When he got home, he texted Oyin because he didn't feel like talking and turned on a football game as a deterrent because he didn't feel like being talked to. When Oyin walked into the kitchen a few minutes later, however, she either did not notice his mood or did not care because she grabbed her food from the island and came to sit next to him.

"What did you get for yourself?" She asked.

He paused the game and looked at her. And that was when Henry realized that he did not get anything for himself. Figures.

"Didn't you get anything for yourself?" Oyin asked again.

"I guess not," he said quietly.

Oyin gave him an endearing smile and offered to share hers with him.

"No, thanks. I am not that hungry."

"Okay."

Henry turned back to his game and was about to play it when Oyin asked if he told Olive that her food was waiting.

"I texted her. She said she will be out in a few minutes."

The words were barely out of his mouth when Olive walked into the kitchen.

"Hey, Olive," Oyin said.

"Hey, what's up?" Olive replied. "Thanks for the food."

Oyin chuckled dryly. "It was all Henry, though I think he forgot to get something for himself."

Olive gave a small, teasing smile. "How St. Henry of him to think of others before himself."

Oyin chuckled.

Henry grunted. "Rather than sit here while you guys talk about me like I am not in the room, I am just going to leave the room. Give you guys space to say more."

"You are such a baby," Olive laughed. "All I hear is *wah-wah-wah*. Oyin, is that what you are hearing, too?"

"Yup."

Henry narrowed his eyes at Olive, a reluctant smile finding its way to his lips. "I really don't like you. You know that?"

Olive beamed at him, her eyes twinkling. "Well, I love you, so deal with it."

Olive could not have heard Oyin's silent gasp or felt the temperature of Oyin's corner of the room drop a few degrees, but Henry did.

Before he could do or say anything, not that he knew what to say or do, Olive said. "Oh, I almost forgot, I am leaving the day after tomorrow."

"What?" was the only intelligible thing he could muster after a couple of moments.

So, she was leaving.

Henry would not be mad about Olive leaving if he were not sure that she was leaving because of Oyin. And that...*that* was not okay.

No, actually…Henry would not be mad if Oyin was not so obviously happy that Olive was leaving. While he had been agonizing about Olive's sudden departure and badgering Olive as to why she had to leave early, Oyin was conspicuously silent. A silence that said she was fine with the sudden departure.

Olive had dissembled, claiming that she was needed back on campus and that she needed her mentor's help with her thesis.

Nothing he said made her budge. Oyin had said *nothing*.

On the day of Olive's departure, Oyin hugged Olive and told her to come back anytime, but Henry saw the relief in Oyin's eyes. She made no effort to conceal it from him, unlike some other emotions that she was a pro at concealing.

As if his feelings didn't matter.

As if he had not been solicitous of her feelings when her parents left.

Henry sighed. It was just...whatever. Was it too much to ask that she treat him with the same level of respect that he treated her?

To add salt to the injury, she suggested that they go on a dinner date as if to celebrate Olive's departure.

"We have not done one in ages!" she exclaimed excitedly, but what she really meant was they had not done one since Olive had arrived.

He did not have the presence of mind to tell her no.

So, instead of heading home after a long day of work that was made even longer by his state of mind, he was driving to their favorite French restaurant in Old Town Scottsdale.

The rush hour Scottsdale traffic was doing nothing to help with his mood. If anything, he just got more upset so that by the time he got to the restaurant and handed his keys to the valet, all he could say to the hostess was a clipped "Henry Wilson, table for two."

The hostess informed him that Oyin was already waiting for him at the table and began to lead him there. She probably had better traffic, he mused, since she worked near Scottsdale.

When he got to the table, Oyin looked up and smiled brightly.

"Hi, baby," she said.

"Hi," he replied and turned to thank the hostess.

"Of course. Your waiter will be by shortly," she replied and walked away, but not before flashing him a smile that could only be described as flirtatious.

He could not help the slight pink that tinged his ears, and he gave her a polite smile.

"So, are you going to get the same thing that you got the last time?" Oyin asked as he sat down.

If she saw anything of the weird exchange that had just happened, she showed no indication of it. And Henry certainly was not going to bring it up.

"*Le Poulet?*"

"No, babe…remember, you ended up trying the *Le Saumon?*"

"No, I really don't remember. But if I liked it last time, yes, I'll order it this time."

Oyin frowned slightly. "Okay."

The table was silent for a few seconds as Oyin perused the menu. Then she said, "How was your commute here? I think they are preparing for a festival tomorrow."

"It was okay."

"Oka-a-y," she said with a tentative smile. "And how is work going?"

"Fine."

Oyin narrowed her eyes at him. "Okay, spit it out. What's up with you?"

Henry's first inclination was to deny that anything was wrong and try to be more engaging throughout the dinner to keep the peace, but something snapped in him. Maybe it wasn't really a snap than it was a switch, a switch that turned on the light and exposed feelings that had been shoved into the dark recesses of his heart.

"To be honest," he began. "I am upset."

"What? Why? What can I do?" came Oyin's concerned response.

"Just…" Henry sighed. "Why are we having dinner tonight?"

Oyin looked confused. "You are upset we are having dinner tonight? I just wanted us to go on a date. We've been so stressed lately, and I thought it would be a nice getaway."

"A getaway from what?" Henry prodded.

"I'm a little confused and frankly getting a little irritated at having to explain my reasons for wanting a date with my husband. Can you please just tell me why you are upset?"

"I don't think you respect my feelings," Henry blurted.

A look of shock came over Oyin's face, and then their waiter came up.

"*Bonsoir Madame et Monsieur.* Have you decided what you will be having this evening? Let's start with appetizers, yes?"

"*Monsieur? Madame?*" The confused waiter repeated after a few seconds.

"Sorry!" Oyin exclaimed. "No appetizers. I will just have *L'Agneau,* and he will have the *Le Saumon.*

"*Merci.* Any drinks to go with that?"

"Just sparkling water for both of us."

"Your food will be out shortly."

The tension that ensued around Table 19 after Arnold, the waiter, walked away could be cut with a knife.

"You don't think…" Oyin cleared her throat. "You don't think that I respect your feelings?"

"Not as much as I respect yours."

"In what manner?"

"When your parents left, and you were sad, I made sure you were okay and tried to be solicitous of your feelings. But from the moment Olive announced that she was leaving, your relief could not be any more palpable. As if I don't have a right to be sad. Not once did you join me in asking Olive to stay! Not once did you ask how I was feeling."

"Okay…first of all, I was not sad because my parents left. I was sad because, well…it doesn't matter."

Oyin sniffed and continued. "Actually, you know what, it does matter, and if you had spent more time with me instead of with your friend, you'd know that. Would you really blame me for being happy to have my husband to myself again?"

Henry was incredulous. "Really? I am telling you I am upset, and we are back to talking about you? As if we don't do that enough? And you wonder why I say you do not respect my feelings?"

Oyin's face was thunderous for a second, and then it went blank. Go figure. "I don't think this is an appropriate place for us to have this conversation."

Henry pursed his lips, barely restraining his frustration and did not respond.

"We should just go. I am not going to enjoy dinner anyway." To put action to her words, Oyin dug into her purse, placed a fifty-dollar bill on the table, and beckoned to a nearby waitress.

"We just suddenly lost our appetite and would like to cancel our orders."

Oyin pressed another twenty-dollar bill into the waitress's hands and smiled gratefully when the waitress assured Oyin that she would take care of everything.

"I will see you at home, Henry," was her greeting as she stood up and left the table. Henry had no other course of action but to follow her.

A particularly vengeful, adulterous thought occurred to Henry on his way out as the hostess from before smiled at him again, a flirtatious promise in her wink and slightly jutted hip. Henry, of course, did not act on the thought, but he sent the hostess an engaging smile of his own that bothered him all the way home.

CHAPTER 24

Insecure Avoidant (Part 1)

Despite her efforts, Olive could not stop crying, and she hated herself for every single tear. The tears didn't stop falling till the day after Olive arrived in San Diego.

Pining over a married man. How pathetic. How freaking cliché.

She should have based her thesis on a self-case study of her own attachment style, she mused sardonically.

Children brought up in unstable homes are more likely to latch onto emotionally unavailable partners when they become adults.

She kept replaying the whole scene in her mind like a train wreck she could not look away from.

Oyin in Henry's arms. He had cradled her like she was the most precious thing in the universe, and she had fit so perfectly into his arms, her love for him displayed in every motion. Olive could have sworn she heard her heart shattering when she walked from the island where she and Henry had been childishly playing a game of thumb war to the sight of Henry kissing Oyin.

Her traitorous legs had kept her rooted to the spot as Henry and Olive had pulled apart. It wasn't until Oyin had ungraciously wished her off that she was able to get her body to obey her command.

She honestly could not fault Oyin; Olive knew she would have done the exact same thing if she was in Oyin's shoes.

And boy, how she wished she were in Oyin's shoes. That she was the one that put that look of puppy adoration in Henry's eyes. That it was her embrace that Henry craved, that she was...

"Stop it, Olive!" she chided herself, rather loudly into the empty lecture room.

"You know, one of the symptoms of a narcissistic personality type is an inflated sense of self, such as when one begins to refer to themselves in the third person," came Dave Marigold's voice.

Alarmed, Olive looked up. She had thought she was alone in the classroom.

"Dr. Marigold. Hi."

"Hi, Olive."

Somewhere in Olive's Henry-soaked brain, she still absently noted that Dr. Marigold had not reminded her that he was 'Dave,' not 'Dr. Marigold.'

"So, do you have anything to say for yourself? Is narcissism something that runs in your family?" Dr. Marigold continued in a mock-serious tone.

Olive scoffed and laughed despite herself. "Yes, I would say that is pretty accurate, actually."

Dr. Marigold knew her story. He knew her mother's pipe dream to be the world's best soprano voice had led her to abandon a five-year-old girl to an emotionally absent father. He knew her father had focused his attentions on finding a suitable bed partner under the guise of finding her a mother.

So, yes. It was safe to say that narcissistic tendencies ran rampant in her family. But Dr. Marigold had encouraged her to laugh it off, to treat her childhood as the stereotypical bad-childhood fodder that it was.

"Ah, there you go. Your first laugh since you came back."

"Is it?" Olive demurred, a little surprised.

Not answering, Dr. Marigold asked instead, "How is your thesis coming?"

In a lighter mood than she had been all week, she replied. "It's funny. I can come up with a topic on basically every other scenario in the world but my research thesis."

Dr. Marigold drew closer, his setting up for the class momentarily abandoned. "That's good. That's how you know you have the right topic. That's how you know you have stumbled onto something that has not been touched before. Your brain just needs to adjust to the new information you are asking it to process and analyze."

Olive sunk her chin onto her elbow. "I guess."

"So, how was it?" Dr. Marigold asked, switching topics on her again.

It should have been totally weird that she knew what he was talking about even though he did not use any nouns, but it wasn't.

"Harder than I thought it would be," she heard herself admitting.

"I am not going to say, 'I told you so,' so don't let that affect your answer to this next question, but do you think studying their relationship made it harder?"

"To be honest, no… I was just…you know, never mind."

It was pathetic enough to admit to herself that she was in love with a married man. It would be downright embarrassing to admit to someone else that she had feelings for a man who was seemingly happy in his marriage.

Dr. Marigold didn't push. Instead, he asked, "So, what can we do to get you out of your funk? Go hiking? A spa day? Shopping? A movie montage of a makeover?"

Olive found herself laughing again, as was obviously Dave's intent. "How guy of you."

Dave just smiled, an eyebrow raised in anticipation of an answer.

Olive thought for a second. "I think I just need to take a good nap, put on my big girl pants, and get on it. I have not even looked at their questionnaires."

"Okay, we can schedule sometime after next class to go over what you have come up with."

"But our next class is in two days!" Olive exclaimed.

"Well, I guess you better have read through their answers before then."

Olive smiled, shaking her head as she packed up her bag. Dave was such a... She stopped. Literally. She froze. When did he become *Dave*?

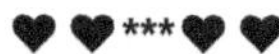

She did what she said she would. She took a nap and... opened her laptop. That was as far as she got.

"You are being ridiculous, Olive."

Uttering that statement out loud reminded her of Dave's comment about narcissistic personality types from the previous day, and she smiled. Heaven only knew how he knew what she was feeling and exactly what to say to make her feel better.

Still smiling, she took a deep breath and opened the questionnaires.

Forty minutes later, Olive could not believe her eyes. Henry presented with an *anxious-preoccupied attachment style*[24]. He craved intimacy with his partner that he was terrified she would not give.

---

[24] *Anxious-preoccupied attachment style* - One of the four adult attachment styles, anxious-preoccupied attachment style presents with *high anxiety* and *low avoidance* in their relationships. Read more at psychologytoday.com

Olive re-analyzed the data, but the results remained the same. The data was obviously not lying, but something was not right.

While they were in college before Henry had met Oyin, Olive had forced him to take an adult attachment test, and he had presented with a secure attachment style!

It made sense. He had grown up in a stable two-parent home that fostered a secure attachment.

So had Oyin, she realized with a start.

Another forty minutes later, Olive had Oyin's results, too. Oyin presented a *fearful-avoidant attachment style*[25] because she was anxious that her partner would not give her the intimacy she wanted, she repressed her feelings, giving off an uncaring air.

The MFT Therapist in Olive despaired of the Wilsons' marital future with both partners presenting such opposing forms of insecure attachment.

While Olive did not have pre-marriage results for Oyin, the likelihood that she might have previously presented with a secure attachment style was high.

How did two individuals with secure attachment styles become insecure in a relationship? Could their attachment styles have been affected by the extra stressors of having family around, making it a false positive?

Olive sighed. She only had questions, but she could not see a way to bring them together to form a coherent hypothesis.

She would just ask ~~Dave~~ Dr. Marigold for help, she decided. He always knew how to make sense of her nonsense.

---

[25] *Fearful-avoidant attachment style* - One of the four adult attachment styles, anxious-preoccupied attachment style presents with *high anxiety* and *high avoidance* in their relationships. Read more at psychologytoday.com

Olive's mental mouth popped open at that statement. She dismissed the thought immediately, not willing to analyze and re-analyze *that*.

CHAPTER 25

Oyinbo

O ga o.[26]

That was the sentence rolling around in Irene's mind as she and Dele taxied to their upscale Buckhead hotel in Atlanta, Georgia.

The opulence around her was loud, demanding to be noticed from the sprawling mansions in the neighborhoods to the glass skyscrapers proudly reflecting the hot Atlanta sun.

Next to her, Dele scrolled through his tablet, reading an article.

She nudged him to get his attention. "Dele, are you seeing what I am seeing?"

He just grunted and kept on scrolling, ignoring her.

Irene rolled her eyes, *hissed*, and kept gazing out of the window. Dele had been like that since they left Phoenix, ignoring her and only speaking in monosyllables when it was necessary.

She knew he didn't like how she had talked to Oyinkan before they left Phoenix, but Oyinkan was her child too, so Dele was just going to have to get over it.

Everyone was content to paint her as the wicked mother-in-law in this narrative, and that was fine with her as long as she was sure that Oyin was happy.

---

[26] *O ga o* - A Yoruba exclamation that is synonymous with 'Wow.'

"You said the W Hotel, ma'am?" came the heavily accented voice of the taxi driver.

"Yes, is this it?"

"Yes, ma'am."

Irene pulled her wallet out of her purse and began to dig through it for her card, and the taxi driver, in turn, began to eye her suspiciously through the rearview mirror.

"Ah-ah, I just had it," she muttered, perplexed.

Where is this stupid card, now?

She looked over at Dele; he had his fingers crossed, watching her. Their eyes met, and she waited to see if he was going to say or do something. When he kept staring without moving a muscle, she *hissed* and returned to her rummaging.

Really?

Just as her fingers brushed over the telltale edges of an ATM card, Dele wordlessly paid the taxi driver and got out.

Irene harrumphed and followed, fuming as they unloaded the car, checked into their room, and got into the elevator.

As soon as the elevator doors closed, Irene rounded on her husband.

"Dele, what was that outside?" she exploded in Yoruba.

He didn't answer immediately. Then, he said, "Since you know everything and don't need anyone's input, I have decided to let you do what you want. *Nnkan t'oba ba n be, wahala e ni*[27]," Dele said so calmly that Irene wanted to throttle him.

"Oh, what a thoughtful husband," she retorted sarcastically. "This is about Oyinkan, isn't it?"

------

[27] *Nnkan t'oba ba n be, wahala e ni* - the consequences will be yours to face (Yoruba).

Dele shook his head and scoffed. "No, Irene. It's about you and what you want."

"As always," he added in a mutter.

Irene recoiled. Before she could react, the doors opened onto their floor. They exited the elevator and made their way into their room without a word.

"So, I'm selfish now, Dele? Is that it?" Irene asked in a hurt voice, after a few minutes of tension-filled silence during which Irene had unpacked and Dele had picked up an article.

Dele sighed as he took off his glasses and placed them on the bedside table. "Irene, I don't think your problem with Oyin's marriage lies with the marriage. I think it lies with you."

Irene opened her mouth as if to comment, and he held up a hand.

"Wait, let me finish. Yes, you love Oyin, Irie. But her marriage is about what she wants, what is going to make her happy. Not what you think is going to make her happy. And you putting words in her head, turning her against her husband, icing the poor boy out in his own house was wrong."

"Did she seem happy to you, Dele? She was in tears all the time!" Irene cried.

Dele sighed again.

"All I know is I have this bad feeling. Like something bad is about to happen or is already happening. I have been feeling it since that last talk with Oyin."

"Like *we* did something bad," he added quietly.

Irene's eyes widened, fear gripping her heart. As a girl who grew up in a polygamous home, Irene knew the importance of listening to that sixth sense. Listening to that sixth sense had saved many a child from poisonings by envious rival wives. As a Christian, it was even more important because it could be a warning from the Holy Spirit.

Dele must have read her panic on her face because he immediately stood up from the bed and came over to where she sat.

"Let's pray," was all he said.

Irene did not remember much of what she said that evening as she begged God to help. To fix whatever needed fixing.

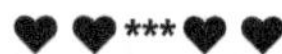

"You are here? Why didn't you let me know you were around? Since yesterday afternoon?!"

Irene could not very well tell Naomi, her former schoolmate, bosom friend, and the mother of the bride-to-be, that she and Dele had spent the entire evening praying for Oyinkan's welfare.

"We turned in early," was as close to the truth as she could get, so she said it.

"*Eeyaa.*[28] You guys were probably tired with that long layover. You are *sha*[29] coming to the bridal shower on Wednesday?"

Irene rolled her eyes in a fond, exasperated manner. Naomi had planned an advice-giving session during her daughter's bridal shower, and no amount of "Naomi, I don't think that's how they do it now" would make her budge.

"Yes, of course."

"Okay, *ose.*"

"*Ba mi ki*[30] Mummy Bose *o!*" Dele called from the bathroom.

---

[28] *Eeyaa* - A Yoruba exclamation synonymous to 'Aww.'

[29] *sha* - Used for emphasis (Nigerian Pidgin English/Yoruba)

[30] *Ba mi ki* - Say hello to (Yoruba)

Irene passed on his greeting to Naomi and cut the call.

"How did you sleep?" Irene asked as Dele padded out of the bathroom, wrapped in the plush hotel bathrobe.

Dele nodded. "Okay."

"You know what I'm asking."

"I don't know," Dele sighed. "I am still feeling a bit strange, but since we prayed together last night, I have definitely felt lighter."

"Me too," Irene sighed. "Why did we ever stop praying together?"

Dele shook his head as he sunk into the bed next to her. "I don't know, but I think we have learned our lesson."

Irene moved closer to her husband and lay her head on his chest. "I think we have."

Irene had never seen so much pink silk and white feathers in one place.

If the purpose of the entryway was to call every female hormone to attention, they could confidently call the event a success.

"Irie-Irie!"

"Na-who-baby!" Irene called Naomi's nickname.

"Wow! How long has it been?" Naomi said as they untangled themselves from a tight embrace.

"Seven years, I think. Maybe more?"

Naomi laughed. "You don't look a day over forty! Uncle Dele is doing his job."

Irene laughed and shook her head. Naomi was really the one who did not look a day over forty with her completely jet-black hair pulled into two Afro puffs, barely existent laugh lines, and eyes so light a brown they were almost gray.

"You look very nice too," was all Irene said, though.

Naomi just waved the compliment away. "Well, you are here now! So, let's go tell these *aimokan-mokans*[31] about marriage."

"Wait, is it just the two of us?" Irene barely got the question out, as Naomi rushed her off to a seat.

It wasn't just the two of them. Naomi had six "aunties" in total at the silk-feather-fest to share words of advice.

And no one held back. From the dos and don'ts of the wedding night to the dynamics of domestic chores, nothing was left untouched. Irene actually found herself enjoying the conversation.

"Now David is a good boy, Abosede, but his mother will not appreciate you turning him into an errand boy."

Bosede, the bride-to-be, pouted. "Mummy, I am not anybody's slave either!"

"All I am saying, my dear," Naomi commented, "is for you not to forget your role as a woman in the house. Don't let modernism creep into your home and rob you of a stable, happy marriage."

Bosede rolled her eyes, clearly unconvinced.

"If I may jump in," Irene heard herself saying, "there is nothing wrong with being a woman in your home."

Everyone turned to look at her, and she flushed a little before continuing. "I know you girls of nowadays don't want to live the double-shift lives that a lot of us, your mothers, lived. But that is part of why a lot of us are still married. It's not the biggest part, but a part nonetheless."

Bosede scooted forward, her full attention on Irene. "But Mummy, your daughter, Oyin, is married to a white guy. Surely, he is not leaving all the house chores and kitchen duties to her."

---

[31] *Aimokan-mokans* – Novices (Yoruba).

It was in that moment that Irene realized just how much she had failed Oyinkan in her duty as a "mother-of-the-bride." She had been so bitter when Oyinkan had said that it was Henry or nobody else. Oh, she had played the part of the happy mother-in-law when in public, but she had seethed and fumed in private, feeling cheated.

Sure, Naomi had been pushy, but at least *her* heart was in the right place. Irene had not called Oyinkan to the side to give her advice, not before her wedding, and certainly not on this last trip. Instead, she had looked only to criticize.

Oh, Lord, I have been so blind. I'm sorry.

"No, he's not," Irene replied. "House duties are not the only part of a woman's role in the house; that's what you girls are forgetting."

"But," Bosede pressed, "who does the cleaning? Who cooks the meals?"

Irene realized with a weary sigh that she had *also* not cared to learn the answers to the above questions while she was in Oyinkan's house.

"I don't know too much, but I know that they have a house cleaner, and both of them cooked for us on separate occasions."

A chorus of "oohs" and "wows" rose from the group of younger girls.

"That's what *me* I want too *oo*. I am not about to be anybody's slave. David knows!" Bosede said determinedly.

Naomi shook her head. "Bosede, your husband is not white, one. Two, what works for the goose is not what will work for the gander. What I am telling you as your mother is for you to be a Proverbs 31 woman. Bring good to your husband, no matter what form that takes."

Irene nodded. "Yes, I agree. Oyinkan and her husband have a system that works for them. Find your own system and be a virtuous woman to your husband; God will lead you."

Bosede pouted slightly, but it was clear that she was pondering the words.

"My dear, even if that system is the typical, you in the kitchen and him mowing the lawn, it's your house. Manage it for the both of you, not for anyone else," one of the aunties chimed in.

"And if it means him cooking because you have a deadline to meet at work, it's your house. Manage it. That is what it means to be a Proverbs 31 woman managing your household," another auntie added.

"Yes," Irene nodded.

Naomi laughed. "Our advice is so good that we should start a *pubcast*."

Bosede rolled her eyes. "You mean a podcast, Mummy?"

Everyone laughed, including Irene.

Naomi chuckled good-humouredly. "It's your father that cannot speak English. Before you were born, *mo ti n s'Oyinbo.*[32]"

Everyone laughed again.

"Okay, Mummy." Bosede snickered.

"Anyway, you see how important this advising session is now? But when I was planning it, you were complaining." Naomi teased her daughter.

"Yes, Mummy, thank you."

"*Oya*, let's pray."

---

[32] *mo ti n s'Oyinbo:* I have been speaking English.

CHAPTER 26

Insecure Avoidant (Part 2)

It was the third time since they had been married that Oyin and Henry did not sleep next to each other on the same bed.

Henry did not think he could bear to be so close to Oyin. So, he slept on the loveseat in their study because he also could not bear to be too far away from her.

She drove him crazy, and he apparently drove her to tears. He had lain awake to the sounds of her sobbing next door.

Oyin was not prone to tears…till she married him. The sentence sounded so much like Oyin's mom that he immediately became angry.

Lord, I can't keep living like this.

The emotional stress was more than he could bear, more than he had ever had to bear. He was the only child of two loving parents. His childhood had been the quintessential American dream – white picket fence, SUV, …the whole thing.

Henry tried to get more comfortable on the couch, but it was impossible. His back and knees hurt from being cramped all night. He wished that day were a weekday, so he could leave for work and give the situation time to cool. But it was a Saturday, and Friday night had not gone well.

When he got home, Oyin was nowhere to be found. Okay, maybe he did not go looking for her… but she was not in the kitchen because that was the first place he walked into as he entered the house. Neither was she in their bedroom and study when he went to retire for the night.

So, they had done it – let the sun go down on their wrath.

The Bible certainly knew what It was talking about because time had only made him angrier.

Henry knew he should pray and ask God to fix this, but his mind was heavy, his tongue felt like lead, and he did not even know what to say. It was like he was swimming through thick muck, and he was too weary, too weighed down by the dirt to look up for help.

Henry shut his eyes as if to block out the thoughts of his failure. He must have dozed off because the next thing he knew, the door swung on its hinges, and Oyin walked in.

She was looking everywhere but at him, and she looked…awful. Not ugly, just a tired beauty like a rose that had not been watered and was quietly wilting.

When she finally looked at him, the depth of feeling in her dark eyes took his breath away.

She sat across from him in one of the straight-backed chairs and said, "Can we talk?"

Henry nodded, unable to say anything.

"Am I not enough for you?" she asked bluntly.

Henry just looked on, still unable to say a word. Oyin took his silence as assent to continue.

"I saw your exchange with the waitress yesterday. And you pining over Olive as if I am not here…"

Henry scoffed, feeling attacked, and he went on the defensive.

"What started this conversation, Oyin, was my being upset with you for not taking my feelings into account. Forgive me if I don't really want to hear about what you think I did wrong for the millionth time when I have not heard an apology."

Oyin chuckled hysterically and clapped her hands three times in that Nigerian gesture that expressed exasperation.

"You realize that you are defending Olive's honor from me? Your wife? Forgive *me* if I feel threatened."

Henry's eyes widened, and he took in Oyin's meaning. He knew he should end this, draw her close to reassure her that she was enough for him, but something stayed him. He was tired of always being the one to apologize.

"I can't pretend to not be happy that Olive is gone, Henry," Oyin said in a quiet voice.

Really? Not even for me? Henry thought, and then he said it out loud to her.

"That's what is driving me crazy, Henry. Why does it matter? Why are you making it a thing? You know how I feel about her, about what she feels for you..." She left the sentence hanging as if she wanted to say more but was afraid to.

"So you keep saying, Oyin, but she has been my best friend since elementary school! How about I feel?"

Oyin's eyes widened, and she looked like she was about to choke on air.

"So, you love her? Is that what this is about? Am I the third wheel in some kind of twisted best-friends-turned-lovers situation?"

Before this statement, there had been a tentativeness in their manner of speaking, as if they were afraid to say anything hurtful to each other. That changed.

"That's ridiculous. You are being ridiculous, Oyin."

"Really?" Oyin said hysterically. "What else am I supposed to think when my husband is mad at me for not comforting him in his despair that his best friend is gone? Did I mention that this best friend is freaking in love with you?!"

Henry shook his head exasperatedly. "Sometimes it feels like we are speaking two different languages."

He continued. "You are not the victim in this situation! It always has to be about Oyin and what she feels; she is the beautiful flower in a garden that must not be allowed to fade,"

Oyin gasped. "Really? Henry, really? You are going to mock our wedding? My culture?"

Anger consumed Henry. "And your family hasn't mocked mine? Or are you going to deny that your mother has not said as much? That's absolute B.S., Oyin."

"Ugh!" Henry stood up and kicked off the throw he had used overnight. Anger, like a wild horse, spurred him on.

"I'm just - I'm just so sick of it! I'm tired of always having to measure up, of always having to struggle to be enough…"

"…I am just over it."

Henry breathed heavily in the silence that ensued. He had exposed it, the bitterness etched in the vilest part of him that he had not allowed love to touch.

"If you had to do it again, would you choose me?" Oyin asked, her face completely devoid of emotion.

"What?"

"Knowing what you know now, feeling what you feel now, would you choose me?"

"That's not a fair question."

"I think it is."

When he didn't say anything, Oyin stood to leave. "Let me know when you figure out the answer to that."

Henry's reaction was instant. "That's it? You are just going to walk out on this conversation?"

"Well, you have expressed your feelings regarding me and this marriage quite clearly. Let me know when that changes."

"I would say that is the most dramatic thing I have ever heard, but your mother takes the cake on that one."

Anger darkened Oyin's face immediately. "Get mad at me all you want, but do not disrespect my mother. Do not bring my mother into this."

Henry opened his mouth to speak, but Oyin interrupted. "No, you got your chance to speak. It's my turn. That you don't see my concern with Olive is baffling to me. You think you are tired? Well, that makes two of us.

"I am tired of having to remind you that I am your wife, that you are supposed to take my side. I am tired of feeling like I have to compete for your attention. I am tired of having to wonder if I am enough to hold the attention of the great Henry Wilson that every girl would kill for. I am tired of feeling inadequate…I – I am just tired."

Without waiting for him to respond, she walked over to the door, opened it, and said without looking back. "I think we need space. I am going to go stay with my parents in Atlanta before they leave for Nigeria."

Thirty minutes later, she, too, was gone.

CHAPTER 27

Bang!

Oyin smelled like blossoms. She didn't.
Oyin's hair was textured and smelled like exotic oils. Hers wasn't and didn't.
Oyin's lips were full and fit his perfectly. Hers didn't.
Oyin always smiled when they kissed. Olive didn't.
What the hell did I just do?

PART THREE

CHAPTER 28
S.O.S

Twelve hours before…

SOS.

Olive's heart skipped a beat. Then another. Henry never ever sent a trivial SOS text.

Her fingers began to tremble as she picked up her phone to call Henry. She was concerned but hesitant because all his *SOS's* had the same topic in common – Oyin.

"Hello?" Henry's voice came through the phone, soft and quiet.

Her hesitation disappeared at the agitation in his voice.

"Beave? What's going on?"

"I- I don't - I don't know. She's gone."

Gone?!

"Henry, what happened? Who's gone? Where are you?"

"Oyin."

His voice shook as if he was trying to hold back tears. "Oyin's gone, and I don't know if she is coming back, Olive."

She knew they were arguing, but separation? So early in their marriage?

"Henry, I am so sorry."

A broken sob came through the phone in response, and Olive's heart thudded at the sound.

"I don't know what to say, Henry. Where are you right now?"

Olive wrung her fingers in distress. She wished she could give him a hug.

"I'm home. Olive, I don't want to be alone right now. Can you…" He broke off. "I'm sorry. That was a stupid thing to ask. You have your thesis to worry about. Sorry I even asked."

"No! Wait, Henry. Of course, I can come. I will take the next flight out."

As soon as the words fell out of her mouth, she felt a pang of regret.

"No - no," Henry protested. "You don't have to do that. Focus on your thesis. I just needed someone to talk to for a minute."

Olive hesitated. Indecision plagued her. What good were their years of friendship if she could not be there for Henry? A part of her heart whispered that he was more than a friend, and maybe she should stay away for the sake of her sanity, but she couldn't. Henry was in pain.

"No, I am coming. You shouldn't be alone right now."

"Okay," he said, giving up his protest.

This only assured her that she was making the right decision. He needed her.

As soon as the call ended, Olive burst into a flurry of frenzied activities. She was feeling a sense of urgency unlike anything she had ever experienced. Part of her thought that it was because Henry was hurt, and she needed to be there for (and with) him as soon as possible, yet deep down, she knew that it was because if she did not hurry, she might succumb to her misgivings. So, she hurried.

Her traitorous heart skipped at the thought of seeing Henry again, but her head screamed No! She threw her toiletries into a bag.

This is crazy, Olive. Stop.

She flung her nightclothes and packed a toiletry bag into her recently unpacked suitcase.

Olive, this is crazy. Are you really doing this? You can't keep running to him. This is not healthy.

She zipped her suitcase, wheeled it out to the front door, and pulled out her phone to call an Uber.

Olive, what are you doing? STOP IT!

She froze. But she couldn't stop her fingers from trembling.

What *was* she doing?

Was she really about to fly to Phoenix on Henry's request? For the second time?

Olive let out a shaky breath.

Yes, yes, she was. Because that's what a good friend would do. It wasn't his fault she was in love with him.

She rested her head heavily against her front door. She would always be there for him, healthy or unhealthy, Phoenix or San Diego.

An hour and thirty minutes later, she sat in front of her boarding gate, waiting for her flight to be called. She kept trying to convince herself that she was doing the right thing.

Right?

Right! She needed to be there for him. That's what a good friend would do.

Just then, her ringtone blared through the uncharacteristic silence of the waiting area.

The middle-aged lady sitting across from Olive, who had a sleeping mask on, sneered in Olive's direction.

"Sorry!" Olive whispered.

In her haste to silence the phone, she picked up the call without looking.

"Hello?" she whisper-yelled.

"Olive? Are you okay?"

"Dave?"

Dave chuckled before saying, "Yes, it is me. What is going on? Why are you whispering?"

Olive rolled her eyes. "I am at the airport. Just text me."

"What? Why are you at the airport? What's going on?"

"Text me!" Olive replied before she hung up the phone. She threw an apologetic glance at the lady, who had taken off her sleeping mask and was now openly glaring at Olive.

Her phone buzzed loudly against the metal handle of the chair as a text came in, and Olive quickly picked it up.

Of course, it was Dave.

Are you okay? Why are you at the airport?

Olive rolled her eyes.

I'm okay. Had a family emergency.

It wasn't really a lie. Henry was family...ish.

Her phone buzzed a second later. Although her palm helped to muffle the sound, Olive quickly switched her phone to silent mode with a chuckle. Cranky Lady looked about ready to murder her, and Olive wanted to at least earn her master's degree before she died.

I thought your dad lived in Malibu.

Oh my goodness, Dave...

Yes, he does. I am going to Phoenix.

She knew it was going to happen, so she was not surprised when her phone lit up with a call from Dave.

Olive rolled her eyes again and cut the call.

I can't talk.

You can't or you won't?
Olive, why are you going to Phoenix?

Why *was* she going? Olive asked herself.

Henry and Oyin are having trouble. He needs a friend.
Then he should call his mother or his father.
YOU could call his mother.
You don't have to go.

Olive put down her phone, not knowing what else to say. Her misgivings tripled in size. She wanted to go, but she didn't at the same time. She needed to go, but she didn't at the same time.

Her phone lit up as another text came in. It was Dave again.

At least call his mother, Olive.
You shouldn't be there alone.

He was right, Olive sighed. So, she walked away from the seating area to avoid Cranky Lady's wrath and dialed Patricia.

Patricia Wilson picked up on the third ring.

"Ollie, sweetheart, it is so nice to hear from you."

As always, Patricia's voice brought a smile to Olive's face.

"Hi, Patricia."

"Hi darling, it's been so long. You barely text anymore."

"I'm sorry, Patricia. This last year of school has been brutal."

It was only partly true. Olive knew that Patricia knew that she was in love with Henry. And Patricia was Team Oyin. She had been since she heard how excited Henry was about Oyin. Of course, Patricia had never actually said anything to Olive, but Olive knew that she knew, and that was worse.

"That's okay, honey. I understand. So, what's been going on with you?" Patricia asked conversationally.

Olive hesitated for a second. Patricia did not sound like someone who knew that her son and his wife had just separated. Olive almost cut the call right then. She did not want to have to be the one to tell her, but Dave was right. She *could* not be there alone.

If she told Patricia, she could leave a couple of days earlier than was on her return ticket and not feel guilty about leaving Henry by himself.

"Olive? Hello? Are you there? Greg, I told you this phone is acting up. We should call that nice lady at the phone store and -"

If the situation weren't so grim, Olive would have chuckled.

"I'm here, Patricia. Have you spoken to Henry today?"

Patricia paused for a second before saying, "No, I haven't. But he did tell me that you were in Phoenix, visiting. How is that going?"

Olive nodded as she took in Patricia's spoken and unspoken words.

"Oh, I left some days ago. Patricia -" Olive took a deep breath. "Henry called me earlier this morning. There was an argument, and Oyin left. He sounded really bad."

Patricia gasped. "Left? What do you mean?"

"He said he didn't know if she was coming back."

"Oh, my baby!" Patricia exclaimed.

"I am at the airport now, waiting to board a plane to Phoenix," she added as an afterthought.

"Oh, that's great, Olive, thank you. He shouldn't be alone now. Greg and I will be on the next flight out. Thank you for letting me know."

"Of course. You are welcome."

"Have you...uh, tried to reach out to Oyin?" Patricia asked.

"No, I haven't. I think maybe we should...um, hold off on that until we talk to Henry?" Olive suggested.

Olive had "nothing" against Oyin, but her allegiance was to Henry.

"Of course. Of course. Thank you, Olive. We will see you soon."

Olive hung up, feeling lighter. She would only be down there for a couple of days, and they would be fully chaperoned. What could go wrong?

CHAPTER 29

Iced Heart

This is crazy.

Henry had not moved from the couch since Oyin walked out. He had not done much of anything except stare into space, all the while wishing he could lay back on the couch and restart the day. He could not believe Oyin was gone. She left.

Like...she was gone.

It had taken an hour after Oyin walked out for all the rage to evaporate, but as soon as it did, pain solidly took its place. He had never been so angry in his life. He had never felt so much pain in his life. It was like his heart had been ripped from his chest like it walked out the door...possibly never coming back.

He considered calling Oyin, but every time he started to, he couldn't. When he finally picked up his phone, he texted Olive instead. That was hours ago, and Henry had still not moved from the couch.

When did everything go so wrong?

Just then, as if in response, his phone rang. Out of habit, he glanced at the screen. It was Mom. He let it go to voicemail. What was he supposed to say when she asked about Oyin?

Oh, she's fine. I mean, we got into a fight, and she left, but it's all good.

The phone stopped ringing and started up again. Henry closed his eyes, took a deep breath, and picked it up.

"Henry?"

"Hi, Mom."

"Honey, I just got off the phone with Olive. I am so confused, Henry. What's going on?"

The worry in her voice was palpable, but the pain in his heart was tangible, so Henry did not have it in him to explain, reassure, or comfort her.

"I don't know, Mom. I don't know," he said in a tired voice.

Mom had always been adept at deciphering his feelings, so he was not surprised when she didn't push it. Instead, she said, "Okay, well, your Dad is working on getting us tickets. We could not get anything for today, but we should arrive on the first flight tomorrow. Okay?"

"Okay."

"Okay. Just...tell me this. Do you know where she went? Is she safe? Do we need to worry about her?"

Henry scrubbed his hand over his face as a sudden weariness overtook him. "She said she was going to be with her parents in Atlanta."

Mom let out a breath. "Okay. Okay. Good. Good. Have you...um, have you had anything to eat today?"

Henry gave a bitter chuckle as he realized that he hadn't. His appetite had apparently walked out the door with Oyin.

"Promise me that you will get up and eat something, Henry. Please. I don't want to have to worry about that, too."

"Okay, I promise."

"Okay, sweetie. We will see you tomorrow, okay?"

"Okay."

"Maybe just talk to God a little today before you go to bed?"

"Okay, Mom."

"Bye, sweetie."

Henry hit the End button, and his phone's lock screen popped into place. It was a picture of him and Oyin. (Of course, it was). She had just come back from the salon, and she had been extremely excited about her new hairdo. She kept going on about how important "protective styles" were for her hair, and the light in her eyes drew him in like a moth to a flame. He had tried to pull her in for a kiss, but she ran away laughing. He had chased her and gotten his kiss as well as multiple selfies.

"Ugh!" He pushed his phone away, along with the memory.

He wasn't ready to face the magnitude of what had just happened.

But his brain won't listen. He had been able to shut it off for the past hours, but now he couldn't stop the onslaught of memories. The most painful one, of course, was playing on repeat:

"That's ridiculous. You are being ridiculous, Oyin."

"Really? What else am I supposed to think when my husband is mad at me for not comforting him in his despair that his best friend is gone? Did I mention that this best friend is freaking in love with you?!"

"Sometimes it feels like we are speaking two different languages...you are not the victim in this situation! It always has to be about Oyin and what she feels; she is the beautiful flower in a garden that must not be allowed to fade,"

"Really? Henry, really? You are going to mock our wedding? My culture?"

NO!

He got up suddenly, ready to outrun the memory if that was what it took. He decided to make good on his promise to his mom. He walked out of the study, grabbed a Pop-Tart from the kitchen, and collapsed onto the bed.

Of course, the pillows smelled of Oyin, rose blossom water and argan oil. They always did. Once, he had told her that he would bottle her scent, label it 'Honey,' and sell each bottle for $5000.

Watch how bees would be out of business because everyone prefers Oyin's Honey, he had proclaimed.

It was so cheesy, but it had evoked the desired effect. Oyin rolled her eyes and gave him the smile that he loved so much, the one that lit up her eyes and usually rendered him speechless.

Stop!

Henry put the last of the Pop-Tart in his mouth and, in a swift motion, stripped the pillowcases and lay back down again. He fell into a fitful sleep after a few minutes.

The piercing sound reached Henry in the deepest realms of sleep and yanked him out with all the gentleness of a hawk snatching its prey. Henry jolted upright, his head groaning at the sudden movement.

His phone started ringing again, and Henry swore. Henry never swore, but apparently, today was a day of firsts.

He picked up his phone to look at the caller ID. It was Olive.

"Hello?"

"Oh, thank goodness! I have called you like three times now. I was starting to get worried."

She truly sounded concerned, and a twinge of guilt - the first emotion he had felt all day that wasn't rage or pain - flitted through him.

"Sorry. I'm fine. I was asleep."

"Oh, Beave. You don't have to apologize. It's okay. I am just glad you are okay."

Henry nodded and repeated. "I'm fine."

Olive cleared her throat. "I am in an Uber right now. I should be at your front door in like ten minutes."

Henry stifled a sigh and ran his free hand through his hair. He shouldn't have asked Olive to come. He did not want anyone to see him this way, not even Olive. But he should have known that she would come. He hadn't even gotten the entire sentence out before she agreed. Tears pricked the corner of his eyes. Olive was always there for him.

"I, um - thank you so much, Olive. I- uh, I... just, thank you."

"It's nothing. Truly," he could hear the smile in her voice, see the smile on her face as if she were right in front of him.

"Okay. See you soon."

"See you soon."

Although his eyelids were heavy from weariness, he rose out of bed and headed to the bathroom to freshen up. His breath stank of sleep and Pop-Tart remnants.

It felt like it was only five minutes later that he heard the doorbell ring. He pulled a blue U of A sweatshirt over his head and walked to open the front door.

Olive stood there, the early evening sun creating a halo of light around her. She had a slight smile on her face as she greeted him. He hadn't realized just how much he needed somebody until the somebody he needed stood in front of him. As soon as she and her luggage were safely inside, she threw her arms around him and wrapped him in a bear hug.

His arms rose to her back, and he hugged her just as tightly. Soon, the hug ended, and Olive pulled him by the hand to the nearest sitting area.

She settled a no-nonsense gaze on him as they sat down.

"Talk to me," she ordered, brooking no argument.

A slight smile cracked Henry's face as he regarded her. "Don't you want to take your stuff into your room and freshen up?"

"Are you saying I stink, Beave?"

Henry rolled his eyes automatically. "No, I am saying you traveled hours to get here. The least I can do is to make you comfortable."

Olive waved his concern away. "That's unimportant. Talk to me, come on."

Henry got up, effectively eliminating any possibility of an immediate conversation. "I will, I promise, but let's get you settled in first."

He extended a hand to help her up, and then paused as a thought struck him. "How long were you planning on staying?"

Olive's cheeks reddened, before she said, "I can only stay for a few days. That's why I called Patricia, which I hope you are not mad about, by the way."

Henry nodded, his hand still outstretched. "Then, we still have time, and no, I am not mad." He waved his palm up and down in an exaggeratedly impatient manner. "Come on, up you go!"

It was Olive's turn to roll her eyes. "I concede this round to you, but you are going to cave, Beave Wilson!"

Henry chuckled, warmth flooding his heart and thawing the ice that had started to form since Oyin walked out.

CHAPTER 30

The Stupidest of Them All

Once upon a time, there was a girl, and she knew she was stupid. In the history of stupid people, she was sure she was the stupidest of them all. Three hours in the air had given Oyin plenty of time to ponder and wonder, and the only reasonable explanation for her behavior was idiocy of the highest level.

She fingered her flight ticket stub, the serrated edges lightly grazing her fingertips. She looked out the window onto distant treetops as the plane descended toward Hartsfield-Jackson Atlanta International Airport.

Five hours ago, Oyin had been sure Henry would call her back as soon as she had walked out of the room, so she sat on their bed, waiting. Five minutes went by. Ten minutes. Twenty. Nothing. A blinding anger consumed her, and she made good on her threat. She grabbed her purse and phone and left the house. Although anger spurred her on, her heart cried, trusting that Henry would call. When she got to the airport, she loitered around the waiting area for several minutes before heading to the ticket counter.

He's going to call, her heart had pleaded.

He never did. She had sat at the boarding gate, waiting for ~~his call~~ her flight. She had to have been the last one to put her phone in Airplane Mode, waiting until their plane was literally off the ground. He never did.

Oyin rested her head against the window, a bitter smile crossing her lips. Most of that anger was gone now, replaced by a weariness that made her bones rattle and her heart whimper. Every time she started to pray, she couldn't. What was she supposed to say?

Dear Jesus, help my marriage. My husband might be in love with his best friend, and I am running to my parents. But still, help my marriage.

Oyin shook her head. She was not even sure what she wanted. This morning, she found out what it meant to truly hate somebody. Not caring about a person was not hate, that was indifference. No, to hate someone was to love and to have that love shoved back in your face like a prank birthday cake. Hate didn't hurt, it stung. Because for every part of her heart that hated Henry for siding with Olive, every other part loved him just as fiercely.

"Ladies and gentlemen, we will be landing in a few minutes. Thank you for flying Strong Air, and we hope you choose us again."

Oyin looked up from the window and felt the wetness on her cheeks. As quickly as she could, she tried to wipe them off, but not before the guy sitting next to her noticed and said,

"Are you okay, miss?"

Oyin wanted to scream. There was so much concern in the random stranger's voice.

Was it too much to ask that her husband cared too?

"I'm okay. Yes, thank you."

As soon as the plane's tires hit the runway, Oyin pulled out her phone and switched it off Airplane Mode. She promised herself she was not looking for a call or a text from Henry, but her eyes ran down her Messages and her Call Log, frantically searching for something, *anything*, from 'Babe ♥.'

There was nothing.

Oyin opened her WhatsApp application and called Mummy, instead of screaming in frustration like she really wanted to.

Mummy picked on the first ring.

"Oyinkan, you called at the exact right moment. I was just walking into the bathroom. If I was in the event hall, I would not even have heard my phone ring."

Oyin frowned. *Event hall?*

Then she remembered. Mummy and Daddy were in Atlanta for a wedding. The scream of frustration almost slipped out as she realized that she was going to have to put on a happy face. Mummy and Daddy could not know - no one could know - until after the wedding. Oyin would die first before she saw smug looks on those aunties' faces as they whispered behind their wedding programs:

Didn't they tell her not to marry a white man? Children of this generation, they get what they are looking for.

"Hello? Oyinkan? I think the network here is bad."

"I am here. I can hear you. How is the wedding going?"

"Oh, pshhtt…" Oyin could just see Mummy waving her hand in the air.

"They were supposed to start at five *o*! They just started the wedding a few minutes ago. A whole two hours behind! The groom has not even entered yet. I *sha* hope they are not late for the Thanksgiving service tomorrow too. Anyway...*bawo ni*[33]?"

"Fine. Fine…" she trailed off.

"Ah-ah, you don't sound like yourself. What's wrong, baby?"

The pilot's voice came through the speakers just then, cutting Oyin's response off.

---

[33] *bawo ni* - how are you? (Yoruba)

"Wait, are you on a plane?" Mummy's incredulous voice came through the plane, somehow managing to be louder than the plane's speakers.

Oyin sighed. "Yes, mummy. That's why I was calling. I came to surprise you and Daddy."

"Oh…"

Oyin could tell Mummy was not really pleased with the 'surprise,' but she could not bring herself to care. She had told Henry she was going to Atlanta out of spite to hurt him like he had hurt her. The fact that he hadn't even tried to stop her only helped to make Atlanta seem like the Maldives.

"I will see you soon, Mummy."

Oyin hung up the call without waiting for Mummy's response.

Maybe she should not have called.

CHAPTER 31

Beave

Henry placed two plates of mac and cheese onto the kitchen island, shaking his head.

"I can't believe you are just sitting there. You came here to help me, remember?"

Olive placed her elbows onto the island, rested her chin on her interlaced fingers, and batted her eyelashes dramatically.

"But, like, I am, like, totally helping!" she mock-protested in a valley-girl accent.

Henry snorted in response. "You are behaving just like …"

Oyin.

It felt like it was only yesterday that her parents were around, and his biggest worry had been getting them to like him.

Olive placed her hand on his. "It's okay to say her name, Beave. It's not a curse word."

Henry raised his head to meet Olive's gaze and was floored by the concern in her eyes. "I know. I just…"

Olive rubbed his hand sympathetically. "I get it. But remember, you love her."

He did. With every breath in his body, he did.

Henry sighed. "I do."

Olive nodded. "I know."

"Wait, you just said you get it. What did you mean?"

Olive removed her hand from his and blushed slightly before waving his question away. "Ha. Nice try. We were talking about you. Not me."

Henry shook his head. "I can't believe you are holding out on me. I tell you everything!"

Olive just rolled her eyes and put a forkful of food into her mouth.

Henry insisted. "I am not telling you anything until you fess up."

Olive rolled her eyes again. "It was nothing! It was just a silly crush that never went anywhere. Not important at all."

Henry narrowed his eyes at her.

"Beave," Olive began in what he had come to recognize as her therapist voice, "your marriage is more important right now. Tell me what happened."

Henry sighed. He did not even know where to start. After a few minutes of contemplation, he finally said in a careful voice, "I think issues had been simmering beneath the surface for a while, and they finally just came to a head this morning."

He expected a hug, a sigh of sympathy, anything other than a solid punch in the arm.

"Ow!"

"You sound like you are giving a business presentation. This is your marriage we are talking about. Can you give me more real and less...stiff?"

How could everyone see into him so clearly? Olive, Mom, *Oyin*. Was he really that transparent?

Henry buried his head in his hands. "I'm scared to feel it, Olive. I don't want to go there in my mind. What if this is the end?"

Olive sighed. "It's not... just tell me what happened."

Henry took a deep breath and recounted the events from last night to this morning – the dinner that did not happen and the morning-after conversation.

"She kept saying I was defending you but is it too much to ask that she considers my feelings too? The worst part is that this is what always happens! All the darn time. I always have to bury my hurt and apologize. All the time. Olive, all the time. I was just so done!"

Henry concluded his monologue-turned-tirade with a grunt, his chest heaving up and down.

Olive's mouth was slightly agape. "Wow, just wow."

"Yeah."

"That's a lot."

"I know."

"Did you really say her mom takes the cake on being dramatic?"

Henry closed his eyes, mortification coloring his cheeks. "Yeah…"

"Wow."

"And she asked if you would choose her again?"

"Yep."

Olive shook her head, visibly perplexed. "Like, doesn't she know how much you love her? *Everyone* can see how much you love her."

"That's what drives me crazy, you know? Because then…I, I - like, I get in my head that, is it really about me loving her or she just wanting to control me?"

Olive shook her head. "Yeah, I don't know about that."

"Do you think I'm being crazy?"

"I think she's just scared to lose you, Henry. And you are scared to lose her, too. I don't think that's crazy."

Henry scrubbed his hand over his face. "So, what now? What am I supposed to do, Olive?"

"Well, what do you want to do?"

"I don't know," Henry sighed. "I mean, I love her, but I am so tired."

Olive nodded. "Then take some time. That's okay, too."

Henry let out a breath. Olive was right. Of course, she was. She was always right. He needed time to think – to just breathe. So much – *too* much – had happened over the past few weeks.

Maybe giving each other space isn't the worst idea...

He felt like he always had to be something for Oyin that he never really got to be himself. But now, here with Olive, he could just be Henry.

"How about this? No marriage talk or *thoughts* for the rest of the night?" Olive suggested, after many minutes of silence.

"Am I that transparent? Is my face a jumbotron for my thoughts?"

"Yes. One hundred percent." Olive said with a laugh.

Henry laughed. "Wow."

"Good analogy, by the way."

Henry laughed some more. "Thanks."

"But you've always been really good at analogies. You remember the olive oil incident?"

Henry's eyes widened as he recollected the "scandalous" incident that had been the talk of their fourth-grade class. "Wow! I have not thought about that in years. Remember how I vowed I was going to call you Oil for the rest of our lives?"

"Yes, I remember. And I remember threatening to shave all your hair if you did."

Henry chuckled, his heart feeling lighter and lighter. "But *my* threats didn't stop you from calling me Beave!"

Olive rolled her eyes. "Okay, first of all, Beave is cute. Literally, everyone goes 'aww' whenever they hear me call you that..."

Not Oyin, Henry could not help but think. Just as quickly, he pushed the thought away.

No more Oyin-related thoughts tonight.

Olive was still talking, "...quite different than Oil. Oil is a terrible nickname. Besides, the origin story of Beave is way less embarrassing than Oil."

Henry scoffed. "Maybe for you. It was horrible for me!"

Olive laughed. "No, it wasn't. It was cute. You wore a suit and tie!"

"Yes, I remember. But I also remember you saying that you were going to wear a ballgown."

"I was kidding! We were twelve! Who wears a ballgown for their first kiss?"

"People who say they are going to. We were the only ones in seventh grade who hadn't had a first kiss, and we decided to do it with each other. You said you wanted it to be special!"

Olive laughed some more. "I did, but not nerd-special."

"Wow, you suck."

"I do not! I mean, you show up at my door in a suit and tie and say, 'Who is ready to smooch?' Forgive me for not wanting that."

Henry mock gasped. "You love Game-show Henry!"

"I do, but that was tacky."

"And so was the kiss," Olive added as an afterthought.

"I was twelve!" Henry protested.

"So was I!" Olive retorted, "But you didn't see me biting your lips off in a pathetic attempt at a kiss."

"I did not bite your lips off. It was a little nib, and it was only because I was nervous. It was totally a mistake."

"Tell that to my mortified twelve-year-old self. You and your beaver teeth totally deserved the nickname."

"But I apologized over and over!"

"And that's why I changed the name to Beave instead of Beaver! You should be grateful."

Henry laughed delightedly as euphoric elation flooded his senses. He retorted carelessly, "It doesn't matter. I do better in the kissing department now, so you can stop calling me that."

There was something in the air between them. Something dangerous. It twisted and taunted and danced and laughed as Olive responded with twinkling eyes. "There is no way for me to confirm that statement, and I can't just take your word for it. So, I'm just going to have to keep calling you Beave."

Heedless of the fire alarm ringing in his head, Henry said, "Well, there is a way…"

Olive's eyes widened, and she glanced at his lips.

The atmosphere in the room changed, so suddenly that Henry would have thought he was dreaming if his eyes were not wide open.

CHAPTER 32

OH

Now

Pastor Greg Leard knew something was wrong. Something was terribly, horribly wrong. It started as a slight concern when he did not see them arrive for the church workers' meeting. Oyin and Henry never missed the meeting, but his concern did not grow into a worry until both morning services were over, and they were nowhere to be found. No one seemed to know where they were, either.

As soon as the last "Amen" was uttered, Pastor Greg knew something was up. It wasn't like people didn't skip church some Sundays, but the Wilsons' absence sat heavily on his heart. Having spent almost 15 years in a relationship with the Lord, he knew this meant the Lord wanted him to do something.

But what?

Pastor Greg whispered a quick prayer to the Lord for guidance before getting up from his seat to greet the other parishioners.

"That was a great sermon, Pastor G!"

"Are you still coming to the game this Saturday, Pastor?"

"Happy Sunday, Pastor Greg!"

Pastor Greg's face was the definition of happiness by the time he reached the church doors. There were only a few people still left milling around, either in deep conversation or yelling last-minute brunch plans as they headed to their various cars. He waved at the few who looked in his direction as he headed to his office. Just as he rounded the corner, he ran into a group of ladies by the bathroom.

A chorus of "Hey Pastor" greeted him.

"Hi ladies, how is it going?" Pastor Greg asked politely.

As a male pastor, he had to remain conscious about maintaining a respectable distance with his female parishioners. Even more so that he was a single pastor and many women saw him as their personal project.

"It is a good thing you're here, Pastor!" Margot, one of the ladies, responded. Margot was, well, an attractive woman. Her mocha skin, white smile, and big brown eyes gave off a warmth that made people want to be around her. But it was her heart for the Lord and her compassion for people that made them stay around her.

"We were just talking about maybe going to visit Oyin and Henry since we did not see them in church."

"Oh, okay," Pastor Greg said as he nodded approvingly.

"Yeah, I texted with Oyin on Tuesday, and we talked about getting brunch after church today. It's not like her to be MIA," Penny, a children's teacher on Oyin's team, offered. Penny was a force of nature. Although her own children had long since left the coop, she hadn't lost her motherly nature, and that made her a great children's teacher.

"I agree. It's quite unlike them, but you know they have house visitors, so maybe something came up," Millie, one of the members on Henry's ushering team, added.

Millie was, well, Millie. She was a very capable usher who never let anything slip through the cracks. A fiery redhead with icy blue eyes, her strong-willed personality made her the "one who got things done," but that also meant that she did not like when things did not go her way.

Pastor Greg frowned. "But without calling or letting someone know? That's unlike them."

"Pastor, would you like to go with us?" Margot offered.

"Yes, of course. When were you planning on going?"

"I texted Oyin earlier this morning when she did not show up for workers' meeting, and she has not responded, so we are not sure yet," Penny said.

"Yep, so they might not even be around," Millie chimed in, maintaining her stance.

"But they could be," Margot said.

All three women turned to Pastor Greg expectantly. Waiting for his verdict. To go or not to go. It was a simple decision, but not really. Leading a church was never simple. Leading a church as a single, white pastor in a mixed-race church was even harder.

"It wouldn't hurt to go," he said after a quick word to God for wisdom, "worst-case scenario, they are not at home, and we could leave a note. Their house is not far from here."

"But we don't all have to go unless you all feel up to it?" He looked around, meeting each one of their gazes.

They all nodded.

"Okay, then. It's settled."

Fifteen minutes later, two cars drove into the Wilsons' driveway.

Pastor Greg had been to the Wilsons' house a couple of times before, but he still shook his head as he parked his car in their driveway, a wry smile playing on his lips.

At least Oyin and Henry never had to worry about money causing issues in their marriage.

"Oh, wow! Their house is nice!" Margot exclaimed as she disembarked from her car with Penny and Millie in tow.

Pastor Greg just chuckled in response.

"Oh, I am sure they have a pool!" Penny said in wonder.

"Yeah, Pastor, this is where we are hosting the next church barbecue, no question," Millie added.

Pastor Greg smiled and waved for them to follow him. "We would have to ask Oyin and Henry about that."

"Oh, we don't need to ask. We taketh it by force."

Pastor Greg rang the doorbell as Millie continued, "Haven't you heard where the Bible says, 'the violent taketh it by force?'"

Penny laughed and responded, "So, in this misuse of Scripture, Millie, would their house be the kingdom of heaven that that verse refers to?"

Millie stuck her tongue out at Penny, and everyone burst out in laughter.

"Hello! How may I help you?"

A tall, beautiful middle-aged woman stood at the door with a small smile on her face. It took Pastor Greg a couple of seconds to recognize her as Mrs. Wilson, Henry's mother.

"Oh, good afternoon, Mrs. Wilson!" Pastor Greg greeted.

Mrs. Wilson's eyes widened as she recognized him.

"Oh hi, Pastor Greg, right? I am sorry I didn't recognize you immediately. My eyesight is not what it once was. Actually, my *everything* is not what it once was. I tell you, my dear, don't age past 45."

Pastor Greg chuckled. "This is Millie, Margot, and Penny. We missed Oyin and Henry in church, and we came to check on them."

"Oh." Mrs. Wilson paused.

"O - or is this a bad time? Because we can go?" Pastor Greg quickly interjected.

Mrs. Wilson took a second to consider before she said, "No - no. Come in. I will get Henry."

Mrs. Wilson stepped back and waved them in, a warm smile on her face.

"Please make yourself comfortable," she directed them to a family room area. "I hope you all like tea. I just put on a pot."

"Of course, thank you so much, Mrs. Wilson," Margot answered.

Everyone else either nodded or politely smiled as they took their seats in the large family room.

"Please call me Patricia. Let me get Henry."

"Wow!" Millie exclaimed as soon as Patricia Wilson exited the room in search of Henry.

"I know, right?" Margot squealed

"This is a very nice house," Penny added, obviously impressed.

"I wonder how much it went for on the market," Millie said.

"Does anyone know if Henry Wilson has a younger brother because I am single!" she added with a cheeky grin.

"Oh my gosh!" Margot suddenly exclaimed. "Is that the original Psalm 85 painting?!"

Pastor Greg turned to look at the painting and missed Henry walking into the room until Henry said, "Actually, it isn't. That's a reprint of the original."

"Of course. Wow." Margot responded.

"Thank you for coming, guys. I feel very loved," Henry said with a small smile as he sat down on the three-seater next to Pastor Greg.

Pastor Greg smiled back at him and opened his mouth to speak.

Ask about Oyin, the Spirit gently prodded.

"Of course," Pastor Greg replied to Henry. "We were just concerned about the radio silence from your end. I guess you guys couldn't make it because of your Mom visiting?"

Henry attempted a smile, but because of Pastor Greg's proximity, he could see the strain in Henry's smile.

"I guess you could say so," was all Henry said, though.

Then Henry changed the subject. "So, how was church? I will definitely be on the lookout for your sermon on the church podcast. It's still the Paths of Love series?"

"Yes, it is, and it was such a great sermon!" Margot answered. She flashed a smile in Pastor's Greg's direction, and his heart skipped a beat. "I am truly in awe of God's anointing on Pastor."

Penny nodded. "Oh yes, I am definitely re-listening to it later in the week. I learned so much. Especially for us married couples."

"And for us singles, too! Right, Pastor?" Millie said, a teasing smile playing on her lips.

Pastor Greg smiled back politely, unable to stop himself from comparing her smile to Margot's.

Ask about Oyin, the Lord said again.

"Speaking of which," Pastor Greg blurted out, "where is Oyin? Is she feeling okay?"

"Oh." Henry paused.

A sense of déjà-vu, along with a strong sense of wrongness, hit Pastor Greg as he remembered Patricia Wilson had had the same reaction earlier.

"Yeah, I texted her, and she didn't respond. Is everything okay?" Penny added.

Henry crossed, uncrossed, and then crossed his legs again, clearing his throat. "Yeah. No. Every - uh, everything is fine. Oyin is...um, she is out of town."

"Oh." It was Pastor Greg's turn to pause.

Penny frowned slightly. "That's strange. She and I made plans to go out for brunch after church today. She didn't say anything about being out of town. I hope everything is okay?"

"Yeah. Yeah, she is fine. I believe the trip was impromptu."

Ask about Oyin, Pastor Greg heard again.

Okay, Lord, I am not sure what to do here. He said she is on a trip...

"Oh, okay. I hope she will be back soon. She has been really excited about the Noah's Ark project we are working on with the kids," Penny said, looking at the hallway Henry walked in from as if expecting Oyin to materialize.

Henry smiled, the first genuine one all day. "That does sound like her. I am hoping she will be back soon. Maybe text her so she does not forget about the project in church."

Pastor Greg frowned. That was weirdly vague and did nothing to help him feel at peace.

"Oh, okay. Great. We are glad to hear you guys are fine," Millie said with a note of finality. It was obvious that she was ready to leave.

"Tea is ready!" Patricia Wilson called out. "Henry, can you direct our guests over here?"

Henry got up and led them out of the family room into a breakfast nook that could have passed as the dining area of a smaller house.

Pastor Greg and the ladies spent another hour with Henry and Patricia, talking and laughing about everything and anything but Oyin.

Pastor Greg threw his car keys on the center table in his living room and sank onto his couch. "Lord, I don't understand."

He truly didn't. He had gone to the Wilsons' house expecting to see them. Instead, he met Henry and his mom. He never did find out where Oyin was and what prompted her trip. He never did find out why Henry missed church. As if that was not enough, he kept getting the impression to ask about Oyin. And Pastor Greg had tried. But every time he had brought her up, the topic was changed either by Henry or by Patricia Wilson.

But something was wrong. Was Oyin sick? Henry had looked like he hadn't had a good night. His usually glossy hair had been lacking in luster, and his eyes were heavy and out of it. Why was his mom around? Maybe Oyin was pregnant? But Oyin's parents had just been around. They would not have left so quickly if Oyin was pregnant. Besides, a pregnancy just didn't make sense with how he was feeling.

"Lord," He prayed, "I know something is wrong. I know You want me to do something, but I don't know what. Lead me."

After uttering that prayer, he felt more at peace. Even if something was wrong, it was in God's hands now. Just like pursuing a relationship with Margot was in His hands.

Pastor Greg made himself a sandwich and parked himself on the couch for a *Cold Cases* marathon.

An hour later, his phone rang. It was Henry.
"Hello?"

"Pastor, hi. Thank you so much for coming over. My mom says hi, as well."

"Oh, yeah. Thank you for having us. I will pass on your greetings to the ladies."

"Oh no, it's okay. I already reached out to them."

Ask about Oyin.

This time, Pastor Greg did not mince words. "Henry, talk to me. Where is Oyin? Are you and Oyin really okay?"

"I - I…"

"Henry, it's me. Talk to me."

"Oyin is in Atlanta with her parents…"

Okay, that didn't sound bad.

"We had a fight, and she left."

"Wait, what? Was she already going to Atlanta?"

"No, she, um...she thought we needed a break."

"Henry!" Pastor Greg could not help but scold. "When did this happen? Why didn't you call me?"

Henry sighed. "Yesterday, it happened yesterday."

"Oh, wow. I am so sorry. I guess that's why your mom is around, huh?"

"Yeah...I didn't really know what to do. I was in shock for most of yesterday."

Pastor Greg sighed in concern, "So, what do you want to do? Do you want me to talk to her and get her back here?"

"I don't know. I am still trying to figure it all out."

Pastor Greg was taken aback. "I don't understand. You don't want her to come back?"

"No - no. It's not that. I just - um, I - I did something stupid. Pastor G, I am so confused!"

The despair in Henry's voice alarmed him. Henry had put up a good enough front while they were in his house, and if not for the Lord's prompting, Pastor Greg probably would not have thought twice about the whole situation.

Lord, teach me what to do here.

"Okay. Okay. Let's just pray for a second?" Pastor Greg suggested.

"Okay."

"Lord, we are asking for wisdom. We are asking for clarity. We are asking for You to come and intervene. In the Name of Jesus, we ask. Amen."

"Amen," Henry repeated.

"Why don't you come over for dinner tonight or tomorrow? We can continue this discussion then, okay?"

"Okay. I can come over tomorrow."

"How long is your mom around for?"

Henry gave a dry chuckle. "In her own words, 'until you are happy, I am not moving an inch.'"

"Good. Good." Pastor Greg breathed a sigh of relief. "I will see you tomorrow."

Wow, Lord, thank You.

CHAPTER 33

Hope

Oyin missed her husband. She missed Henry so much it wasn't even funny. She was sure he would reach out before the end of the day. She kept reminding herself that Phoenix was two hours behind Atlanta. He would call. He had to call.

She woke up on Sunday morning, and there was nothing from him. Not even a freaking emoji. Out of anger, she had turned her phone off and left it in the room when she left for church. Was this him picking Olive over her again? This question plagued her all through church. It didn't help that it was a Thanksgiving service for the newly wedded Bosede and David, who were so obviously in love it hurt.

As soon as the final Hallelujah was chorused, Oyin got up to leave. Before she could escape, Mummy and Daddy invited her to go to lunch with them. Wanting to just lick her wounds in private, she declined, saying she had a headache. Mummy and Daddy quickly acquiesced, sending her off with instructions to rest.

As Oyin made her way back to the hotel, which was walking distance from the church, Oyin wondered at the level of restraint Mummy, and Daddy had exhibited since she arrived in Atlanta. They had welcomed her as soon as she arrived at the hotel yesterday, no questions asked. They had not put up an argument when she said she would be checking into her own room. They had not asked why she was in Atlanta and Henry was in Phoenix. They had not even complained when she left the wedding reception early because Auntie *This* and Auntie *That* would not stop asking where her *Oyinbo* husband was.

Not too long after, Oyin walked into her sixth-floor hotel room. The first thing she did was grab her phone to turn it on. Several emails from work and texts from friends came in, but nothing from Henry. She responded to her texts and turned off her phone again. Without meaning to, she fell asleep.

Three hours later, she woke to the sound of her hotel phone ringing. When she picked it, it was Mummy asking if she had had anything to eat. The call ended with Oyin promising to join her parents in their room for dinner in about an hour.

She hung up the phone and sat in silence, waiting but not waiting. She sent off an email to work requesting some time off for a family emergency, but she didn't even know when she would be back, so she hadn't given them a return date. Her heart wanted her on the next flight to Phoenix. She just wanted to see his face. Her head argued back. Did he want to see her?

Oyin breathed deeply. She had to admit that she was miserable. She flew across the country just to prove a point. She hadn't talked to her parents, hadn't talked to her friends, had barely spoken to God.

She was so ready to end this. She thought about texting him, but she really wanted to hear his voice. She wanted to call him.

God, I am so scared.

A blast of courage came out of nowhere, and she dialed his number.

Just as Oyin began to dread leaving an awkward voicemail, Henry picked up.

"Hello?"

Tears immediately sprang to her eyes at the sound of his voice. How did they - no, how did *she* let things get this far?

"Babe," she said softly.

"I miss you," she added a second later, unable to help herself.

"Me too," Henry said, his voice husky as if he had just woken up.

"I'm sorry we fought, Henry."

"Me too. I hate this."

Happiness flooded Oyin's heart, and it brought hope along with it. She and Henry were going to be okay.

"So… you really flew to Atlanta, huh? I didn't think you would," Henry continued with a wry chuckle.

Oyin had to chuckle along with him. It *was* pretty dramatic of her to fly across the country. "Yeah, I didn't think I would, too."

But I was expecting you to ask me to stay, she wanted to add, but she didn't.

"So, what do we do now?" she asked instead.

"I don't know. I am still processing, trying to just...wrap my head around it all. You?"

It was a lot, no doubt. Henry had said a lot of hurtful things, and she still hated his relationship with Olive with the passion of a freaking supernova, but she wanted her husband more.

"I agree. I mean, I am still processing. There is a lot we have to work through, but I just - I just really want to see you. I was thinking maybe I would head back tomorrow?"

Henry paused. Oyin literally heard Henry pause, and her heart started to thud.

"Maybe that's not such a good idea…"

What?

"What?"

"Maybe time apart is not the worst thing for us right now."

What the actual heck?

Oyin had promised herself she wouldn't get angry, but there it was, the red-headed monster rising from the ashes.

"So you think I should stay in Atlanta?"

Oyin knew Henry could hear the incredulity and irritation in her voice, and it destroyed the tentative ground that they had been walking on since the call began.

"You went there, Oyin, of your own accord," Henry shot back, his voice rising a half-decibel higher.

Henry sighed and softened his voice. "I just think time apart is necessary right now. I am still very hurt."

Tears fell down Oyin's cheek, and she hastily wiped them off. "Okay, if that's what you want."

"It is."

"Okay. Alright. Bye, then."

"Wait, Oyin, wait. I - I love you."

The stupid tears just won't stop falling. She didn't even think she had any left.

"I love you too."

She hung up before he could stop her again. How could she love someone so much yet want to throttle him at the same time? She was hurt too. She was mad too. But she was willing to put it aside. Henry, obviously, was not. She hadn't considered that Henry could still be mad, mad enough to not want to see her.

"Lord, it wasn't supposed to go like this," Oyin grumbled out loud, wiping her face clean of tears.

She pushed her phone away and lay back on the bed, curling into a fetal position. Humiliation flooded her face, making her ears hot. How could Henry tell her to stay away? She had done what he didn't. She reached out. She extended the olive branch, and he all but shoved it back in her face. So, was this it?

Was this the end for them? Had he made his choice? Had he decided that he didn't want her?

"Oh, God..." Oyin whimpered.

She was spiraling, and she knew it. But she couldn't stop. She had no reason to, no incentive to. It could be true. It could all be true. Henry could decide that she was more trouble than she was worth, and what was she supposed to do then? Separate? Be a divorcee in her mid-twenties?

She looked around at the functionally decorated hotel room just then as the magnitude of what she had done hit her.

They were already separated!

"Jesus, we are not even in the same time zone. Oh God, Jesus, what did I do?" Tears filled her eyes as a heaviness clogged her throat, and her voice broke.

She should have stayed! She could have gone to the park to take a breather. But no, she had to fly almost 2000 miles.

Oyin got into a kneeling position, her knees on the bed, but her head still on the bed as if she could not bear to lift it up.

I want my husband back, Daddy, her heart cried.

You know I got you, Oyin heard in her spirit. Although Oyin was feeling a panic unlike anything she had ever experienced, the Lord's voice was enough to bring her back from the edge. There, she stood on the edge of the precipice about to dive into the tumultuous waters of depression, regret, and guilt, and His voice drew her back.

Her phone buzzed as a notification popped into view. It was from her Bible app, reminding her about the verse of the day. It read:

The Lord will guide you continually, giving you water when you are dry and restoring your strength. You will be like a well-watered garden, like an ever-flowing spring.

Oyin lay back down on the bed, her eyes fixed on the ornate ceiling, taking in the words from Isaiah 58:11.

"I know I need You now more than ever," she sighed.

She picked up her phone and hit the hamburger icon to display all the verses from Isaiah 58

It was gradual, but as Oyin lay on that bed, her heart taking in the Word, panic began to ebb, and peace took its place. She still had no idea what the future held, but at least the Lord was with her. He *got* her.

By the time Oyin finished the chapter and got ready to join Mummy and Daddy for dinner, a small smile had appeared on her lips.

CHAPTER 34

Exposed

Irene Johnson was not going to panic. She promised herself she wasn't going to panic. Not when Oyinkan arrived in Atlanta alone with red, swollen eyes. Not when everyone was wondering where Oyinkan's husband was, and she heard people whispering about Oyinkan's 'failed' marriage. Not when Oyinkan refused to spend any time with her and Dele, the people she claimed she flew to Atlanta to see.

Thank God for Dele. He saw through her not-panicking and insisted that she compel Oyinkan to eat dinner with them after church.

As Oyin walked into their room that evening, a small smile on her lips, all the carefully crafted walls that Irene had built around her panic began to crumble. Oyinkan was here. They would finally find out what was wrong, and Irene did not know if she was strong enough to handle it.

"Good evening, Mummy," Oyinkan genuflected as their eyes met across the room.

"How are you, my dear?" Irene asked.

"Fine," Oyinkan replied, sinking into the couch that took up almost half the living area. "Where is Daddy?"

"He went to quickly take a walk, but he told us to order for him."

"Ok-a-ayyy...but does he even know where he's going?" Oyinkan said as her smile turned teasing.

"Don't ask me *o*. You know how your father is."

Oyinkan chuckled dryly, and Irene joined in with a half-hearted chuckle of her own.

"As long as he has his phone with him," Oyinkan said.

"He does."

"Okay, then," Oyinkan stood and walked over to the bed where Irene sat and picked up the hotel phone on the nightstand.

"So, what does Daddy want?"

"Order spaghetti for both of us," Irene replied.

While Oyinkan dialed the restaurant and placed their orders, Irene prayed for God's guidance. Whatever was going on with Oyinkan, she asked God to take control. She asked for strength. She asked for patience. She asked for guidance. She kept asking when Dele walked in and when the food arrived. She kept asking until they were all sitting in the living room eating, and Oyinkan blurted out, "Henry and I fought."

Irene's eyes flew to meet Oyinkan's, and she could have sworn she *heard* Dele's do the same.

"A big fight," Oyinkan added.

"Oh, okay," Dele said with a calm voice that Irene so envied at that moment. She, on the other hand, was through-the-roof panicking.

Oh, God, what have I done? Oh God, oh God, oh God!

"It's why I came to Atlanta."

Dele looked at Irene as if he were expecting her to say something. When she didn't, he asked Oyinkan to tell them what happened.

Oyinkan shook her head as if she were trying to determine what, if anything, to say. "Henry was...we were...um, we were ...uh..."

"Was it because of what happened when we were there? Was it because of me?" Irene blurted out.

Oyinkan looked away. "It was part of it."

"*Jesu.*" Irene placed her palms on her face, cupping her mouth and nose.

Oyinkan sighed and reached across the small center table to gently pry Irene's hands off her face. "Mummy, stop."

"Henry said that you don't like him, that you don't approve of him...and after everything that has happened, I have to ask, Mummy, is he right? Do you really not like him?"

Like?

Like was such a trite word to describe her relationship with Henry. It had never been about not liking Henry per se. He … just never fit. But could Irene tell Oyin that? Or would that just make everything worse and destroy whatever was left of Oyin's chance at happiness in her marriage?

Lord, teach me what to say.

"He's white, Oyinkan," she heard herself saying.

Oyinkan rolled her eyes and shook her head incredulously. "Okay, Mummy, cool. So, we are back to this? Seriously? Okay. Cool. Cool."

Dele reached across the table and patted Oyinkan's hand gently. "*Ni suuru* [34]."

"He was never what I planned for you, Oyinkan. You knew that from the beginning! I did not want someone I could not talk to for a son-in-law," Irene explained with wide eyes.

Oyinkan's face was thunderous. "So, you are punishing him? You are punishing *me*? You are punishing me for not marrying who you wanted, who you 'planned' for me?" She raised her fingers to make air quotes. "It's been over a year, Mummy, and you still have not accepted Henry? You have

---

[34] *Ni suuru* - be patient (Yoruba)

not gotten over it? Because he is white? What happened to 'we are all one in Christ'?"

Every word from Oyinkan's mouth was a little dart fired at the dartboard of Irene's heart, each one of them hitting dead center.

"What did you expect me to do, Oyinkan?" Irene cried out, feeling attacked. Suddenly, the spaghetti in front of her looked as desirable as a plate of worms.

"Calm down, Oyinkan. *Ni suuru,*" Dele interjected, trying to diffuse the situation.

"No, I just want to understand what Mummy's plan was for this summer. If you hated Henry so much, why did you come? Was it to break me and Henry up so that I could finally marry your chosen one, Mummy? So I can marry Dee?"

Oyinkan spat out the name *Dee* like it was poison.

Irene jerked back as if she had been struck. She was mortified, horrified because that was exactly what she had hoped. It was not a plan, per se. Of course, she had not planned for them to break up, but she had been sure they would - that Henry would mess up - and she had *planned* for her and Dele to be there to take Oyinkan home to someone who would treat her like she deserved. Hearing Oyinkan voice the thoughts that had been swirling in her head made Irene feel lower than scum.

What kind of a mother am I?

What kind of a Christian am I?

Quite uncharacteristically, Irene found herself unable to say a word in response.

"That's enough from you, Oyinkansola!" Dele exploded in Yoruba, his face otherwise calm, except for the telltale vein throbbing in his temple. "I understand you are angry, but that does not give you any right to talk to your mother like that," he added in perfect English.

Oyinkan shut her eyes. "I am not angry, Daddy. I'm sad." There was a break in her voice. "Henry and I could be over, and I just let it happen, Daddy. He kept telling me, and I didn't listen. I just..."

Dele sighed and rubbed Oyin's arm. "Why don't you tell us what exactly happened, *oyin mi*?"

A tear escaped Oyin's eyelids as she opened her eyes and scoffed. "I don't even know where to start."

"Anywhere is fine."

"You remember Henry's friend, Olive? From the first day I met her, I immediately knew that she was in love with Henry."

"What?!" That revelation swiftly untied Irene's tongue. She had had her suspicions, but to have them confirmed so blatantly…

"What?!" Dele said, a few seconds later, as if shock had stolen his words only to belatedly release them.

"Yeah," Oyinkan confirmed with a world-weary sigh. "I told Henry that I was not comfortable with their friendship because of her feelings for him. He didn't believe me that she had feelings for him, but he agreed to keep a distance. And he did until you guys said you were coming for the summer. All of a sudden, Olive wanted to come spend her vacation with us too. Before I knew it, it became Olive-this and Olive- that. I think he started to take comfort in her because -"

"My God, Oyinkansola, are you telling me that Henry cheated on you?" Dele cut in, his eyes wide with shock.

Irene was sure her face mirrored Dele's as her eyes fixed on Oyinkan for an answer.

Oh, God. This was it. Irene felt like her heart was about to fall out of her chest.

"What? No! No! No, he didn't. Henry would never do that. What I was saying was that -"

"So, why did you fight then?" Irene cut in, unable to help herself, confusion and relief, making her head light.

Oyinkan pursed her lips before responding, "we fought because he kept taking Olive's side over mine."

Stupid boy, Irene could not help but think. That old, but familiar, resentment rose in her as she remembered Olive and Henry smiling at each other like idiots. Right in his matrimonial home!

Irene wrinkled her nose, the ugliness of her thoughts showing on her face. "Are you sure that Henry is not sleeping with her?"

"Irene!"

"Mummy!"

Irene waved their exclamations away as one would an annoying fly. "What? I am just asking *na*! How can he be siding with her over you? And I suspected that Olive girl *o*, but I was not sure. You know how women can be."

Dele dropped every attempt to be calm, his eyes bulging as he spat out in Yoruba, "What kind of nonsense are you saying? Are you really trying to split these children up for God's sake, *ehn*?"

Irene sighed, her indignance evaporating as suddenly as it arose. She just wanted Oyin to be happy, but it seemed like she kept making things worse. She clamped her lips together, saying nothing.

Oyinkan dropped her fork on the table and began to get up. "You know what, it's fine. I am full now, anyway. I will call room service to come and clear up. *Odaaro*[35]."

Irene sighed. "Oyinkan -" She stopped, still not knowing what to say.

---

[35] *Odaaro* - good night (Yoruba)

"Oyin, sit down. We have not finished talking," Dele said firmly.

"No, Daddy, it's fine. There is no point. I- I'm tired anyway."

"Okay," Dele relented. "We can continue tomorrow?"

There was something in Oyinkan's eyes as she left their room, something Irene had only ever seen once before. It was written boldly on her face when she told them, in no uncertain terms, that she was getting married to Henry. Seeing that look again, more than anything else, terrified Irene. The first time, that look had meant Oyinkan did something that was so out of character. She had always been an obedient child. Rather than disobey her parents, Oyinkan would convince them to see the value of what she wanted to do. That day, that look meant that she didn't care whether Irene and Dele were on board. She did not care what they thought, she was going to pick Henry, and that was it. Seeing that look again, more than anything else, terrified Irene.

As soon as the door closed behind Oyinkan, Dele rounded on Irene.

"Irene, for God's sake!" he cried in exasperation.

Somehow, as if she had been subconsciously holding them back when Oyinkan was in the room, tears began to roll down her cheeks.

"You didn't see what I saw, Dele. Oyinkan doesn't deserve a cheating husband or a loveless marriage."

Dele sighed and moved closer to Irene. He wrapped his arms around her. "It will be fine. God is in control."

CHAPTER 35

Here

Henry woke up groggy. He had been sleeping a lot the past few days, yet he never truly felt awake when he wasn't sleeping. It was weird to wake up in a bed without Oyin in it. No warmth next to him, no satin scarf lying at the foot of the bed because it had come off during the night, even the smell of rosewater and argan oil that was so Oyin was beginning to fade from the sheets. Washing the sheets was definitely out of the question even though he had been waking up in a sweat the past few days and the sheets stank.

But did he even deserve to feel this way? Did he deserve to long for her and wish she were with him? After what he had done?

Without looking at the time, Henry guessed it was around 10 am. Sometime between Saturday and today, Mom had helped him reach out to the office and make excuses for his absence. Henry rubbed his eyes wearily as he looked around the dimly lit room. Maybe he should just have gone to work. At least, there would be something else to focus on. Here, everything reminded him of Oyin. He missed her so much that he could not even remember why they were arguing. Many times last night after her call, he contemplated just flying to Atlanta, but he couldn't. He didn't deserve to. He didn't get to do what he had done and then play hero-husband.

Henry turned and faced the wall, away from Oyin's side of the bed. His eyes landed on their couples' devotional, and at that moment, Henry wanted to vomit. There it sat, looking cheery and smug with its blue and yellow cover, mocking him.

If only you and Oyin had spent more time reading me instead of arguing, it taunted.

Henry didn't just miss Oyin. He missed God too. He missed that comforting Presence that somehow always made everything okay. But how? How could he talk to God after what he had done?

If only he had listened to Oyin about Olive's feelings for him. No, Henry shook his head. On some level, if he were being honest with himself, he knew, or at least suspected. In a weak moment, he had taken advantage of those feelings and messed everything up.

Henry closed his eyes. He just wanted everything to go back to the way it was. He wished he had a time machine so that he could go back to Saturday morning. He would throw himself at her feet and apologize as soon as Oyin walked through the study door. He would kiss her until they both didn't remember why they had been arguing. Oh, how he wished...

Oh God, what had he been thinking? He loved Oyin. What the hell had he been thinking on Saturday night? Would Oyin ever forgive him for Saturday night? Would God ever forgive him? Would Olive ever forgive him? The only person who was still around was Mom, and that was only because she didn't know what he had done, how stupid he had been. Once she did, she would leave and tell Dad not to bother flying in anymore.

Maybe you should just end it, the thought came unbidden yet solid. He had pushed everyone away. Maybe it was better for everyone if he just...wasn't here anymore. Then, he wouldn't hurt Oyin again; he wouldn't hurt Olive again; *he* wouldn't hurt again. He looked around the room. It would be so easy to slip away. Everything he had was also in Oyin's name anyway. She would get everything without needing a will. She still had a chance to be happy. She could be with Dee. He could just see it now...

No!

"I shall not die, but live, and declare the works of the Lord." The words from Psalm 118:17 tumbled out of his lips from years of recitation.

The dangerous thoughts disappeared as quickly as they came, and Henry gasped in relief.

Thank You, Lord.

"Sweetheart," came Mom's voice from behind the door. "Are you up yet? How are you feeling?"

After a breath, she said, "I'm coming in. I don't care if you're naked."

For all the pluck in her voice, Mom still opened the door tentatively as if she didn't want to spook him.

"Henry? Sweetheart?" she called as she walked closer to the bed and sat down on the edge.

"Hi, Mom," Henry said in a small voice.

"Hey, how are you feeling?" Mom rubbed his foot affectionately.

"Tired." It was true. Even his bones seemed to hurt.

Mom sighed. "Yeah, I can see it on your face. I am making chamomile tea. Come sit with me and Dad in the kitchen."

"Dad is here?" Henry asked, a small smile gracing his face. He had not seen Dad in person since Christmas, which was several months ago.

Mom answered with a smile of her own, "Yeah, he came in on the first flight this morning."

"Okay, get up," she stood as if to punctuate her words, "take a shower and join us in the kitchen, alright?"

"Okay, Mom."

As soon as Mom shut the door behind her, Henry closed his eyes.

"Thank You, Lord," he said again, this time out loud. Even in his darkest moment, the Lord was here. Protecting him. What would have happened if that verse hadn't come in time or his parents weren't here?

He was glad Dad was here, but that also meant he had to face the music. He couldn't get away with monosyllables and "I'll be fine" anymore. Dad would get everything out of him. Henry smiled. Yes, he was glad Dad was here.

Less than twenty minutes later, Henry walked into the kitchen, a small smile dancing on his lips.

"Hey, Dad," Henry greeted as soon as he saw him.

As their eyes met, Dad smiled widely, his blue-green eyes crinkling at the corners. "Hey, little man."

When they embraced, it felt like everything, and it took every ounce of the little strength Henry had not to cry. Henry held on longer than usual, and Dad let him, patting his back.

Henry finally withdrew from the embrace and sat down. "I am not so little anymore, Dad."

Dad smiled teasingly. "That's not what that hug said. You're sending me mixed signals here, little man."

Henry laughed and poured himself a cup of tea.

"I'm glad you're here, Greg. I have not been able to draw more than a small smile from him since yesterday." Mom said.

Dad snickered. "It's okay, Pat. I think we both know who his favorite parent is."

Mom rolled her eyes and asked Henry, "how's the tea?"

Henry smiled. "Very good. Thanks, Mom. You added honey?"

"Yeah," Mom said as a puzzled look came over her face. "You guys have several bottles of honey. I didn't really have a choice…"

Henry chuckled dryly. "Yeah, it was a running joke between me and… Oyin."

Mom raised her eyebrows questioningly.

Henry took Mom's expression to mean that she was asking for more details, so he continued, "Yeah, um…sometimes after work, I would stop by the grocery store to get a bottle of honey. Then I would give it to Oyin and say, 'honey for my Honey.'"

When both Mom and Dad kept staring at him, Henry added, "you know…because her name means Honey?"

Dad nodded. "No, Hen, we get the joke. I think we are both more concerned with the fact that you just used *was*."

"What?"

"You said it *was* a running joke."

"Oh."

"You don't expect it to be a running joke in the future?" Mom asked, her face arranged into a worried frown.

Before he could answer, Dad asked more bluntly. "Are you expecting this separation to be permanent, Henry?"

"No!" was his first reaction. Then, "Well…I don't know. I mean, um. I think it's possible."

"What?"

"What?"

Two pairs of eyes stared back at Henry in shock.

"So, it's that serious, huh?" Dad asked.

"I don't know, I mean…I g- I guess, it's just that…ugh, I don't know."

"Hen," Mom began, "you said that it was just an argument that got out of hand. I don't understand. What happened?"

"Hen, why don't you start from the beginning?" Dad said in a gentle but firm voice that brooked no opposition.

He gave them the abridged version of the events from Friday night to Saturday night, glossing over the horrible things that they had both said to each other and skipping over what happened on Saturday night.

"Surely, you don't think Oyin would leave you because of Olive?" Dad exclaimed incredulously.

Henry started. "No, I -"

"Of course not! She married you knowing that Olive was your best friend, didn't she?" Mom answered for him quickly, as if afraid he would say something contrary.

Henry could only nod. If only they knew what had happened on Saturday, what he had foolishly wanted to happen…

"Did you consider that, maybe, Oyin was right to be jealous?" Mom asked in a careful voice.

As much as Henry wanted to deny it, he couldn't anymore. Oyin had been right. Saturday night was proof. What else had she been right about?

"What do you mean?" Dad asked.

Mom sighed. "It has always seemed to me that Olive liked Henry as more than a friend. Do you think, maybe, Oyin saw what I have always seen?"

Dad ran a hand through his still-full-but-more-grey-than-red hair. "Darn. Really?"

Mom just nodded.

Henry closed his eyes and groaned. It was all starting to make sense now. Why Mom had disapproved of Olive being around this summer, why Mom had skipped on her duties in church and flown in on the first flight on Sunday.

It was so he wouldn't be alone with Olive. He almost chuckled.

Too little, too late.

"Why didn't you ever say something, Mom?" was all he said out loud.

"They were only suspicions, Hen. What was I supposed to say, 'I think your best friend is in love with you, but don't let on that you know since I am not sure?'"

"Wait, is that why Olive is not here? Didn't you say she was staying for a few days?" Dad asked.

Henry's heart skipped a beat and then another until his chest began to hurt physically.

"Henry?"

He dissembled, "Yeah, I told Mom before. Um...she had to get back to school."

"You're lying. You lied to your Mom before, and you're lying to me now," Dad countered simply.

"Henry, we've taught you better than this. Come on." Mom said, a disapproving look on her face.

"Sorry," Henry said apologetically, his face heating up. "Olive and I, we...um - there was, we had a moment."

"What happened?" Mom asked, her face deceptively calm.

Henry shook his head. "It was so stupid. I was so angry and sad, and Olive was there...and I -well, we almost...I just wish I could redo the night."

If Henry was hoping that this acknowledgment of guilt would deter his parents from making a fuss, he was wrong.

"Henry, oh God, Henry. What were you thinking?" Mom cried, her voice a full octave higher than normal.

"I almost don't recognize you. Lying to your parents, cheating on your wife. Henry, what has gotten into you?" Dad said, almost simultaneously.

Henry groaned and buried his face in his hands. What could he say? He could barely recognize himself. Everything was getting out of hand, and he felt powerless to stop it. This must have been how King David felt as he slipped deeper and deeper into the clutches of sin. A leisure walk had turned into an adulterous act, which had turned into plotting another man's murder. In Henry's case, an argument had turned into a separation, which had turned into a disastrous moment with his best friend.

Oh, God. Oh, God. Oh, God.

Dad broke the strained silence that had descended upon the room. "So what do we do now, Hen? What do *you* want to do?"

Henry raised his eyes to meet Dad's. The disappointment he saw in them hurt. Apparently, there was still some part of his heart left to hurt after Oyin had walked out the door.

"I don't know, Dad," he said in a small voice.

"You don't know?" Dad said, irritation evident in his voice and clear in his eyes.

Henry sighed and ran his hand through his hair. "I don't know, Dad! I know I messed up, okay?" he cried out in frustration.

"Good. At least you and I can agree on that," Dad said coldly.

Henry looked at Mom to see if maybe *she* would understand. She wasn't looking at him. Though her head was faced in his direction, her eyes were averted as if she could not bear to look at him.

Jesus, Henry found himself praying, *please*.

When she finally brought her eyes to his, she said, "I think we need some time to process this, Henry. We are both very disappointed."

She tapped Dad's hand lightly, and Dad grunted out a "Yeah."

"I think we will head over to the country club for a few hours. Maybe we can talk when we get back?" she added.

"I was going to meet Pastor Greg later in the day for dinner."

Mom looked at Dad, who still remained stonily silent, his eyes fixed on a spot on the wall. When he didn't meet her eyes, she said to Henry, "That's a good idea. Why don't you invite Pastor Greg over instead, and I can make dinner for all of us? Sound good?"

"Okay."

An hour later, Henry had not moved from his seat at the kitchen island since he heard his parents' rental car back out of the driveway. Henry placed his head on the cold marble countertop, the coolness helping to soothe the headache that had lodged itself in his skull since Saturday morning. He had hoped he would garner sympathy from his parents. But it seemed like they were taking Oyin's side, too. So, had she been right all along?

At the moment, standing in their study, Henry had felt so right, so justified in his anger. Oyin *did* withdraw from him without regard for his feelings, and she *did* handle Olive's presence and absence poorly. Her parents *didn't* like him, and her mom *did* show her disapproval quite clearly. But now, as he sat by himself, alone (and lonely) in a huge house, none of those things seemed to matter. He had always known that Oyin's parents preferred Dee, but he had promised himself that he was going to win them over and prove to them that he was a better husband for Oyin, a better son-in-law than Dee could ever hope to be. When had that changed? When had it become a battle of them versus him?

He had met Dee a couple of times, and he had been simultaneously intimidated and disgusted each time. The first time Henry met Dee was the day after Henry had taken

Oyin out on a first date. He was already crazy about Oyin by then and had never thought to ask if another guy was in the picture. In hindsight, Henry knew that he hadn't thought to ask because he hadn't cared. He had floated into their Cultures and Religion class that day, his eyes searching the room for a beautiful pair of dark eyes and a head full of thick curls. What he had seen brought him crashing back down to earth. It was Oyin; he wouldn't have known it was her if not for her expressive eyes and beautiful umber skin. Her hair was straight and long - a far cry from the ear-length curls she sported the day before. A guy (who he would come to know as Dee) leaned on her desk, their faces inches apart as she beamed at him. Something had made her look up in Henry's direction, and their eyes met from across the room. Dee had looked back as well, and Henry watched Dee's posture change from flirty to possessive as he raised his palm to caress Oyin's cheek. Henry hadn't waited to see anymore. He turned around so fast and hightailed it out of the class. He had skipped class that day, unable to face Oyin and so, so envious of Dee. It had taken him weeks to work up the nerve to ask her for that first date. That was the face he had so badly wanted to touch the night before but was terrified of doing anything to mess the night up. To see Dee touch her so carelessly, so freely made him sick with envy.

The second time had been at a Christmas dinner party at Oyin's parents' house in Texas. Although he and Oyin were officially dating at the time, Oyin was not ready to introduce him to her parents as her boyfriend. Just happy to be around her for the holidays, he had agreed to attend the dinner as a "friend." He had not anticipated how hard it would be to see Oyin and be unable to give her more than a perfunctory hug, and he certainly had not anticipated the amount of self-control it would take not to punch the ever-present smirk off Dee's face that night. Everyone had thought she and Dee were together, and although Oyin vehemently denied it each time it was insinuated, no one listened. They all thought she was being coy. Everyone kept referring to her as *Ayaba* and to Dee as *Omoba*. Oyin had later confirmed to him what he had already suspected – because Dee was a prince, Oyin was being called his princess. Dee had, of course, basked in the royal adoration. He had sat in the living room with Oyin's dad and the other older men instead of helping to get dinner ready like a real man would. When dinner was finally served, and Dee made his way to the table, Oyin's dad's arm around his shoulders. Oyin had been asked to serve him. Henry had clenched his jaw so hard as he watched anger mar Oyin's beautiful face. Dee was the only one served that night; everyone else, including her parents, had served themselves. That was the night that Henry decided he was going to marry Oyin. She deserved better, and so did her parents.

Why had he lost that resolve? He could have tried harder to win her parents over, but he didn't. After the semi-disastrous trip to Nigeria for the traditional wedding, he had consoled himself with the knowledge that he only had to see them a few times a year. Oh, he had been so blind, so self-righteous…

His phone dinged then, interrupting his reminiscences. He unlocked his phone and saw a text message. It was a GIF of a teddy bear holding a heart out with the words "I heart you" inscribed on it. It was from Oyin. Tears immediately sprang to his eyes. Henry chuckled and then sniffed, wiping his face clean of the tears that had fallen without his consent.

He had been making mistakes since he first laid eyes on her. He was the one who had messed everything up, yet she was the one offering her love on a platter. Henry didn't know much of who he was or anything else for that matter, but he knew he loved his wife, Oyinkansola Wilson.

He typed back,

I love you too, Oyin. So much. You will always be my oyin

Henry closed his eyes tightly and begged God.

Lord, I promise that if You fix this, I will be better. I will love Oyin's parents like my parents like they deserve to be loved.

CHAPTER 36
On/Off Fleek

Oyin was tired. Not physically, no. The abrupt ending to the dinner yesterday meant that she got more than the recommended eight hours, albeit fitful. No, she was freaking tired of all the drama. It was like she was living out an especially melodramatic Nollywood movie. She could only hope that when the "To God be the Glory" credit rolled across the screen, it would be to a happy ending. If she could, she would get on the next flight to Phoenix, but she wanted to give Henry the space he asked for. It killed her to think that Henry needed space from her, but it was the least she could do.

This was all her fault. If she had stayed in Phoenix, she and Henry would have made up. But no, she had to jump on a cross-country flight like the hapless heroine in a freaking Hollywood romcom. She felt so powerless. She was not where she wanted to be, and there was nothing she could do but wait. What scared her more than anything else was that their separation could be permanent. If only she had stayed...Darn!

Oh God, how stupid could one person be?

Okay, that's it. Get up.

There was no doubt in Oyin's mind that the Lord had just asked her to get up, but...

"What? Why?" Oyin whined, content to lie there, drowning in her thoughts.

Oh, Oyin, how long of a pity party can one person throw?

Oyin's mouth popped open as a startled laugh escaped her. She continued to chuckle, unable to say anything.

That's enough self-pity for today. Get up.

This time, Oyin didn't ask again. She got up from the hotel bed and walked into the bathroom. She almost jumped out of her skin when she saw her reflection in the mirror. She looked, to put it mildly, washed out. She hadn't brought her satin headwrap or pillowcase from Phoenix, so her braids looked lifeless. Her eyes were bloodshot from stress-influenced sleep, and her eyebrows were off fleek. Crashing the wedding party had necessitated an emergency dress-shopping trip to Lenox Square on Saturday, but she had refused to buy any makeup products. Buying makeup had meant accepting that she was going to be in Atlanta for more than a couple of days.

Oyin did not like the girl she saw in the mirror. The Lord was right. (Duh, of course, He was.) This pity party was over. If she was truly over the drama like she claimed to be, then she had to act like it, starting with a shower and then an emergency trip to Lenox Square for a gallon of foundation and mascara, please.

As soon as Oyin walked back into her hotel room around 12:30 pm, her phone began to ring. She placed her shopping bags onto the floor, careful not to break her newly manicured nails. She pulled out her phone from her purse. It was a WhatsApp Video call from Daddy. Oyin sat on one of the chairs in the living area and picked up the call.

"Oyin *mi*, good morning."

"Good morning, Daddy."

"How are you? Oh, are you going somewhere?"

"No..." Oyin paused, "I just came in. Why do you ask?"

"No, when you look like you are going out *ni*, with your makeup done and... did you change your hair?"

Oh. That.

Oyin might have gone a little overboard with the "emergency trip" to Lenox Square since she came back with a made-up face, freshly painted nails, and braids now washed and curled.

"No, I just went to Lenox Square for a little while."

"Oh," Daddy paused. "So, you're fine?"

Oyin rolled her eyes. How typical for her Dad to think that going to the mall meant that she was fine. She *was* fine, though.

"Yeah. I think so."

"Oh, okay. Do you want to talk to your mother?"

What Mummy said last night had hurt, and it still stung that Mummy thought what she thought, but Oyin was OVER the drama, so she said,

"Daddy, we are in the same hotel. I can just walk over to your room."

"Ah, *maa binu*[36]. Come then."

"Okay. I'm coming."

Oyin ended the call, grabbed her room key, and walked over to her parents' room.

"Lord," she prayed when she reached their door, "please take control."

It was Mummy who opened the door when she knocked. Oyin smiled and genuflected as soon as she saw her.

---

[36] *maa binu* - don't be angry (Yoruba)

"Good morning, Mummy."

"How are you, my dear?" Mummy moved to hug her, and Oyin hesitated for a second before she returned the hug.

Soon, Mummy released her and ushered her into the room.

"Have you eaten?" Mummy asked when they were both sitting.

"Yeah, I had a croissant when I went to the mall. Have you and Daddy eaten?"

"Oh, we went down for the continental breakfast. We tried calling you, but it was going directly to voicemail. I thought you might still be angry about yesterday."

No, Mummy. Why would I be angry? It's not like you called my husband an adulterer.

Oyin cleared her throat, but before she could respond, Daddy opened the door to the bathroom and walked out.

"Oyin *mi*, you're here."

"Good morning, Daddy."

"Good morning, my dear," Daddy replied as he sank into the couch next to Mummy with a grunt.

"So, what did she say?" Daddy said, turning to Mummy.

Years of experience with Mummy and Daddy's dramatics informed Oyin that she was the "she." Oyin tried to tamp down the irritation she felt at being spoken of as if she was not in the room.

"I was just about to tell her when you came in," Mummy replied.

"Oh, okay. Do you want me to go back into the bathroom and -"?

"No, please!" Oyin blurted out exasperatedly. "Please don't go anywhere, Daddy. Mummy, can't you tell me what you want to tell me with Daddy in the room?"

Mummy regarded her for a moment before saying, "I wanted to talk to you woman-to-woman and explain what I meant last night."

"Oh, okay. I don't mind Daddy staying in the room. Is that okay with everyone?"

They both nodded, and Oyin breathed a sigh of relief.

"Oyinkansola," Mummy began. "You know I love you, and everything I say comes from a place of love."

"Yes, Mummy," Oyin said in a monotone voice.

"If you say that Henry is not cheating on you, I believe you. I'm sorry I insinuated otherwise. He is your husband, so you know him better...but just keep your eyes open, you hear?"

Oyin knew that was the best Mummy could give, and she appreciated it. Although Oyin knew that Henry would never cheat on her as well as she knew that the sky was blue, she said, "I've heard," because she knew that Mummy needed to hear that.

"For what it's worth, Oyin, I don't think Henry would cheat on you. You know us, men. Sometimes we can be daft and stubborn when we don't get our way. He had Olive as a friend before he met you. He probably just needed to throw his weight around a little," Daddy added.

Oyin nodded.

"So, it looks like you are ready to go back to Phoenix?" Mummy said with a questioning lilt at the end of her sentence.

Was she?

She was. Dear God, she was so ready.

"Yes, actually," Oyin acquiesced.

"So you and Henry have finished your fight? You spoke?" Mummy asked.

Define finish.

"Yes, Henry and I spoke," was all she said, though. It wasn't a lie, not technically. She and Henry had spoken. Sure, the call only lasted a few minutes, and he had basically asked her not to come to Phoenix but *po-tay-to, po-tah-to*.

"So, when are you planning on leaving?" Mummy asked.

Oyin paused. She didn't actually have any plans to leave, not until she really spoke to Henry. "I don't have any set plans yet," she hedged and then quickly changed the subject.

"When are you and Daddy leaving?"

"Tomorrow," Daddy supplied. "Remember, we are going through Abuja to see Baby K before we go back to Lagos."

Oyin didn't remember, but she nodded anyway.

She and Baby K kept a running streak on Snapchat, so, of course, Oyin knew that Baby K was in Abuja, but Baby K hadn't said anything about Mummy and Daddy coming to see her.

Silence reigned in the room as everyone retreated into their individual thoughts.

Oyin saw Mummy open her mouth to talk several times, but each time she closed it. Out of the corner of her eye, Oyin saw Daddy subtly reach out to take one of Mummy's hands in his, and he began to rub it gently. That touch seemed to give Mummy the courage that she needed, and she squared her shoulders. The beauty in what Oyin had just witnessed took her breath away. Quite literally.

"I know I don't always say things right, Oyinkansola," Mummy said, "but your happiness is important to me."

She took a deep breath and continued. "I failed you when you first got married, Oyinkan. I was not there to put you through, to be the mother you needed. This past weekend, I saw what Naomi did for Bosede, and I am ashamed of myself. I was bitter, very bitter, and I didn't understand why you didn't want Dee. My dear, will you please forgive me?"

Mummy was the stereotypical Yoruba warrior-mother. She supported her husband solidly and fought for her children valiantly, all while looking so put-together, so it was rare to see the vulnerable woman beneath. Only Daddy ever got to see that woman. Seeing Mummy make such confessions broke Oyin's heart. Yes, she wished Mummy had been more present when she was a new bride, but that was over a year ago. It was fine. Really.

"Mummy…" Oyin muttered feebly. "I'm - I... Of course, I forgive you."

She added, "And in fairness to you, I never explained what happened with Dee."

Oyin continued, "We did date, but only for a little while. The rest of the time, we were just friends. At the time, I didn't understand what was holding me back from committing to him, but later I found out that he was also with three other girls while we were dating. When I confronted him, he claimed we were never exclusive. Thankfully, by that time, I had already met Henry, so his answer didn't really matter."

"Wow," Mummy sighed. "To be fair, you kept saying that you were just friends, but I did not believe you. Why else did you keep bringing him around?"

"Because you and Daddy liked him so much! Whenever we talked, you always asked about him, even after I told you there was nothing going on."

"Whatttt?" Daddy interjected teasingly. "I never liked that boy! First of all, his name is Adediwura. Calling himself, Dee was just pretentious. Secondly, I was really only after his crown."

"Dele!" Mummy exclaimed as she swatted his arm. "Don't say that."

"I wish you had just told me this before," Mummy said.

"Would you have listened?" Oyin asked, her eyebrows raised.

Mummy gave a wry chuckle. "Probably not. That boy was charming."

Oyin rolled her eyes. "*As in.* He oozed charm from every sweat pore of his body. You know, when we first met, he walked up to me after class and said, 'My name is Diwura, but you can just call me Dee since you will be bringing all the shine to this relationship.'"

Daddy burst out laughing, while Mummy just looked confused. "I don't get it."

"Because *wura* means gold…and gold is shiny?"

"Oh, oh, oh! Wow!" Mummy exclaimed. "How many times do you think he used that line?"

"At least three other times," Daddy said before he burst out laughing again.

Oyin and Mummy joined in the laughter as well.

Mummy was the first one to sober up. "It was a good line, though."

"It was. It got me to date him for a while, at least," Oyin replied.

"Can I just say," Daddy said when he had sobered up, "God does work everything out for good? I'm glad you are married to Henry and not him."

"Me too," Mummy said. A surprised look came over her face as if she couldn't believe she felt that way. Then, the expression disappeared as one of calm, genuine acceptance and approval took its place.

Oh, God. Oh, God. Oh, God!

Oyin did not realize how much she needed her parents to be happy with her marriage until she heard those words. She had decided to settle with a grudging acceptance. But for them to approve? To say they were happy that she chose Henry? It was everything.

Tears pricked Oyin's eyes, and she gave them a watery smile. "Thank you, Mummy. Thank you, Daddy."

"Aww, come here, *ọkọ mi*[37]."

Oyin found herself in her mother's arms as Mummy hugged her tightly. Mummy stroked her hair, repeating "*ọkọ mi*" over and over. Finally, Mummy released her but refused to let her go back to her former seat. Oyin positioned herself at Mummy's feet and placed her head in Mummy's lap.

"In hindsight, I should probably have gone back into the bathroom. If I wanted to see water, I would have just turned on the tap," Daddy said.

"Daddy!"

"Oladele!"

Daddy laughed, obviously glad to see smiles on his girls' faces, instead of tears.

Mummy ran her hand through Oyin's braids lovingly. "I want to know everything now. Tell me, what do you love most about Henry?"

Oyin paused as a shy smile played on her lips. "Everything…"

"Okay," Mummy chuckled. "What is your favorite physical feature on him?"

"Okay!" Daddy exclaimed as he began to get up. "And that is my cue to leave. Love you both."

"Dele, don't go anywhere. We need to listen to her."

There was obviously some silent conversation going on above her as Mummy and Daddy locked eyes. Finally, Daddy looked away, sighed, and sat back down.

---

[37] *ọkọ mi* - my dear (Yoruba)

"We are listening, Oyin," Mummy said.

Oyin paused to contemplate the question. There were so many good options to pick from, but …his eyes. Those eyes captivated her, and she told Mummy that.

"Yes," Mummy agreed. "His eyes are intense. It's like he can see into your soul. It's a little unnerving. Sometimes I don't even look into them for fear that he will see what I am thinking."

Oyin chuckled. He *had* seen what Mummy was thinking.

"Your children are going to be a sight to behold. With his eyes and your beautiful hair," Mummy said, smiling.

Oyin blushed, too happy to even feel embarrassed.

"Dele, was there anything you wanted to ask Oyin about her marriage?" Mummy asked pointedly.

Daddy rolled his eyes. "Actually, yes. Just...how rich are his parents?"

Oyin laughed. "I have no idea. They are so humble and God-fearing that you would never even expect that they could buy a house of that value."

"Ah, the reason I ask is because when we went down for breakfast, a manager came over to our table and specially asked if we were okay, offering one thousand extra things that we didn't need. I didn't see him ask anyone else, so I asked him why he singled us out. He said, 'your daughter is Oyin Wilson, right? She called from your room yesterday.' When I said yes, he said, 'the Wilsons are very good friends of the hotel,' with emphasis on friends."

Oyin laughed. "Wow, I would have to ask Henry when I see him."

"Speaking of," Mummy said, "I thank God for this opportunity to get to do what I didn't before you got married."

Oyin nodded and waited for Mummy to continue speaking.

"When you go back to Phoenix this time, stay there. Let this be the first and last time you use distance as a weapon in your marriage, okay?"

Oyin nodded. Mummy's words were blunt but honest. Coming to Atlanta had been an impulsive decision on her side, but in God's fashion, He worked it out for good.

"Neither you nor Henry are perfect. No one is. So, love and success in marriage do not come from perfection in the spouses. No, perfection in marriage, perfection in life comes from love. Your marriage will be perfect if you love like 1 Corinthians 13 says to love."

"Well said, Irie," Daddy agreed, as he nodded slowly. "Well said."

"So, when you get home, my dear, be patient and kind. Don't be jealous. Let go of this Olive thing, if you trust your husband. Let God deal with it. And let this argument go completely. Don't keep any record of anything that he said or did…just let it go! Love him, Oyinkan. Love him, you hear?"

Oyin nodded as she soaked in the words. Mummy was right. For all the I-love-yous she had said to him, she hadn't really shown it. She had been jealous and petty about Olive being around. She knew that he would never cheat on her. Hadn't she defended him so violently to her parents? So, what had she been so worried about? Why had she fought against Olive's presence and made him miserable? It was because she expected him to let Olive go as a "proof" of his love.

Oyin shut her eyes. She always expected him to do what she wanted as if that was what showed that he loved her. She had expected him to be perfect before she showed him love. But how about her? How had she loved him? She had insisted on her own way and thrown a fit when she didn't get her way. Basically, the opposite of love.

Henry had loved her. He had catered to her insecurities even when she hadn't realized that they were insecurities. Oh God, how she loved him and his laugh that ended with a croak. Her very own frog prince! Oh, how she loved his off-key singing voice - her very own nightingale. Oh, how she loved his blazing red hair that didn't match his personality. Oh, how she loved his inability to fry anything. Oh, how she loved him, body and soul.

Wow.

Right then, she plucked her phone from the center table and sent Henry a GIF.

"Did I overwhelm you?" Mummy asked. "I wanted to give you a few minutes, but you have not said anything…"

"No, no, I was just thinking. Yes, I agree absolutely."

Mummy nodded, relieved. "Okay, let's get to the juicy stuff. Dele, it's time for you to go into the bathroom."

Daddy looked at Mummy, and what he saw in her face made his mouth curl up in disgust. "Oh! Ugh! Yeah, it is definitely time for me to leave. I will also turn on the shower so that I don't hear anything that will make me vomit my breakfast."

"Go, *joor*[38]!" Mummy said, giving him a slight push.

The door had barely closed behind Daddy when Mummy asked with wiggling eyebrows,

"So tell me, how are your bedroom affairs? How was the wedding night?"

"Mummy!" Oyin's face grew so hot that she was sure she had to be as red as Henry's hair.

---

[38] *joor* – just (Nigerian Pidgin)

❤ ❤ *** ❤ ❤

Later that day, when Oyin finally came back into her room and lay on her bed, she saw a text that had come in from Henry:

I love you too, Oyin. So much. You will always be my oyin.

Oyin put her head on her pillowcase as she beamed at the ceiling. If it was possible to die of happiness, her heart would have stopped beating by now.

CHAPTER 37

Diagnosis, Prognosis

Olive had stopped crying. Just five minutes ago, she had declared that no more tears would be shed over Henry Wilson.

So far, so good.

It was a waste, she knew, to spend this much time crying over Henry. That hadn't stopped her from spending the entire day in bed yesterday. She had walked into her apartment on Sunday morning, dumped her luggage all over the floor, and tumbled into her bed fully clothed. Of course, she couldn't sleep, so she lay there for the rest of the day, catatonic. She must have drifted off later in the night because it was her stomach's complaints that jolted her awake at 6 am this morning.

She didn't have class until later in the evening, so she gave herself a few more hours to wallow, and finally, at 9:30 am, she placed an embargo on all Henry-Wilson-related tears. No more. She knew it was going to be a Herculean task since her master's thesis was based on his marriage. But, if Hercules could do it, so could she. So would she. Henry Wilson was nothing more than a study participant, an experiment subject. She could do this. She would do this. She had to do this.

Because she had stupidly gone running when Henry had wiggled his little finger, she hadn't come up with angles for her thesis. Dave Marigold would not be pleased if she didn't have anything to show him, especially since he knew she had gone to Phoenix.

Olive shook her head in disgust at herself. She couldn't believe she had planned on missing class. She had put in too many sleepless nights and pizza-fueled weekends into her degree to throw it all away. Yet she almost did. If things had gone the way her heart had so badly wanted on Saturday night, she would have. If Henry had pledged his undying love to her on Saturday night, she would have stayed forever if that's what he wanted.

I guess I should be thankful.

She didn't feel thankful, though. Just angry and cheated. Olive shook her head in a bid to ward off the thoughts. She rose out of her bed. If she was going to have some ideas with a semblance of sense, she needed to begin her day. The only way to avoid thinking and tears was to keep her body and mind occupied. As she freshened up, she mulled over the Wilsons' attachment style results. As she ate breakfast, she wondered if attachment styles were malleable and if there was any research on that. As she unpacked her suitcase, she debated whether culture and religion had any effects on attachment styles. By noon, she was physically exhausted but mentally overcharged. Ideas flitted around her head in a manic-like fashion. She grabbed her laptop and pounded on the keyboard, words pouring out of her onto the Word document.

Do attachment styles predict partner selection?
The chicken or the egg; attachment styles and attraction
Could attraction affect attachment styles?
Can the emotional and physical connection called love render attachment styles useless…

On and on, she wrote. When Olive finally looked up from her computer, two hours had passed. Her eyes hurt from the blue light emitted from her laptop, her head hurt from the intensity of the past two hours, and her heart hurt from rejection, yet Olive's lips were curved into a small smile. She finally had a direction for her thesis, and Dave was going to love it.

He smiled when she walked in, and she felt beautiful. Seen. Not a substitute for someone else, just Olive. She smiled back at Dave and found a seat in the second row. Only two other students had arrived for class, and they both had their headphones on, waiting for class to start.

"Hey."

Olive looked up from her laptop, which was booting up. Dave was standing two desks away from her, his hands resting lightly on the desk in front of him.

"Hey," she said back, a smile on her face.

"You are back."

"I am."

"Talk after class?"

"Sure. Yeah."

"Okay."

"Okay."

Olive's smile didn't slip when Dave turned and walked back to the instructor's desk. It stayed on her face, playing on her lips until thirty minutes after class ended, and Dave was yet to talk to her.

I should just go. I can talk to him about the thesis later.

But she didn't want to. She wanted him to smile at her again so she could be sure that her heart could still feel happiness. She watched Dave as he talked patiently with a fellow classmate, Kyra, whose thesis was due in November as well. Olive had never noticed how attractive his eyes were, but as she sat in that class, half-exhausted, half-upset, and fully on the rebound, that was all she could see. Those eyes crinkled at the corners as Dave laughed with Kyra and handed her back a stack of papers. Kyra smiled back flirtatiously and reached out to collect the papers.

Olive rolled her eyes. It was common knowledge that all the single ladies in the master's program - probably the entire Psychology department - found Dave attractive.

"It's a really good topic, Kyra. I think you've hit on a much-needed area of research," Dave said as Kyra walked towards the door.

Olive felt something akin to jealousy. Dave was her mentor, not Kyra's!

"Thank you, *Dave*," Kyra responded, flashing yet another flirtatious smile before finally walking out the door.

Olive couldn't help herself. "Dave, huh?" she asked as soon as she thought Kyra was out of earshot.

Dave chuckled good-naturedly. "Yeah, Dr. Marigold makes me sound stuffy. I already feel so old teaching a class of twenty-somethings."

She laughed. "I wouldn't say old, just...ancient."

"Ha! Thank you. So, will you please honor this old, ancient man's wishes and call him by his first name so he can hold onto a modicum of his youth?"

He had been Dave in her head for a while now, so that was not hard to do. She somehow found herself wishing that she was the only one granted the privilege of calling him, Dave.

"Dave," she said out loud.

He smiled at her again. She had seen the same smile a thousand times, but just like earlier today, her heart fluttered, and she returned his smile.

Yep, her heart could still feel happiness.

"Olive," he said by way of response as he walked to sit in a nearby desk.

"So talk to me. How did it go in Phoenix? How's he doing?" he asked, once he had folded his six-foot-three frame into the small desk.

Olive's smile slipped, an image of Henry's piercing blue eyes appearing unbidden in her mind's eye. "Fine. It was fine."

"And the truth is?"

Olive sighed shakily; she could feel the tears begin to form at the corner of her eyes. "Can we - do you mind...I'd really rather not talk about it right now."

Dave raised his hand as if to touch her and then seemed to think better of it and dropped his hand. "Hey, it's okay. You're okay."

He cleared his throat and changed the topic, "So did you make any headway on coming up with a thesis topic?"

Olive nodded, trying to discreetly wipe away an errant tear. She sniffed. "Yeah, actually, I think I have some good ideas."

"Good, good. We should discuss those," Dave said, his eyes saying the opposite.

Olive sighed. She wasn't ready to talk. Because talking meant accepting, and she was not ready to do that.

"Yeah, we should," she said firmly. She tapped her mousepad, and her laptop's screen lit up, displaying a Word Document full of disjointed ideas.

"I was thinking maybe attachment styles are more malleable than has originally been posited?"

Dave nodded for her to go on.

"Okay, so I found out the Wilsons' attachment styles. Mr. Wilson presented with the anxious-preoccupied attachment style, and Mrs. Wilson presented with a fearful, avoidant attachment style."

If Dave noticed that she avoided using their first names, he didn't show it. He asked instead, "That's really interesting, actually. Are you sure?"

Olive nodded.

"Wow, that's crazy. So what are you thinking?"

"I am thinking that it is too crazy to be true. It's obviously not the test, so something must have caused their attachment styles to change."

"Hmm...you know you need to have pretest and posttest results for validity? Do you have anything that could show this change you are theorizing?"

"Yes, I tested Mr. Wilson before he got married, and he presented with secure attachment."

"And you think marrying Mrs. Wilson changed that?"

Olive decided to attribute the skepticism in his voice and his face to purely academic reasons. "No, actually, I don't. I think Mrs. Wilson probably presented with secure attachment as well."

"Huh. How do you figure?"

"Mrs. Wilson is an only child, and research shows that only children are likely to be better psychologically adjusted. Besides, there is no basis for her to have formed an insecure attachment – her family is practically perfect."

"Olive, you know that things are not always as they look. It feels like you might be...reaching here."

"So, you don't think there is any merit to this line of thinking?"

"I am not trying to tell you what to explore, Olive. I just want you to consider all angles to whatever topic you decide to pick."

Olive resisted the urge to roll her eyes. "But you don't think this is worth pursuing, do you?"

Dave shook his head. "I don't know enough to think that. Neither do you, honestly."

Olive sighed. That was not what she wanted to hear, even though she had to admit Dave was right. A post-test was useless without a comparable pre-test. For her hypothesis to even come close to suggesting a correlation, she needed more.

"For what it's worth, I think you are on the right track. Take a few more days to think about it and come back to me."

Olive gave a deflated sigh. "Okay."

Dave gave a small chuckle. "Don't look so deflated. You still have time. You've got this, don't worry."

Deflated didn't quite explain what she was feeling, but she pasted on a smile and shut off her laptop. She closed the lid and placed it in her bag. As she made to get up, Dave stopped her.

"Wait, Olive."

There was something in Dave's voice, something *different*. Olive looked up at him, "Yes?"

His eyes, darn, his eyes held so much concern, and they threatened to break her resolve. "Will you not tell me what happened in Phoenix?"

"I - I...," Olive looked down, her fingers entangled in the straps of her bag. Just the mention of Phoenix made her want to cry. Tears pricked the corner of her eyes. "I don't want to talk about it, Dave. Please."

Dave sighed. "I am not trying to pressure you. I just want to make sure you're okay. That's all."

Olive nodded, blinking furiously to stop the tears from gathering. "I will be. I am just...humiliated. I am so stupid. I basically threw myself at him, and he...oh! How could I have been so stupid?"

Dave moved closer and laid a hand on her arm. Olive didn't have time to react because he withdrew it just as quickly. "You are not stupid, Olive. I don't know what happened, but I know you, okay?"

Olive shook her head as she finally lost the battle, and tears rolled down her face. "But you don't know what I did. It was so stupid!"

This time when Dave placed his hand on her arm, he didn't withdraw it. "But I know you. Whatever you did, whatever happened, it will be okay. I promise."

Olive nodded numbly, not knowing what to say. She looked up at Dave and met his brown eyes. There was concern there, but also something else. Something *different*. Something *more*. Something that called to the woman inside her.

Olive, stop it, she chided herself. She had thought there was something in Henry's eyes too, and... look where that got her.

"I need you to be okay, Olive," Dave said, his gaze melting into hers, drawing her in. She could see into his soul, see how much he cared, see that she was desirable to him. It was heady, having this kind of power over someone. It was a powerful feeling to be desired by someone when all she had ever known was unrequited love and rejection. All she had to do was press her lips to his, and this time she knew she would be welcome. But this was Dave. She couldn't lose Dave too.

Olive cleared her throat and looked away, effectively breaking the moment. "I should go."

Dave blinked, and Dr. Marigold appeared in his place, his warm brown eyes replaced with cold steel. "Of course. I understand. Yeah."

Disappointment washed over Olive like a cold shower. She wanted to sit there and watch him watch her with those eyes, but until she was completely over Henry, this would only ever be a rebound. After everything Dave had been to her over the past year, he deserved better.

CHAPTER 38

What Really Happened

Pastor Greg Leard turned off the engine of his 2017 Toyota Camry and placed his head on the steering wheel. He hated this part of his job. He was always terrified about saying the wrong thing. It was a constant battle to make sure that the words coming out of his mouth were the Lord's. Pastor Greg shut his eyes tightly as if that would somehow loosen the tightness in his chest.

"Lord, teach me what to say here. Please."

Pastor Greg sat there in silence for a few moments, waiting to hear something from the Lord. He heard nothing, but in that stillness, he felt the unmistakable calm that characterized the presence of the Lord. Pastor Greg smiled as he exited the car and walked up the expansive driveway.

Just as he raised his hand to ring the bell, he heard the door being unlocked. He dropped his hand as the door swiveled to reveal Henry on the other side.

"Pastor Greg," he greeted with a warm smile. "Thanks for coming on such short notice. Come on in!"

Greg gave a small chuckle as he walked into the house. "It was no bother at all. I'm honestly glad I didn't have to make dinner."

Henry smiled. "My mom will be grateful you think that. This way, please."

Henry led him down a central hallway. Large frames of Scripture verses were arranged on one of the walls. Pictures of Oyin and Henry and extended family members (Pastor

Greg assumed) dotted the other wall. They went past the living room he had sat in on Sunday and past the kitchen with the adjoining breakfast nook and finally arrived in a cozy dining room area. Patricia Wilson beamed at him as they walked in.

"Hello there! Come on in," she said by way of greeting.

"Good evening, Mrs. Wilson."

"Oh, bother! Please call me Patricia." She motioned to the gentleman with salt-and-red-pepper hair seated to her right. "This is Greg, Henry's father."

Pastor Greg smiled. "Hello Mr. Wilson, I'm also a Greg."

Greg Wilson chuckled. "I know! Welcome. It's very nice to finally put a face to the name. Henry would not stop talking about you. It was always Pastor Greg this, Pastor Greg that. You know..."

"Dad..." Henry interjected, taking a seat at the table.

"Oh, where are my manners?" Patricia Wilson exclaimed. "Please take a seat, Greg. You can sit there, right next to Henry."

"Thank you, ma'am," Pastor Greg replied, just as Greg Wilson said, "But I am already sitting!"

Patricia Wilson shook her head, smiling. "That's going to get old, Greg. Stop it right now. Do you hear me? You know what, we are just going to call him Pastor. Okay?"

Pastor Greg smiled as he watched Greg Wilson make a show of clamping his lips together, padlocking them, and throwing away the key.

"Just ignore him," she said as she rolled her eyes. Then she said, "Pastor, can you please bless the food?"

"Of course," he said, standing up.

"Father, we come to You this evening to thank You for giving us this meal. We are grateful for it, and we pray that You provide for all those who don't have. Bless the hands that have worked for and on this meal. All this we ask in Jesus' Name. Amen."

"Amen," they chorused back.

Silence reigned on the table as bowls of potatoes and sautéed vegetables were passed around.

Pastor Greg was not surprised that Greg Wilson was the one to break the silence.

"So, *Pastor*, Henry never said if you were married."

Greg smiled. "No, I am not married, sir. Never been."

"Oh, really? Do you intend to?"

Greg found that he could not get mad at Greg Wilson's bluntness. Greg Wilson was so utterly guileless that his words had no sting behind them whatsoever.

"I do, actually. Just waiting for the right lady."

"Good for you, son. Don't settle for anything less."

Ask about Oyin.

"Thank you, sir. Speaking of the right lady, Henry, what happened between you and Oyin?"

Henry coughed loudly, and his entire face went red. If the situation wasn't serious, his reaction would have been comical.

"Yeah, um...we had an argument, and she left for Atlanta. She is still over there."

Pastor Greg nodded. "I remember you said that. I also remember you saying you did something stupid. Can you tell me what the argument was about?"

Henry glanced at his mom and dad and then sighed deeply. "I should probably start from the beginning. This whole thing started when Oyin's parents arrived. Her mom has this way of treating me like an interloper. But Oyin doesn't see it. When I learned her parents were coming, I - I invited Olive to come spend her break here -"

"*You* invited her?" Patricia Wilson cut in, an incredulous expression on her face.

Henry closed his eyes in mortification. "Yeah."

He continued. "Oyin was angry that Olive was coming over because she was convinced Olive was in love with me. But it was like, she could see that, but she couldn't see that her parents didn't like me? I thought she was being unfair and selfish. To cut a long story short, hosting Oyin's parents and Olive started to put a strain on our relationship. I felt like Oyin wanted me to be okay with her parents being here even though she was not okay with Olive being here. The last straw was when she wanted to go out for dinner after Olive left as if to "celebrate" her departure. When I brought it up, she just got defensive, and we ended up having a huge argument about it. We both said some pretty awful things and she...um, she said she wanted space.

"You have to understand, as angry as I was after Oyin left, I was also really sad. I needed someone, so I called Olive. She flew in that same day, and we hung out for the rest of the day. It was really nice to just laugh when all Oyin and I had been doing for weeks was argue. And I... very stupidly, started to compare Oyin to Olive. One thing led to another, and as we walked to our rooms that night, I don't know where it came from, but I remember telling her that I wished she was the one I married. I think because hanging out with her had been so effortless and drama-free, and it was such a stark contrast to what I felt like my marriage was like. I don't know. I still can't believe I said it. It wasn't even true, and I knew it wasn't, yet I said it. I think I just wanted to hurt Oyin. Oh God, I was so stupid… how could I have said that?"

Pastor Greg reached out and gave Henry a soothing pat on his back. "Hey, it's okay. You are going to get through this, okay?"

Pastor Greg glanced at the elder Wilson couple. Both had pensive looks on their faces, their eyes on Henry as if waiting for him to finish.

"Is that it?" Greg asked, looking at Henry.

Henry grimaced. "No, I - um, I…" He glanced at his parents and sighed. "I had a very vivid dream about kissing her. It felt so real. I can still smell her perfume –"

Pastor Greg could feel the displeasure emanating from the other side of the table, but he was determined to let Henry finish his story before saying anything.

"As soon as I woke up from the dream, I felt so guilty. I couldn't go back to sleep, so I went to grab a glass of milk. Olive was in the kitchen when I got there…"

Oh, God.

"…one thing led to another, and she tried to kiss me. And for a second, I wanted to kiss her too."

If Pastor Greg had any pearls on, he would have clutched them. But he could also see the vulnerability and self-loathing in Henry's eyes. There was nothing he could say to scold Henry that Henry had probably not said to himself. There was a collective gasp from the other side of the table. Determined to allow Henry to say his piece, Pastor Greg jumped in quickly.

"What happened, then?"

"I ended up pulling away, and I told her I couldn't do that to Oyin. She got very upset and accused me of leading her on. And she, too, left."

Drained by the story, Henry pushed away the already-forgotten plate of potatoes and placed his head on the bare surface of the mahogany table.

"Is that all, Henry?"

"Yes," he mumbled.

Patricia Wilson cut in quickly, "Wait, I am confused, Henry. Did you guys kiss or not?"

Henry raised his head. "No, we didn't. I turned away, and it landed on my cheek instead. But the guilt is killing me."

Patricia Wilson only nodded in response.

"Okay." Pastor Greg said a silent prayer for guidance and looked up at the elder Wilson couple. Pastor Greg was impressed at the picture of calm and unity they presented. Their plates of food also forgotten, Greg Wilson had his hand around Patricia Wilson, and he rubbed her shoulder comfortingly, her nearness obviously comforting him as well.

Greg Wilson spoke up, his face resolute. "Henry, raise your head and look at me."

Henry obeyed and lifted his head from the table. He looked awful, red-rimmed eyes that held unshed tears, hunched shoulders, and trembling hands.

"I asked you before, and I am asking again. Man to man, father to son, what do you want to do?"

Henry shut his eyes, and twin tears rolled down his cheeks. "I want a do-over, Dad. I want you to look at me without disappointment in your eyes. I want to not have called Olive over. I want my wife back."

"We don't get do-overs, Hen. We can only try to fix what has been broken. Are you willing to fix what has been broken?"

Henry turned to glance at Pastor Greg, and Pastor Greg nodded in encouragement.

"Do you think she will ever forgive me?"

Pastor Greg sighed. "I think Oyin loves you very much, Henry. Love forgives."

Pastor Greg continued. "But before we talk about Oyin, I think it is important that Henry knows that you forgive him, Mr. and Mrs. Wilson. He obviously knows that he made a mistake."

Greg Wilson regarded Henry for a moment before he stretched out his hand and curved it in the universal sign for "come here."

Henry got up and walked over to his dad. As soon as Henry fell into his father's arms, he began to sob. Greg Wilson held his son up as Henry sobbed into his shirt.

"It's okay. You're okay," Greg Wilson repeated as he patted Henry's back comfortingly.

Thank You, Lord.

There were a thousand ways the dinner could have gone, and Pastor Greg had walked into the house afraid that he had a potential divorce on his hands, but the Lord had gone ahead of him and done the work.

"Thank you, Pastor," Patricia Wilson said as she too gave Henry a tight hug.

Pastor Greg gave a small chuckle. "I didn't do anything. Thank *you*, guys, for being here for Henry as a good example."

Greg Wilson shook his head slightly, deflecting the praise. "Thank God."

"How are you feeling, Henry?" Pastor Greg addressed Henry, who had just returned to his seat.

Henry smiled. It wasn't a beaming smile of joy by any means, but it was a hopeful one.

"Hopeful," Henry simply said.

He added, "And I know I didn't really say this before, so...I'm sorry, Mom and Dad, for everything. I wish I could go back and... well, you know."

Patricia Wilson answered for both of them. "We know, honey. We love you. Of course, we forgive you."

Pastor Greg nodded. "Wow, thank you both so much for being willing to listen to Henry and for making my job easier."

Everyone chuckled at that, and much of the tension in the room since Henry began his story dissipated.

"Pastor G, how do I get Oyin to come back?" Henry asked.

"Just tell her," Pastor Greg replied. "Tell her to come back. That you want her to come back. You do, don't you?"

"I do, but what if she doesn't want to come back? I don't want her to come back if she doesn't want to, you know?"

"Henry, Oyin loves you. Of course, she wants to come back," Patricia Wilson said softly.

"Mom, you weren't there. You didn't see the look in her eyes when we argued. And nothing had happened between Olive and me then. She will never look at me the same way once she finds out."

"First of all, Hen, nothing really happened between you and Olive. You didn't cheat on Oyin. Yes, you guys almost kissed, but you pulled away. Remember that *you* pulled away," Greg Wilson added.

"But what about what I said to Olive about wishing I married her? What about the dream? It felt so real. I could still smell her shampoo when I woke up!"

"Yes, those will hurt her, but you have to reassure her like you reassured us that they were mistakes. Not a reflection of your heart or what you really feel," Pastor Greg replied.

"Oh God," Henry whimpered. "She's going to leave me for Dee if I tell her."

Pastor Greg inhaled sharply. "Hey! Stop that. Don't do that. Don't go there. Don't bring Dee into this."

"Um, who is Dee?" Patricia Wilson asked.

Henry looked over at Pastor Greg for him to respond, but Pastor Greg said, "Don't look at me. I've never met him."

Henry gave a small chuckle that was more bitter than mirthful. "Dee and Oyin were kind of together when we met."

"Oh, so he is a former boyfriend?"

Henry snorted derisively. "More like a former betrothed-slash-fiancé."

"What?!" Greg Wilson exclaimed just as Patricia Wilson cried out, "Oyin was engaged before?!"

"No, not really...it was - just, it was complicated. They were not really engaged, per se. It was just assumed that they would get married."

"Why didn't you say anything about this before, Henry?" Greg Wilson asked incredulously.

"Because it was - it was...it was -"

Pastor Greg cut in, "If you don't mind me interjecting here, there is no threat of Oyin leaving Henry for Dee. That's what is important here. Dee is in the past. For you and Oyin. Isn't that right, Henry?"

"Yeah, I guess," Henry mumbled.

"We'll trust your word on this, Pastor," Greg Wilson capitulated.

"Thank you, sir. I appreciate that vote of confidence. It's just...the subject of Dee almost came between Henry and Oyin before, and I would hate for the enemy to use that as a tool again."

"Of course, we understand."

"So, Henry," Pastor Greg looked at Henry, "have you and Oyin communicated at all since Saturday?"

The transformation that came over Henry as his frown quite literally turned upside down was fascinating. "Yeah, we have talked and texted a little."

Pastor Greg tried not to smile as he asked, "And?"

"She said she was sorry and that she loves me."

"I'm sorry," Patricia Wilson paused dramatically. "Isn't that what we have all been saying? You heard it from Oyin herself!"

"She doesn't know what I did, Mom!"

"Call her tomorrow, Hen," Greg Wilson said, brooking no argument. Greg Wilson had this unique *dad*-gift of saying things with a tone of finality and authority that made you just agree. Pastor Greg was very thankful for that dad-gift.

"Okay, Dad."

"We'll hang around for a couple more days, if that's okay, Henry?" Patricia Wilson added.

Henry nodded.

Pastor Greg felt at peace, and he knew the night had come to an end. A small smile graced his lips as he rose, "Shall we seal this with a prayer?"

CHAPTER 39A

The Perfection in Love

There was no instruction manual for it, no FAQs, or how-to articles to consult on what he was supposed to say to Oyin. Henry Wilson could not sleep throughout the night. He kept waking every hour with the distinct fear of Oyin never walking back into their house. He would then drift back off into sleep only to be jolted out of sleep again by a nightmare of Oyin getting married to Dee. By 5 am, Henry gave up every attempt to sleep. He sat up in bed, his eyes bleary and bloodshot, and his head pounding. Sighing, he reached for his phone on the nightstand to go through his personalized devotional app.

Thirty minutes later, he was feeling slightly better. He still had no idea what to say to Oyin, though. His devotional content had talked about kindness, so no help there, but at least he knew that the Lord was on his side.

Maybe he should write what he wanted to say?

Henry almost burst out laughing at himself. He was a horrible writer. He was lucky with Oyin; she always thought his lines were cute even though they were incredibly corny.

Lord, if you could just turn back time to Friday, that would be great.

Doesn't work like that, Henry. You can face this - I will be there with you.

"But I can't!" Henry whined. "I just know I'm going to say the wrong thing." He paused as an idea came to him.

"How about this? How about You tell me exactly what to say right now, and I will write it down?"

As opposed to trusting that I will be there?

"No - no. It's not really like I don't trust You. I just want to be sure that nothing will go wrong. Can You at least promise Me that Oyin will come back, and we will go back to the way things were?"

I am your Surety, Henry.

That was totally a non-answer, Henry thought, grumbling.

As if in response, the words in Psalm 24:10 floated into his mind.

Even if my father and mother abandon me,

the Lord will hold me close.

Henry sighed. The Lord was right. Of course, He was. He had to trust the Lord to take control. This was so important to his happiness, and Henry was terrified that he would mess it up like he messed up the past few days, but...he had to trust in the Lord. He had to trust in the Lord's love because...

My perfect love casts out fear

It was a eureka moment. The Lord had been speaking to him through Pastor Greg, through his parents, even through his devotional passage, but he hadn't understood. But as he heard the Lord utter the words from 1 John 4:18, it began to make sense. The Lord loved them perfectly, but he and Oyin's love hadn't been perfect; fear had crept in and debilitated them. They hadn't been kind to each other or loved as they should have...as Jesus did.

Henry grabbed his phone and pulled up all the verses on love that he could find. Romans 8:38-39 serenaded him. Jeremiah 31:3 threw him a wink. 1 John 4:19 smiled at him. John 15:12 waved him over. 1 Corinthians 16:14 and

Matthew 5:43-48 made him stop in his tracks as the words washed over him.

As long as he loved Oyin...no, as long as He loved them, and they loved Him, they would love each other perfectly. They would love the way love is supposed to love.

Good boy.

Henry looked up at the ceiling, beaming as he soaked in the rediscovered Love.

"Video-call my wife," Henry voice-commanded his phone's digital assistant. While the phone rang, Henry smoothed down his hair though it was already slick from his shower, smelled his armpits though he had applied deodorant, and blew into his hand to smell his breath even though he had just finished brushing his teeth.

Finally, Oyin picked up the phone. Henry paused and took her in. She had a white towel wrapped around her head, and she wore a white bathrobe. He had never seen a more beautiful sight in his life. They continued to stare at each other until Oyin realized she was wearing a bathrobe. She yelped and turned off her phone's camera.

"Hold on!" she shouted.

He wanted to say she was beautiful as she was and didn't need to change a thing, but he didn't know how that would be received considering *everything*, so he settled on, "Okay."

Her phone camera came back on, she realized he had lied before. This was a more beautiful sight. She had on a teddy bear nightshirt, and her braids fell around her shoulders in a mess of curls. He had never seen...well, you get the idea.

"Hi," he said with a smile.

"Hi," she smiled back.

"You look beautiful."

Oyin rolled her eyes fondly before she said, "Thank you. Do you like the hair?"

As far as he was concerned, she looked good with every hairstyle, but braids had a special place in his heart.

"I love it. You look really good, Oyin."

It was true. She looked happier than he had seen her in several weeks. Was she doing okay without him? Was she better off without him? That familiar fear began to rise in his heart as he sat there.

"You too. Did you just shower?"

Henry ran a self-conscious hand through his hair. "Yeah."

"Oh, okay," she said.

Henry started to freak out. He should say something. He knew he should say something. But where to start…

TEACH ME WHAT TO SAY!!!

"Can I go first?" Oyin rushed out quickly.

"Of course," Henry replied just as quickly.

"You were right," she sighed, "about Mummy and kinda Daddy too. She truly didn't like…well, she was having a hard time accepting you as her son-in-law, but we've been talking since I got here. Like, really talking and she…well, let's just say, the exact words were 'I'm glad you are married to Henry.'"

"Really?" Henry asked, hope blossoming in his heart.

"Yes," Oyin nodded. "I am sorry for anything they might have said or done that hurt you, Henry. They had to leave early for their flight, but they promised to call and apologize to you as soon as they got to Nigeria."

"Oh." Henry paused. "Did they know about - that we…about what happened?"

"Yes," Oyin said. "And they basically ended up taking your side and scolded me for leaving Phoenix."

A warmth grew in Henry's heart and spread to his face. This was what it felt like to be accepted. To be loved.

"Wow," was all he said though.

"Yeah," Oyin laced her fingers together. "She basically said that if I truly trusted you like I claimed to, I should drop the Olive thing."

Henry raised his eyebrows so high that they almost formed a halo above his head. He didn't know what to think, feel, or say. Oyin's mom was taking his side, actually defending him!

"So…this is me dropping it. I'm sorry for how I allowed the Olive thing to come between us. I really am, Hen."

Henry shook his head. She couldn't be apologizing, shouldn't be apologizing. She had been right, mostly. Olive had been in love with him, or at least had feelings for him.

"Oyin, you don't have to -" he started to say, but Oyin cut in, her eyes bright with unshed tears.

"No, please. Just say you accept my apology, please."

"Of course. I do. I accept your apology."

She sniffed. "Thank you, Henry. Sorry, you can go ahead now."

LORD, TEACH ME WHAT TO SAY!!!

"So," he started, "um...how are you?"

Henry wanted to chew up his tongue and swallow it.

How are you? How ARE you? That's the best I could come up with it?

Oyin raised an eyebrow. "I don't know, Henry. I miss my husband, so there's that."

Henry couldn't help it. He smiled widely. "Really?"

"Of course, I do! The real question here, Henry, is whether you miss me."

How could he explain that he felt like half his heart was missing? That he missed every single thing about her? That seeing her felt like seeing a beautiful sunset over the ocean, calm and euphoria wrapped up in one?

"Of course, Oyin! I miss you."

"Then why didn't you want me to come back?" She challenged. "And don't give me that 'it's not you, it's me' crap."

Oyin's eyes were on fire, and Henry found he could not look away even if he tried...which he didn't.

"But it *is* me. I -" he stopped.

This is it.

"What, Henry?" Oyin asked evenly.

"I didn't think you would want to come back, that you would want *me* back if you knew what happened."

Oyin shut her eyes and sighed. She ran a hand across her forehead and pursed her lips. Henry could not tell if she was frustrated, disappointed, or holding back tears of hurt. Maybe it was a combination of all three.

Oh, I can't do this.

He had barely said anything, and she was already like this.

"Henry," Oyin said, her voice quiet, almost inaudible. "What happened between you and Olive?"

His eyes widened like saucers, and his lips formed an 'o'.

How did she know? Oh God, how?

"Oh my God. Oh. My. Goodness. Henry, your face..." She buried her face in her hands. "...it says it all."

"Wait, Oyin. I -"

"You know what, don't answer that. Answer this, instead: do you want to be with her?"

"NO! No. No. No, I don't want to be with her. I want to be with you, Oyin. Always have and always will. You asked before if I would choose you now, and the answer is yes. I love *you*."

Oyin scoffed, "but you love her, too. Isn't that what started this whole thing?"

That wasn't fair. This wasn't just about Olive.

Oyin sighed again. "I'm sorry. That wasn't fair. It's just...this is not what I expected us to be talking about."

"I know," Henry shook his head. "I am sorry. I just want you to know everything. I think you *need* to know everything before we can move on."

Oyin chuckled dryly, "Do I have to? Can't we just skip to the kiss and make up part?"

Henry raised his eyebrows, hopefully as his lips curved in a small smile. "Wait, really?"

Oyin sighed. "No, it's better I...wait, you didn't have sex with her, did you?"

Henry coughed, then coughed again as blood drained from his face. "What?! No! Of course not! No."

Ew, he almost added.

Oyin nodded. "I didn't think you would. Not even if you were in love with her -"

"Which I'm not," Henry interjected.

"Which you are not," Oyin acquiesced.

This conversation was taking on a life of its own, and he was definitely not in control of it, but he was glad Someone was.

"Did you kiss her, then?"

"No, but there might have been a dream about it…"

Oyin raised an eyebrow and pursed her lips, saying nothing.

The act itself was nothing but a dream, but he was afraid of what Oyin would think it signified that he wanted Olive. But he didn't. He wanted Oyin, no one else.

"Please say something, O. Please."

"What do you want me to say?" she asked in a tired voice, her eyes averted.

"That you believe me when I say it was a nightmare. Literally."

Oyin gave a startled chuckle. Then she asked many seconds later, "You promise?"

Henry nodded vigorously. "Cross my heart."

"Is that all? Did anything else happen?"

"She tried to kiss me. For real, this time. But nothing happened. I didn't kiss her."

"Did you want to kiss her?"

"I - I did. But only for like a second! It was a mistake, a complete, utter mistake. You have to believe me, Oyin."

Oyin clenched her jaw and bent her head to the left and then to the right. "When? When did this happen?"

"On Saturday. Saturday night."

"Saturday?!" Oyin said incredulously, her voice a half-octave higher than normal. "The same Saturday I left?"

"Yes."

"Henry Christopher Wilson, what was Olive doing in my house on Saturday?"

Oh, how stupid he had been.

"I called her."

"You didn't!"

It was Henry's turn to shut his eyes and sigh. He ran his hand through his hair. "I did. It was so stupid. I was so mad -"

"Obviously!"

"- but that is no excuse," he continued. "I - I am really sorry, Oyin."

"So, what? You invited her, and she tried to kiss you. Just out of the blue?"

Henry reddened. "Not really...she said she thought I wanted to kiss her, too."

"And she was right, wasn't she, Henry?"

Henry sighed. "Looking back now, I see how - well, it doesn't matter. I had made a stupid joke about kissing that she must have taken seriously."

Oyin stared at him for many seconds, and he tried to meet her gaze unflinchingly. She had to know he was being truthful. For the first time since the call began, Henry really wished they were having the conversation in person. He wanted to hold her hands in his. He wanted to cradle her face in his hands and assure the heck out of her.

"Are you telling me the truth, Henry?"

Henry nodded. "I promise, Oyin. I am."

"Okay," she nodded.

"You believe me?"

"Yes."

He had to tell her what he said about wishing he were married to Olive, but he hesitated. That was the one that would hurt her the most.

Oh, God.

"I also –," he started.

"There's more?!" Oyin exclaimed.

Henry sighed. "I said something to Olive that I think you should know."

Oyin shook her head, "No, no more. It does not matter what you said. I don't want to know. It's all in the past now. Let's just move on."

Henry stopped. Really?

"Really? You forgive me?"

"Yes."

Henry had thought it would be easier to have this call over the phone because he was scared. Now, all he wanted was her in his arms.

"Thank you, Oyin."

Oyin's quiet voice came through the phone just then, "Can I come home now?"

The sun would have been jealous of the brightness of Henry's smile when he said, "Yes, Abso-freaking-lutely, yes!"

Oyin's smile matched his. "Then I will see you in five hours."

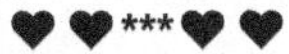

Henry shuffled his feet as he stood in the airport receiving line. He was equal parts excited and nervous. It was very akin to how he felt as he watched the closed church doors just before the bridal march began to play at their wedding. Right now, he stood in a crowded airport with a bouquet of chrysanthemums in his left hand, and his right hand was nervously worrying a piece of lint in his pocket. Oyin preferred white roses, but he hoped the story of the chrysanthemums would make her smile. On their second date, he had taken her to a flower garden to pick a flower to be her favorite. She had initially picked white chrysanthemums, but she kept pronouncing the flower wrong, calling them *chrys-saint-ze-mum*. After failing the tenth time, Oyin had given up.

"This is so humiliating!" she had exclaimed as she covered her face with her hands. "So not attractive."

Henry had gently pried her hands from her face and said. "On the contrary, I am attracted. I'm mesmerized." And then, he had kissed her. It was their first kiss.

An announcement coming through the overhead speakers jolted him out of his reverie, and Henry gave a small smile at the memory.

Lord, I just want...I want us to be happy

I got you.

Henry smiled widely, grateful that God really "got" him through all the temper tantrums, complaining, and mistakes. He sighted Oyin just then, and the smile stayed put. She saw him, and her face lit up. Henry could hardly believe his eyes when she started running. Like, actually started running *to* him. She had barely reached him when Henry was already scooping her into his arms, the bouquet of chrysanthemums forgotten. He hugged her with everything he had, their bodies molding into one.

Oyin drew back to look into his eyes and eased to the ground.

"Hi," she breathed.

"Hi," he repeated, his eyes lost in the dark-chocolate goodness of her eyes.

"Aww, you bought me *kiss*-anthemums," she smiled.

Henry tore his eyes away from hers to look at the bouquet. It was smushed.

"I'll buy a thousand more just to see you smile."

"Henry!" Oyin laughed and hit his chest playfully.

"Come on," he grabbed her tote from her and put an arm around her shoulders. "Let's go home."

CHAPTER 39B

As It Should Be

Henry didn't take her home immediately. Oyin was too busy relishing the feel of her husband's hands in hers to realize that Henry had not gotten off the highway onto their exit. It wasn't until they entered downtown Scottsdale that Oyin realized where they were.

Oyin looked out of the window, confused. "Hen?"

"Yeah?"

Oyin turned to look at Henry. His lips were twitching as if he was trying to conceal a smile. She couldn't help it – she started smiling too. "What are we doing here? I thought we were going home."

"We are. We're just going to make a small detour first."

Oyin shook her head, her smile so wide it hurt. "Babe, what do you have planned? You know I hate surprises."

"No, actually, you love them. You only claim to hate them."

Oyin gasped dramatically and squeezed his fingers that were still interlaced with hers a little too tightly. "I do not!"

"Yes, you do."

"Do not!"

"Yes, you do. Babe, if you hate surprises so much, why are you smiling so much right now?"

Oyin laughed, "Because."

"Because what?" Henry asked teasingly.

In the early sunset, Henry looked like an angel, his red hair blending with the reddish hue of the sunset to cast a halo around his head. In her distraction, Henry suddenly brought their joined fingers to his lips and kissed the back of her palm, "…you were saying?"

It was so attractive. The way he was trying, the way he was wooing her, the way he was totally focused on her – it was so attractive. It was why she fell in love with him.

What were they even talking about again?

She was still trying to answer when Henry said, "we're here."

Oyin looked up. It was their favorite French restaurant – the scene of the dinner-from-hell.

Henry put his Mustang in Park and gestured to the valet to give them a few minutes. He produced a single white rose from God-knows-where and turned to face her.

"We never got to have that dinner date that you were so excited about. Every day with you is worth celebrating. I am sorry that I was so blinded by me that I didn't see you. I promise not to ever let that happen again. I promise to always see you and Mummy and Daddy. I love you, Oyin."

Oyin was speechless. Her heart was singing and floating and screaming and swooning as she sat there motionless. Tears welled up in her eyes as she stared into his.

"Babe...you did this? For me?"

"I just wanted to show you that I meant everything I said on the phone."

Oyin placed her head on the headrest, still blown away by Henry's thoughtfulness. How could she ever have doubted that Henry Wilson loved her?

"But I didn't do anything for you. Henry, this is so thoughtful...I don't even know what to say."

Henry gently took her unoccupied hand open, placed the rose in it, and wrapped her fingers over it. "Say you will go to dinner with me."

Oyin chuckled and brought the flower up to her nose. "Of course, I will go to dinner with you."

Henry did not let her hand go as they walked into the restaurant. He was still holding her hand when Arnold, the waiter, walked up.

"Oh! *Madame, Monsieur*, you're back."

Arnold's French accent made it hard to tell whether he was pleased that they were back.

"Yes, we are," Henry said, giving Oyin's hand a quick squeeze, "and we plan to eat what we ordered this time."

Arnold nodded and took their orders.

It was like a first date all over again. But this time, Oyin didn't hold back. Henry wasn't the only one who had something to apologize for. He wasn't the only one who had to make changes. When their appetizers arrived, before Henry could say grace, Oyin quickly spoke up.

"Can I say something really quickly before we start eating?"

Henry nodded, "Of course."

"Hen, I am sorry too. I am sorry I wasn't... Here's the thing. I promised myself that I would never be a nagging wife, and I wasn't. But I did the complete opposite. I ran away from you, and I am not just talking about flying to Atlanta. I – gosh, this is so hard for me to say – I starved you of my love. I promise never to do that again."

Oyin didn't look at Henry while she spoke, so she was surprised when she looked up, and his eyes were watery.

Henry nodded and brought her palm up to kiss it. "Thank you."

The way he was looking at her made her blush. In the past, she would have just accepted the attention, but this time she gave it back. From the time they said grace, she flirted shamelessly with him so that by the time Arnold brought their desserts, Henry was so red from blushing that Arnold almost did a double-take.

Oyin couldn't believe it, but by the time they had paid the check and walked outside to get their car, she had fallen deeper in love with Henry. All this time, she had thought she was guarding her heart by not letting Henry all the way in. She had really just been holding herself back from experiencing love as it should be.

"I have one more surprise tonight," Henry said as he opened the passenger door for her.

"Henry, seriously?" She chuckled. "I don't think I can take any more surprises today."

"It's okay. You'll love this one."

Oyin just shook her head and smiled.

Fifteen minutes later, they arrived at The W Hotel in Old Town Scottsdale.

"You're kidding!" Oyin exclaimed.

Henry laughed. "I knew you would love it."

"I do love it. So we are staying here overnight?"

Henry nodded, "Since Mom and Dad are still around, I thought it might be good to have the night to ourselves."

He was so thoughtful. Oyin leaned over the console and Henry sighed as her lips touched his.

"You thought right," she whispered in his ear before she pulled back.

Henry's gaze melted into hers, "I have been waiting for you to do that since you landed in Phoenix."

"Why didn't you just kiss me?"

"I wanted it to come from you. I wasn't sure if you were holding back because of...Olive."

Oyin chuckled. "Her name is not a curse word, Henry, and no, I wasn't holding back. I guess I am just used to you making the first move. That's definitely going to change."

She kissed him again for effect and then said suggestively. "Who knows, if you get us checked in fast enough..."

"Say no more," Henry said. He skipped the valet line and drove into the on-site parking himself, Oyin laughing all the way.

CHAPTER 40 (EPILOGUE)
Diagnosis: Love; Prognosis: Perfection

To: Henry Christopher Wilson <henwilson@mail.com>
CC: Oyin Felicia Wilson <ojohnson@mail.com>
From: Olive Sadie Roberts <olivesr@mail.com>
Subject: FW: Final Copy!
Attached: Master_Thesis_Olive_Roberts.pdf

Hen & Oyin,

Wow. I can't believe I am finally done. So much has happened, and as I sit to write this, I can't help but be thankful for every single thing that has happened. You and Oyin were invaluable to this process. Thank you for still being a part of this, in spite of all that has happened. Anyway, I thought you and Oyin would like to see the final product! The full thesis is attached. For the sake of your sanity (because I know that your sanity might be threatened by reading 58 pages of psychological jargon - mine certainly was!), I have copied a somewhat abridged version below. Just FYI, I cut out some parts from all the sections below, so don't be confused! And don't judge the whole thesis based on the below, okay? Unless you love it. In which case, by all means, judge away. Okay, enough foreshadowing. Here goes…

****

The Malleability of Attachment Styles in Marriage
Through The Lens of Faith: A Case Study
By Olive Roberts

Preface

The case study used in this thesis was only made possible by the cooperation of Mr. and Mrs. Henry Wilson. I want to thank them for their time, openness, and willingness to add to the growing body of research on attachment styles in marriage. I want to also thank all the friends and family of the Wilsons who were willing to be interviewed as a part of the study. I strongly hope that they would benefit from the findings of this study.

I would also like to specially acknowledge my mentor, Dr. Dave Marigold, for his invaluable input throughout the development of this thesis. I highly benefited from the very frequent discussions on my progress and next steps. In addition, he gave proactive feedback on the direction of this project before it was written, while it was written, and after it was written. Overall, he helped to improve the overall quality of this final thesis. Thank you very much for being a great mentor. I am a better contributing member of the psychology community because of you.

Personally, I would like to thank Henry and Oyin for their friendship over the past couple of months. I would also like to thank my family (specifically my father David, Patricia, and Greg) for the familial support throughout the years of study.

Working on this thesis has opened my eyes to the incredible power of faith. In the wise words of the first-century faith pioneer, Jesus, "If you had faith even as small as a mustard seed, you could say to this mountain, 'Move from here to there,' and it would move. Nothing would be impossible," including the malleability of attachment styles.

Abstract

Attachment styles is a psychological concept that has been around for many years. Although the concept of attachment styles is one that has always been explored in view of Western medicine and counseling, there is not a lot of research that combines the concept of attachment styles with the faith of the study participants in mind. The researcher analyzed an American interracial couple's attachment styles and how their attachment styles have undergone changes. This study documents their pre-married and married lives extensively, including their childhood, previous attachment styles, and of course, their faith.

This was an instrumental case study that sought to provide more insight into attachment styles, especially through the lens of faith. The study was conducted by one researcher and took place both in-person in the couple's home and virtually via video teleconference. Data collection methods included semi-structured interviews, audio recordings, couple observation, multiple participant testing, examining pre-existing recordings of the couple (i.e., home videos), and document analyses.

Based on the findings of the study, the researcher concluded that the attachment styles of the couple participants underwent changes as they transitioned from single individuals to a married couple and then some more during the first couple years of their marriage. This phenomenon is not unlike the settling of water when it is first poured into a container. It tosses and turns, shifts and moves, until it finds its place and then settles. It is this researcher's opinion that this couple has finally settled with regards to their attachment styles.

The study has opened the door for more research into the malleability of attachment styles, especially in the context of faith and marriage. Recommendations have also been made (page 49) on further research areas.

CHAPTER SIX: Summary, Discussion, and Conclusions
Conceptual Framework and Discussion

Both Mr. and Mrs. Wilson were the only biological children of their respective parents. Both Mr. and Mrs. Wilson went through their early developmental years as the only child of their respective parents, although Mrs. Wilson's parents eventually adopted a younger child. Research shows that singletons (i.e., the only child in a family) are more likely to be better psychologically and behaviorally adjusted. (Liu, Lin, & Chen, 2010). Furthermore, analysis of home videos acquired from the parents of the couple shows that both individuals exhibited secure attachment. Subsequent testing of the couple participant as unmarried adults produced the same result. However, testing the couple participant about a year into marriage produced completely different results. The husband presented with the anxious-preoccupied attachment style, and Mrs. Wilson presented with the fearful-avoidant attachment style. Analysis of the interviews conducted prior to the testing also lent to the same conclusion. There was trouble in paradise, it was evident - but enough to completely alter an attachment style?

Conclusion

On entering marriage, as with recently married couples, Mr. and Mrs. Wilson struggled to be individuals and a couple at the same time. Over time, they stopped struggling and forgot to be individuals. As a result, their Christian faith suffered. Tied as their faith was to their sense of self, their self-esteem suffered, and so did trust and love in themselves and their partner. Both individuals handled this change differently, as discussed extensively above.

It took a physical separation - where they could learn to be individuals again, where they found their faith again, for the water-in-the-container to settle. In rekindling their Christian faith, they found what it means to truly love. In truly loving, in the paraphrased words of Mr. and Mrs. Wilson in their final interview, they found perfection.

****

Dun! Dun! Dun!

I hope this gives you a good understanding of what the other pages say, but you are welcome to read the entire document. I know it couldn't have been easy reading about yourselves in a journal article, so I just want to say thank you again for trusting me.

The way you guys have handled this whole thing has been, quite frankly, saintly. I am still a long way from being called a Christian, but you guys have opened my eyes to the incredible power of faith in God. I'm not there yet, Henry, so don't go ordering cross-shaped balloons, but I'm certainly warmer. 😊

Oyin, I remember you saying Uncle Dele would love to read this thesis. Will you please forward it to him for me? Thank you.

Dave says hi, and I hope you guys have fun at the Thanksgiving parade.

Lots of love,

Olive.

Author's Note

I can hardly believe it's over. Thank you for going on this journey with me. Together, we have swooned, cried, and laughed through Oyin and Henry's imperfect journey to perfection.

Over the past few years, I have learned that perfection can only be found in love, in God's love. Yet, it is not like you become a Christian and instantly become perfect. It is more like God's perfection rubs off on you.

The perfection that Oyin and Henry find in this book is the perfection in the Love of God. They learn to stem their love for each other from that all-consuming Love, and that's where their perfection comes from.

I guess what I am trying to say is that mistakes might trail your path like Hansel and Gretel's crumbs, that's okay. Your perfection does not come from you, but from experiencing the Love of God. It is my prayer that you fall in love (or deeper in love) with the Lord when you read this book.

Kisses and cheers,
Ronke

ACKNOWLEDGMENTS

To you holding this book, thank you. After all, who is an author without a reader?

To all my Facebook writer support groups, I found you when I needed a community, and I thank God for every minute I spent scrolling, commenting, and posting.

To all my family, thank you for the prayers and proud expressions I see on your face when I tell you that I wrote a book. Aunty Dami, Aunty Yetunde, Iya P, Daddy Amoo, (to mention a few), thank you for being my champions.

To all my friends who supported me (Becky, Krissy, Rachel, Tobi, Emmanuel, Elijah, and so many others), I am beyond grateful for you all.

Mummy, you are my rock. Very little compares to the happiness I feel when you ask, "Have you not finished writing *ni*?" I love you. Of course, I would be remiss if I don't mention the years of belly fuel you have supplied. Thank you.

Daddy, if Mummy is my rock, you are my breeze. Thank you for always making me laugh. You bring out the kid in me, and I love you.

Alice/Gbemi/Adesoji (tell me you did not expect this), I could not ask for a better sister. You pushed and prodded until you saw a gem. Well, guess what? I think you are a treasure.

My brother, for the one-line sentences that hold so much thought behind them, no one could replace you. I love you.

Aunty Jummy, thanks for your support and encouragement. Words cannot adequately express how grateful I am for you. I pray that the Lord shows you. You are a star, and I love you.

To my girls (Jojo, Debo, and Alice), I am glad you are in my life. Thanks for the support, love, and many hours *not* wasted in video calls. Y'all are my heart.

Incredibly grateful to my favorite YouTube couples and YouTube series for loading me up on the feels I needed to get through the lovey chapters.

To the ones who got away, thanks for the fuel I needed to get through the angst-filled chapters.

A big thank you to Jake James, Beckah Shae, Limoblaze, Sabrina Carpenter, V.Rose, Niniola, Simi, Hyper Fenton, Okey Sokay, Gil Joe, Nkay (and so many others!) for getting me through those all-nighters.

Finally, Jesus, my darling Jesus, I don't have enough words. You. You. You. You. Thank YOU. You are, quite literally, the Best.

DISCUSSION QUESTIONS

1. The novel begins with an idyllic picture of Oyin and Henry's married life. If they did not entertain visitors that summer, do you think their marriage would have continued in this idyllic manner?

2. Both Oyin and Henry are products of healthy, loving marriages? Why do you think that they were both so insecure in their marriage?

3. Although the verbalized differences between Oyin and Henry are mostly cultural (he is American and she is Nigerian), do you think race played a role in their relationship? Might their insecurities have stemmed from that?

4. It's so frustrating to see Henry and Oyin go back and forth between anger and love. Do you think that he could have prevented her from walking out by answering yes when she asked if he would still choose her? Or had it already gone too far?

5. Clearly, Olive had feelings for Henry. Do you think Henry ever suspected Olive had feelings for him? Why? Why not? Do you think Henry had (or ever had) feelings for Olive?

6. Do you think Olive finally moved on at the end now that she is starting to find faith in God? Is there a connection between her and Professor Dave? Can she finally be happy for Henry and Oyin? And will Oyin be able to see her as a friend, without jealousy, now?

7. Who would you consider the villain of this story? Why?

8. Is it ever appropriate for married people to have best friends of the opposite sex?

9. How can you show Christ-like love to someone who does not share your beliefs or values? Should you minister to someone who might threaten your covenant relationship?

10. What is the role of an individual's parents in a Christian marriage? How much does a couple owe to one another's culture as they build their own family?

11. Can an unmarried pastor serve as a reliable marriage counselor in 2020?

12. If Oyin and Henry were not Christians, do you think they could have gotten through this hurdle in their marriage?

13. It is the love surrounding Oyin and Henry (from their parents, their church and from God) that gets them through this difficult time? How important would you say it is for a new couple to have a support system around (and to some degree, in) their marriage?

14. Pulling from questions 1) and 8), it is arguably Oyin and Henry's "support system" that lit the match and widened the gulf in their marriage. How does a new couple navigate being a couple while also wearing other hats, like best friend or daughter? How does Oyin and Henry's story help point to what to do and what not to do?

15. What lessons, if any, have you learned from Oyin and Henry's story?

16. Who is your favorite character? Why?

ABOUT THE AUTHOR

Ronke Abidoye is a Nigerian-American living in sunny South Florida. She fell in love with Jesus when she was 15 and hasn't looked back since.

When she is not pulling an all-nighter to finish a paper for her master's degree, she is dreaming up new star-crossed characters. *The Perfection in Love* is her debut novel. Connect with her at:

Website: ronkeabidoye.com
Twitter: @ronke_abidoye
Instagram: @ronke_abidoye

www.ingramcontent.com/pod-product-compliance
Lightning Source LLC
Chambersburg PA
CBHW021109110726
47900CB00007B/2107